THE BEST OF THE WEST 2

THE BEST OF THE WEST 2

NEW SHORT STORIES FROM THE WIDE SIDE OF THE MISSOURI

Edited and Introduced by
James Thomas and Denise Thomas

PEREGRINE SMITH BOOKS
SALT LAKE CITY

For Jesse and, this year, Christopher

First edition

90 89 3 2 1

Acknowledgments of previous publication and permission to reprint the stories in this book may be found on pages ix and x

This is a Peregrine Smith Book; published by Gibbs Smith, Publisher, P.O. Box 667, Layton, Utah 84041

Design by J. Scott Knudsen

Printed and bound in the United States of America

Library of Congress Cataloging-in-Publication Data

The Best of the West 2 : new short stories from the wide side of the Missouri / edited and introduced by James Thomas and Denise Thomas.

p. cm.

ISBN 0-87905-162-0

1. Western stories. 2. American fiction—20th century. 3. Short stories, American—West (U.S.) I. Thomas, James, 1946- . II. Thomas, Denise, 1954- .

PS648.W4B47 1989

813′.087408—dc20 89-6255

CIP

The paper used in this publication meets the minimum requirements of American National Standard for Information Sciences—Permanence of paper for Printed Library Materials, ANSI Z39.48-1984 ∞

CONTENTS

ACKNOWLEDGMENTS

Our thanks to Evelyn Belcher, Ginger Bohn, Kristin Brucker, Tom Hazuka, Christopher Merrill, and Dan O'Brien—and to the Miami Township Fire Department—for their critical help and timely assistance with this second edition of *Best of the West.*

"Meat," by Ken Smith, first appeared in the *Atlantic Monthly.* Copyright © 1988 by Ken Smith and reprinted by permission of the author.

"Bitterwater," by Ann Cummins, first appeared in *The New Yorker.* Copyright © 1988 by Ann Cummins and reprinted by permission of the author.

"Cowboys," by Fenton Johnson, first appeared in a somewhat different version in *The Greensboro Review.* Copyright © 1989 by Fenton Johnson and reprinted by permission of the author.

"Ah Love, Remember Felis," by Olive Ghiselin, first appeared in the *Western Humanities Review.* Copyright © 1988 by Olive Ghiselin and reprinted by permission of the author.

"Wickedness," by Ron Hansen, first appeared in *Sonora Review.* It was subsequently published in the book *Nebraska.* Copyright © 1989 by Ron Hansen. Used by permission of the Atlantic Monthly Press.

"The Golden West Trio Plus One," by David Horgan, first appeared in *Quarterly West.* Copyright © 1988 by David Horgan and reprinted by permission of the author.

"Matchimanito," by Louise Erdrich, appeared in the *Atlantic Monthly.* It is from the novel *Tracks.* Copyright © 1988 by Louise Erdrich. Reprinted by permission of Henry Holt and Company, Inc.

"Dust," by John Bennion, first appeared in *Ascent.* Copyright © 1988 by *Ascent* and reprinted by permission.

"The American Dream: The Book of Boggs," by Gordon Weaver, first appeared in the *Kansas Quarterly.* Copyright © 1988 by Gordon Weaver and reprinted by permission of the author.

"Hermitage," by William Kittredge, appeared in the *South Dakota Review.* Copyright © 1988 by William Kittredge and reprinted by permission of the author.

INTRODUCTION

He flung himself on his horse and rode madly off in all directions," a writer wrote of his confused hero some years ago, and in trying to describe the rich and immense diversity of the stories gathered in this second volume of *The Best of the West,* I find myself, initially, of similar mind. If the region of this country which we call the West is one where a good sense of direction is essential to one's credibility and durability—yes, in the long run still, one's very survival—it is equally true for the author journeying in the territory of the short story: direction is everything. And what you will find in the seventeen stories here is instance after instance of surefootedness and clarity of vision, but greatly varied destinations.

What the stories have in common is that they are all set in the West, were all published in 1988, and were the very best we could find in the 175 periodicals we regularly screen. But what we notice most about them is the very different ways in which they are told. Gordon Weaver's lighthearted and satiric "American Dream: The Book of Boggs" stands in sharp contrast to Ken Smith's grim and brutally realistic "Meat," but they both move with relentless grace to their life-reversing resolutions.

The dark, surrealistic delivery of Charles Frazier's "Licit Pursuits" is, in mood, many miles from the brightness and bounciness of David Horgan's "Golden West Trio Plus One," but both veritably sing in the execution of their prose. Ron Hansen's collage rendition of that most dangerous element, the weather, and its impact on a "civilized" West of a hundred years ago in his story "Wickedness," is wildly different from Rick Bass's look at the defeat of contemporary civilization in the back country of "Choteau," although both are clear in the conclusion they draw: in the West the wisest man is he who takes the least for granted.

Nor should the reader take anything for granted in these stories; while there is much that has not—and will not soon be—changed about the West, these stories, in their own ways, defy assumption and deny stereotype. Fenton Johnson's "Cowboys" do not ride the range, but neither are they the dime-store drag queens we begin to suspect they are; and the Native Americans in Ann Cummins's "Bitterwater," Jim Harrison's "How It Happened To Me," and Louise Erdrich's "Matchimanito" are not Indians whose heritage has prepared them—or disprepared them, as another conventional wisdom would have it—for the deleterious effects of white civilization; rather they are individual human beings confronted with particular problems of transition—difficult transitions to be sure, but not confiningly native.

William Kittredge, an articulate spokesman for western writers and whose story "Hermitage" appears here, might have been speaking of the stories in this collection when he said (in *Owning It All*): "Thank God we are mostly free of the so-called 'western,' the official story of the West, which embodied sexist, racist, imperialistic mythology of lawbringing (which is to say conquest) in a comic opera about nonsensical gunfighters and their showdown foolishness. We are starting to experience a wave of stories as various and unique as the lives actually lived in our part of the world, at once shuddering with vitality and so perfectly beautiful, and sometimes terrifying."

The stories here are various and unique, in part because they are about people (not about the West). Their characters have been tempered by their environment, for the better (as we would like to think in "Where You Have Been, Where You Are Going"), or for the worse (as would seem the case in John Bennion's "Dust")—but it is to the individual lives that we as readers pay attention. And we look in those lives for evidence, even proof, of the old notion that a single well-wrought fiction can speak more forcefully of human realities, human nature, and human values than does the simple "truth" of our own isolated real experience.

But if location of a story is secondary to the characters who people it, it is also true that setting can be a good deal more than simply a place for something to happen. Olive Ghiselin, in her lovely story "Ah Love, Remember Felis," finds locale to be a way of expanding, not limiting, a story. "Writers write about the world they know," she says, "but hope to bring to life a world that everyone will recognize as real. Their hero may wear boots and a wide-brimmed hat but be appreciated for what he is by a lady reader in a sari or miniskirt. A trip down the Colorado may be more, to a writer and reader, than an adventure through transitory rapids. When Joseph Conrad wrote about the Congo, he was writing about the vast geography of the human soul. My story is overtly western in fauna and flora . . . but I hope my central character, avowedly a westerner, is perceived as generic in her humanity."

Geography is indeed relative, and the West—like the Congo—has been for many readers, including many who live there, as much an imaginary place as a real one. This has made the western storyteller's job more difficult. The notion that westerners are all tough and flinty and self-sufficient is a product of that imagination, for instance—and on its face obviously false—yet only writers as skilled as Gladys Swan and Jim Finley could persuade us and move us with the extremely poignant human dependency we encounter in her "Lucinda" and his "Leaving on the Wind."

And still we encounter those "tough" characters also. Tom McNeal, whose "Goodnight, Nebraska" is one of those fictions, says that "the West is the ideal place for seat-of-the-pants characters to set up shop. They're given more room to set their own standards, make up their own rules. These are the characters who in both fiction and real life have the capacity to grab you by the shirt, pick you up off the ground, and put you back down in a different place."

The West is, in fact, relative as a geographical region in part because of our enduring perception of it as "new" or young, although even as we say it we instantly think of the old. That the two contrary images can somehow so easily coexist, like a lake on a desert, perhaps accounts for the fact that almost universally we think of the West as exciting.

Thus the imaginary West and real West, the new West and the old, all converge in these stories: the best of the West. And both individually and as a group, they do what fiction does best, they lead us to the truth, which it pleases me to rediscover and note, is a direction—a direction and destination these stories do have in common, despite their very exciting variety.

And so it goes, from story to story in this volume: our own imaginary West projected on the screen of our mind as we read related narratives about people who confirm what we know about life, but not necessarily life as we had it pictured. This is, of course, the trick of all good fiction: to both reinforce our expectations and surprise us with new information, new understanding—constantly and simultaneously.

James Thomas

KEN SMITH

MEAT

John Edward Walker was sitting over his second cup of coffee when he heard the rifle reports. With the windows closed against the cold wind, the sounds came to him only faintly, so he wasn't certain of what he was hearing until the third or fourth shot. He had overslept and had awakened with a bloated stomach that caused him so much pain he cried out in the still house. He was seventy-two years old, and he had been born in this ranch house and had lived in it all his life, alone the past six years. Whenever he thought of Martha, he was surprised, again, that she had been gone so long.

First thing this morning he had walked out to feed the horse kept in the corral overnight, hoping the activity would loosen him up. But later he had spent so much time in the bathroom that he'd let the coffee perk too long, and it was strong and bitter. He knew that whatever men were firing upcountry were up to no good—here in the middle of January—unless they were bear hunters. But bear hunters would have stopped by his place, wanting to know where he'd last seen track or sign.

If I was any good anymore, he told himself, I'd get my rifle and go see about this. But he was cold and his guts churned and growled and threatened to grow beyond the boundaries of his skin and burst, like the stomach of a cow that had eaten dewy alfalfa. At that moment all he wanted to do was sit and wait for his coffee to cool.

Four days ago, along the highway to Young, he had found signs that someone had killed and butchered one of his yearlings. They had worked right from the road, and at night. This made the third cow he'd lost this way in the past few months, and he had taken a few minutes to look over the hide and head, discarded near the pile of viscera, not forty yards from the road. He studied the tire tracks where a vehicle had pulled off the hard-packed surface. He found the tracks of three men, a cigarette butt, and two shell casings from a 30-06. They weren't too particular, he thought. And not very damned skittish about getting caught.

Walker called the sheriff again, just as he had after the first two killings. The same young deputy came out. He stood around for a while and then picked up the cigarette butt and the shell casings and shook his head.

"It's the damned strikes," he said.

Walker nodded. He knew the copper mines in all the little towns around had been out on strike for a long time, some as long as eight months.

"I'm sorry, Mr. Walker, but we can't watch everybody's cows twenty-four hours a day." The deputy gazed down the embankment at the pile of hide and guts. "Sheriff's going to hire a couple more men, and we'll pick up our patrols along some of these out-of-the-way places."

"Yeah," Walker had said. Then he had climbed into his pickup and driven off, leaving the deputy standing by the side of the road.

The coffee, cool enough to drink now, tasted good to John Walker, despite its bitterness. He wondered if the shots he'd heard earlier could have been aimed at his cattle, but he couldn't believe that men would do such work by daylight. He sipped his coffee and waited, his eyes watering against the pain in his gut and his ears as alert as he could get them for the sounds of more gunfire.

Fifty years ago the Walkers had caught two rustlers, men from up north of the Sierra Ancha, where that sort of thing went on all the time. John Edward and his brothers, Vince and Tom, had found a hole cut in the north boundary fence. He and Vince started trailing what looked to be about a dozen head of cattle and two horsemen, while Tom rode downcountry to where Grandfather and Father were branding.

The trail was easy to follow, but he and Vince rode slowly, waiting for the others. In an hour or so, when the older men and Tom caught up to them, Grandfather said, "Why, that trail's plain as your nose. Why aren't you boys spurring those horses?" Neither Vince nor John Edward had known how to answer so they just looked at Grandfather and he back at them, until finally he kicked his horse out ahead of all the rest, shouting, "Come on now, let's go get the thieving sons-a-bitches."

They came upon the rustlers' camp early that evening. They had spotted smoke a mile before, and they had come in quietly and looked things over. The camp was in a long, low saddle, the two men working over a cook fire, and the cattle—eleven long-yearling heifers that Grandfather was planning to keep as breeding stock—grazing nonchalantly through high grama grass inside a rope pen.

It was fall, the start of roundup, and Grandfather decided that with the oak leaves already fallen, they wouldn't be able to sneak up to the camp on foot.

"We'll go in fast," he told the others. "Fast and hollering and with our handguns out . . ."

"No," Father said. "Let's try just one rifle shot from out here, Dad. That's all it should take."

The old man looked at his son. John Edward sat on his horse nervously, waiting for the older men to decide on a strategy. He wondered how tough the rustlers might be, whether they'd put up a fight. He touched the wooden grip of his handgun. He was dry-mouthed, wanting everything to go along smoothly and hoping nobody was going to get killed.

In a few seconds the old man said, "Okay, but be ready to get in there fast if things don't go right." He lifted the Winchester from his saddle scabbard and, still sitting astride his horse, fired once into the rustlers' fire pit.

The men jumped up and whirled around, confused and wondering where the shot had come from. Grandfather chambered another cartridge and was getting ready to shoot again when father said, "Hold it, Dad. I think that's all we need."

But the old man fired once more, and John Edward heard the bullet singing off into the still evening air.

Father spurred his horse through the brush so that he was on the open hillside, above the camp and in clear sight of the rustlers. They were standing on opposite sides of the fire now, their empty hands held up and away from their bodies. Father yelled, "We're Walkers, up from the Tonto, and you'll be okay if you don't get stupid."

The two rustlers stood perfectly still while the five Walker horsemen rode down into their camp.

Grandfather looked at the men, the camp, and the cattle. He took his pistol out and leaned over toward the two men near the fire. "I don't believe you can show me a bill of sale," he said.

John Edward studied the two young faces, with dusk just coming on and the firelight and dying sun fighting over how the shadows would fall. One of the men started to say something but then thought better of it. Finally the other one said, "What you aim to do, Mr. Walker?"

Grandfather didn't answer. He tied the rustlers back-to-back in a position that looked like torture, and the Walkers took turns standing guard through the night. The next morning all seven men drove the yearlings back to Walker range, right through the hole the rustlers had cut in the barbed-wire fence. Once on Walker land, Grandfather told the rustlers to dismount.

"Get their horses," Grandfather said, and Vince and John Edward eased over to take the reins. Now, fifty years later, John Edward could still remember the look on the man's face as he handed over his horse, a look that both questioned and didn't want to know. The man pleaded without speaking. To John Edward his eyes said, *I know I'm in the wrong, but I'm young, like you and your brothers.*

Grandfather threw his bad leg over his saddle horn and said to the rustlers, "Get to work on that fence." He took his hat off and the breeze lifted strands of his gray hair. The rustlers worked, and the only words spoken were Grandfather's, when he said once, "I want it tight, now—tight as it was before." When the fence was mended, Grandfather rode over to the horse John Edward was holding and said, "Keep him steady." Then he leaned down with his knife and sliced through both back and front cinches, so that when he gave the saddle a little push, it slid off. The horse sidestepped and turned to look. Grandfather did the same with the horse Vince was holding. Then he rode over to each saddle, leaned way over on the big bay, and picked each one up by the horn. He pitched them over the fence and into the brush on the other side.

That done, Grandfather faced the two rustlers straight on. "Your horses aren't much," he said, "but they'll go a ways toward paying for the time you've cost us." He paused for a long while, looking down at the two men. Neither would meet his gaze. Grandfather straightened in his saddle and looked toward the north. "Your saddles are on the other side of my fence," he said finally. "I'd just as soon you was over there too."

Neither man moved. They looked up into the faces of the riders as if they weren't understanding something about all this.

Grandfather nudged his horse a few steps closer to the rustlers. "Get," he said. "Go on now." And when he started to uncoil his catch rope, the two men turned and ran, going flat on their bellies and eating dust as they crawled under the wire they had first cut and then mended.

One man lost his hat going under the fence, and the breeze blew it back onto Walker range. He stopped just the other side of the fence, stood up, and looked at his hat on the ground. Then he looked up at Grandfather, sitting tall on the bay horse and playing with his rope. A faint smile came to the rustler's face.

The moment always came back to John Edward whole and clear: his grandfather, who had recovered his cattle and not hurt anybody much in the doing, looking across the fence at a man who had for the past few hours thought he was going to be shot, a young man defeated but not shamed, who suddenly felt alive enough to want his hat.

John Edward got off his horse and picked up the hat. He carried it to the fence. Standing there, studying the man and feeling the weight of the others behind him, he felt awkward, as if he should say something, some last word. He thought about sailing the hat off into the brush or throwing it just right, so that it would land at the man's feet. Instead, he handed it across the fence, and the man came a couple of steps forward to take it.

Walker was in the kitchen, trying to decide whether to make biscuits, when he heard a vehicle pull up. He pushed open the curtain by the sink and saw a pickup and two men, who got out, both looking around curiously. One man was very tall. He slouched as he walked around the yard, looking from the truck to the house. The other was shorter, more compact, and harder looking.

Both men looked cold. The smaller one crossed his arms and hugged himself. Walker bent at the window for a minute and watched them talk. Then he let go of the curtain and went through the front room to the door.

Outside, the first thought that hit him was that it was going to snow. The cold on his skin was just the right kind, and the breeze he had felt earlier had died. He looked up at the clouds, low and still. Then he looked again at the men in the yard. He could see now that the shorter man was Mexican.

Coming down the steps he had to hold the banister and watch his footing. One of the men shouted a hello, and Walker looked up, but the way his ears had gotten, he couldn't tell which man had spoken. They were both smiling. He stopped halfway down the porch steps. "Cold morning, ain't it?"

The men nodded. He looked them over closely again. They were young men. Forty, or maybe just shy of that. He asked, "Was that you fellas doing the shooting?"

The men stared at him and then at each other. The smaller man, the one who looked Mexican, said, "Yes, it was us."

"Thought so," Walker said. "You get what you was after?"

The tall man took a step forward. He stuffed his hands deep into his coat pockets and rocked back on his heels. "You a game warden or something?" he asked.

Walker felt like laughing. He shook his head. "Not just no," he said, "but hell, no."

He had expected the men to smile but they did not. There was a tenseness in the face of the larger man, a dark cast to his eyes, that Walker did not like.

"I'm surprised you'd find deer down this low," he said. "I would've thought they'd still be holing up around the base of that rimrock."

"One old doe," the taller man said. "Couldn't stand the cold, I guess."

Walker smiled. "Coffee's on and hot," he told the men. "I'm not promising anything for taste, but it'll be warm going down."

Inside he sat them at the table and then poured coffee all around. The men took off their heavy coats and were rubbing themselves against the cold. The tall one looked around the kitchen and craned his neck as if he was trying to see other parts of the house.

"Don't keep the place up much," Walker said. "Been like this since I lost my wife."

Neither man said anything, and Walker looked the kitchen over, wanting to see it as if he, too, were a stranger. It was fairly clean but cluttered. The living room was worse—magazines scattered about on the tables Martha used to keep so nice with lace doilies and vases and sometimes even flowers. For a long time after she died, he had been bothered by the way his bed smelled. Somehow it never seemed clean, though he washed the sheets often and dried them on the permanent-press cycle, as she used to. She had been proud of the washer and dryer, and even though they'd spent a lot of money for the larger generator, he was glad that in her later years she had had them. He had thought hard, trying to remember exactly all she did when washing, and then he remembered the funny little pieces of papery cloth she would throw in the dryer with each load. The next time in town he bought Bounce, then he tried Downy, then another brand and another, until he realized that what he had missed smelling was not these things but simply Martha's scent. It was a dried-out smell, something like a mixture of white flour and sage. After that he didn't use the dryer anymore but hung the sheets on the line that stretched from the back of the house to the tack room.

"Coffee sure is good," one of the men said.

Walker turned quickly, flustered because he didn't know which of them had spoken. His stomach knotted and turned over on itself. He wanted to go into the bathroom, but he didn't want to leave these strangers sitting at his table.

He smiled at the men and chided himself about his nerves. Then he said, "Hell, I'm forgetting my manners." He stuck his hand across the table toward the smaller man. "Name's Walker," he said. "Front name's John."

He shook hands with both men and listened as they told him their names. Willy was the small, Mexican-looking man. The tall man's name was Arnold. He didn't catch their last name, but he was surprised that it was the same, an odd-sounding name like Gait or Gain. He asked them to repeat it, but still did not quite catch the sound. "Brothers?" he asked.

"Cousins," Willy said. "My mom's Mexican. Our dads are brothers."

Walker poured them more coffee. Knowing their names made him feel better, and he tried to relax and enjoy their company—the first he'd had in several weeks—but Arnold bothered him. He'd sip his coffee and slide his eyes around and talk to you without looking at your face.

Willy seemed more friendly. He said he'd always wanted to be a cowboy and he asked questions about the ranch and the Walker family. He seemed surprised when John Walker told them he'd been born in this house.

"All the rest have gone away," he told them. And he thought for a moment about his brothers: about Tom, the youngest, who had died in the first minutes of the Normandy invasion; about Vince, closer to him in age, who now lived in a rest home in Casa Grande.

"Yes," he said, "been here all my life." Somehow the words made him proud and sad at the same time. He pointed back along the narrow hallway. "Born in that least little room in the back, when the house was smaller and the range bigger. But lots of it's been chopped up and sold and some just plain give away, so I run only a couple hundred head now." He laughed and shook his head. "Even a small herd is work, though—most days plenty for me."

Willy smiled and nodded. His eyes looked kind. "Yes, Mr. Walker," he said, "I guess you've had your share of hard work."

"But you always got meat," Arnold said. He leaned his elbows on the table, looking hard at his cousin.

Walker rocked back slightly in his chair and studied the man. Suddenly he realized that this was a man who would steal and kill his cattle. If he wasn't the man who had done it already, he was a man capable of such things.

Willy said, "It's nice being a boss, I guess. Something appealing about that. Arnold and me have always worked for someone else." He looked down at his coffee cup. "Oh, I'm not complaining. I'm a machinist . . . well, *was* a machinist."

The men were silent for a moment, and then Walker asked how long they'd been out on strike.

"Too damn long," Arnold said.

Walker clicked his tongue in sympathy. He watched Willy light a cigarette. "Yep, it's hell," he said. "A man's got to have work."

"Money," Arnold said. For a long time he stared right at Walker. "You don't need work, you need cash."

Walker's face went cold. Arnold's eyes were bright and round. Walker looked at them until he had to look away. "Same thing to most of us," he said, his voice sounding low and distant.

"Meat," Arnold said. "That's what we came after."

• • •

Walker brewed another pot of coffee. Then he excused himself and went to the toilet. On his way through the bedroom, he eyed the .30-30 leaning in the corner by his bed. You could pick that up and go run them off, he told himself. But what would be the reason? You can't just say, holding men at gunpoint, that they make you nervous and you want them to get. He wished he still had a pistol, but he had never been any good with a handgun, and when the one Vince left began to shave lead, he had taken it to a gun shop and traded it for all the .30-.30 shells he would probably ever need.

When he returned to the cousins at his table, a bottle of whiskey was sitting near his cup. Arnold smiled and said, "Sit down, have a little of that for what ails you."

Since Vince had gone to the rest home, Walker did not keep whiskey on his place. It seemed to him a dangerous thing, especially for a man alone, a man who might use it too much against his many aches and pains, against the cold, against his loneliness.

The smell of it rose strong into his nostrils, the way it had when he was younger and would take a shot with Vince now and then.

He sat down. Under the table his legs began to tremble. Arnold reached over for the whiskey bottle and poured a little of it into Walker's empty cup. "There you go, old-timer," he said.

Walker looked at the brown whiskey and then at Arnold. "I don't like liquor on my place," he said.

Willy started to say something, but Arnold interrupted. "Ah, Mr. Walker," he said, "we didn't know, besides everything else, you were a preacher, too."

"I'm not a preacher."

Walker slid his foot against the table leg to keep it still. He looked at Arnold and then at Willy. Their faces seemed new to him, as if other men had replaced them at his table. He stared at Arnold, vowing to make the big man, this time, avert his gaze first. Arnold's eyes cut away for a second and then came back larger. Walker had been hit by men before, and the look he saw now told him that Arnold was building himself up to that. He wished again that he still had Vince's pistol, something small but powerful that he could put into his pocket.

"I'm not a drinking man," he said. "I just don't hold with it."

Arnold reached over and flicked his cousin's arm with the back of his hand. He laughed lightly, without opening his mouth. "I think this old man's trying to insult us, Willy."

Willy looked at Walker and then down at the table. Arnold said, "You shouldn't do that, mister. You shouldn't bring us into your house and then treat us like trash."

Walker was pushing himself up out of his chair when Arnold reached across and shoved him hard. He went back over his chair and hit the floor. He could hear Willy talking fast, but he was concentrating so hard on getting up that he couldn't make out the words.

Then Arnold helped him up, saying something about being careful, about staying still.

Walker lunged, trying to grab anything he could, thinking only that he would be all right if he could get this big man down.

Then he was on the floor again, his jaw hurting. He saw only the old wood and the legs of the table and chairs. His glasses had come off and his vision tunneled, but inside the tunnel he could see fine.

He sat up and shook his head. The room went dark, as if thick clouds had suddenly come over the sun. Arms began tugging at him, and someone hit him hard on the mouth.

He heard Willy say, "Jesus, don't kill the old bastard." It sickened and enraged him that Willy would call him such a thing.

When his head began to clear, he found himself tied into a chair. He could move his hands enough to touch the crosspieces beneath the seat. He heard his truck start, and he pushed with his feet, trying to move the chair.

It tipped over. Lying on his left side, still attached to the chair, he kicked his feet and pushed against something so that he scooted a ways. He lay on the floor and tried to think. He kept telling himself that he wasn't helpless so long as he could think.

His arms ached, but the rest of him seemed fine. His face no longer hurt, and this both surprised and calmed him. He breathed deeply but easily. He kicked again and moved without much trouble. He kicked more and rolled over as far as he could on his right side, and he was suddenly looking out his front door, across the porch to the yard.

Snow was beginning to fall. His pickup was backed up to the stock pens, and the men had loaded the steer he had been keeping up to fatten. He watched Willy get in and drive the truck out of sight. Walker figured they were taking the steer over to the A-frame he had built and rigged with heavy block and tackle.

The wind coming in the open door was cold on his face. He lay listening, and the sounds—the truck gears grinding when Willy put it in reverse, the clinking of the chains as they lowered the hook, the shot as one of them killed his steer—told him what the men were doing. He closed his eyes and imagined he could see them as they worked to skin and butcher. At times he heard them talking, or thought he did—he couldn't be sure. When he opened his eyes, he could see through the light snow the road that came off the cholla flat and dropped down into the creekbed to wind its way to his house.

For a few moments he lay and looked and tried to remind himself to keep thinking. Then he saw them. Down the red-clay road came vans and pickups and cars, filled with hungry people wanting meat. They came with their children, their old mothers. They had been out of work for years and their clothes were thin and patched. They were skinny and cold and they were coming by the hundreds to kill and eat his cattle. He knew he could stand with his rifle and kill them as they came, but they would keep coming. He knew an old man could do nothing to stop them once they started. He owned his house and his land and his cattle, but these people owned something more valuable.

Following the vehicles came people walking. Young men taking long steps, carrying skinning knives and hatchets and meat saws. Women with baskets and cheesecloth. And then he was back in his house, aware only of the hard wood of the floor pressing against his shoulder and face.

Walker closed his eyes again, and when he opened them he saw Arnold going across the yard with two large metal washtubs. In a while the tall man went to the pickup they had come in, reached into the bed, and pulled out a tarp. Then he came back and drove the pickup away. Walker guessed they were finished with the butchering and were now loading the meat.

He heard their pickup start again. He pulled hard at the ropes around his hands. Before when he had done this, he had felt the ropes cut into his wrists, but by now his arms and hands were so numb that he could feel nothing. He jerked at the ropes, moving his arms first to one side and then the other. The ropes began to loosen. He wriggled his fingers until some of the feeling returned. Then he found the knots and turned his hands over, straining to make his fingers feel the knots and untie them.

When he was free, he stood and watched the men's truck go out of sight along the creek. He heard the engine lug and then the gears shift, and he knew they were beginning the climb out of the creek. He went quickly to his bedroom, grabbed the .30-30, and took it out onto the porch. The snow was heavier now, but he could see the truck's outline as it made its way up the steep road toward the cholla flat. He laid the rifle across the porch railing and knelt down. His hands were cold and sore.

Wind gusted snowflakes into his face, but by squinting he could focus well enough to get his aim. Through the falling snow the truck stood out dark green, deep in the notch of the rifle's rear sight. For a few seconds John Edward felt content simply to watch. They were still within easy range, the hill was long and steep, and he had plenty of time to get off three or four shots. Maybe more.

Then the back of the truck began sliding to its left on the wet clay. When it was nearly off the road, whoever was driving stopped and the other man got out and came around to climb on the rear bumper. John Edward heard the gunning of the engine and saw the man on the back of the truck jumping up and down, trying to help the tires get traction.

He guessed that Willy was on the back, that Arnold was driving. How easy, he thought, to kill these men. They had already forgotten about him. They had no idea he was free and kneeling there with the rifle, the butt of it pulled hard into his shoulder. He looked through his sights at the man he thought was Willy. The tires caught and the truck gave a sudden lurch, and the man on the back almost fell. Walker felt himself tense, bracing as if he too were falling.

"Hold on," he said to himself. "God damn it, just hold on."

In a few seconds he heard the cousins whooping in triumph as the truck eased on up the hill. How easy, he thought, to let them go, to allow them to sit tonight with their grateful wives and children in a warm kitchen, the air dense with the smell of cooking beef.

He lifted the rifle from the rail and sat back on the floorboards of the porch, the rifle across his lap. Trying to uncock it, his hands thick and tingling, he let the hammer slip, and the rifle discharged. The bullet splintered into a post at the far end of the porch.

Walker sat still. The pickup had by now climbed out of sight. He figured the men would be speeding along, snow falling all around them, the pickup's heater warming the cab. He wondered what they would be talking about.

In a few minutes he felt steady enough to eject the spent shell from his rifle and let the hammer down slowly to the safety notch. He pushed himself up and walked to the end of the porch. From there he could see the A-frame where the men had butchered his steer. Half of the carcass still hung from the heavy chain. He looked at it a long time, realizing it would be more than enough beef to see him through the winter. And after that, he told himself, who knows? He pulled out his handkerchief and wiped the rifle where snowflakes had melted and spotted the steel. The beef carcass swung slowly in the breeze. Snow was beginning to stick to the upper parts of the shoulder. He rubbed his eyes and then his arms. Had anyone else been there, he might have laughed.

"They come and rob you, and you shoot up your own place," he said. "You're a dangerous old man, John Edward." His voice faded into the snowy air. He bent low and stuck his little finger into the bullet hole in his post, surveying the damage.

ANN CUMMINS

BITTERWATER

I'm not the sort of person who takes satisfaction in being scared to death. Some like it. They'll go to horror films for pleasure. I can't understand that. I've walked out of nearly every horror film I've gone to. My dad says life is scary enough; he tells war stories about being an Air Force navigator in World War II, how nothing you can imagine actually feels like being up in the air—no boundaries but air, and the bullets coming at you are real. But after I lived a bit with Manny, I thought he *could* imagine it and better. Maybe he had something wrong with him. He was always on edge, like his whole person was this fighter plane with air boundaries and the bullets coming at him were real.

I married Manny when I was eighteen, and it broke my dad's heart. Manny got in my head right away, from practically the first minute my family moved to the Navajo Reservation. I was thirteen. A bunch of us would play softball next to the mining-company housing project. My dad was foreman at the mill where they processed uranium ore. The company mined uranium all over the reservation. Manny wasn't a company kid, but he'd come over anyway with his friends. Manny pitched. I would come up to bat, and Manny would stand on the mound chewing gum, singing crazy country-and-Western songs—"Might as well go to Tennessee," he'd say—and not throw the ball until I was rolling on the ground. Manny could make me laugh.

"It's strike two hundred and three," he'd say. He kept count of all the strikes he'd ever gotten on me.

"You cheat," I'd say.

Manny would walk right up to me in the batter's box. He'd say, "I'm hurt now. You have hurt me very bad, and you have hurt my ancestors. Do you know who my ancestors are?" Manny was Todacheene clan, which means Bitterwater. He told me Manuelito was Bitterwater, too, and that Manuelito was the last great Navajo chief, and that he, Manny, had been named for Manuelito—he had a great chief in his background, and now a great chief's feelings were hurt. "The only thing to do," he would say, "is to get some money from your dad so we can go get a hamburger."

My dad would never give me more than enough for one hamburger. He'd say, "That boy's got money. The government gives them money."

Manny would say to me, "That's all right. You buy the one, and you can watch me eat."

Watching Manny eat was a thing. This was a wide, pancake-sized hamburger—a skinny sliver of gray meat with two tiny dots of pickle and a squirt of mustard packed between two fat buns. I mean, a reservation hamburger is mostly bread. But watching Manny eat—He's got these magic fingers that would lace together over the top of bread like they were comfortable there. He's got his elbows propped on the table and a loose hug on this hamburger, and he looks happy—a boy with an appetite and the time to enjoy it. The way he watched me over that bread—and talked non-stop—and sort of just chewed at the same time, and smiled, and never offered me a bite. The way his jaw worked, man-sized muscles popping near his ears—some secret jaw action communicating something to the brain, and from the look in his eyes it could've been something dirty, like that meat was an illegal thing. I mean, he knew how to get a girl's attention.

One night he called me on the phone. "Hey, Brenda, you know who this is?"

"Yeah, I know who this is."

"This is Manuelito, in case you don't know."

"I already know," I said.

He wanted to know what I was doing, and then he wanted to know what my dad was doing.

What my dad was doing was being a stone in his chair. My mother had been asking him her favorite question. "Do I get a vote at all," she'd want to know, "or am I just here as part of the scenery?" The stone would ask my mother why she always had to have the upper hand. "Look at me," my mother would say. "I'm a tree."

"You don't listen," my father would say.

I told Manny my father was being a talking stone.

Manny asked me if he had a liquor cabinet.

That night was the first time Manny and I broke into my dad's liquor cabinet. What I did was sneak him into the garage. My dad had converted a quarter of the garage into a playroom. I sneaked Manny in when everybody else was asleep, and we listened to KWYK, and drank, and sort of played on the couch.

"Nobody knows I'm here," he said. "We won't get caught." He sang along with the radio—"Don't let me cross over love's cheating line"—and I'm laughing, you know, and Manny is trying to find his way through my clothes, and what are you going to do? He had this way of getting around me.

But then once my dad walked in on us—I guess maybe I didn't have a shirt on—and Dad was pale, like he was seeing a ghost, and he kicked Manny out and told me I was grounded for the rest of my life. Manny wasn't afraid of my dad. He joked when he left, and my dad heard it—"Hey, Brenda, if you ever get off the ground again, come on over."

• • •

When I married Manny, I figured my dad would come around sooner or later. Eventually he did, and he gave Manny a job at the mill. Manny worked the graveyard shift, eleven to seven. Dad said that after he proved himself he could work days. Manny said he didn't mind the grave. Dad said Manny had an attitude problem. I told Dad that he said things like that as a joke. Dad told me to tell Manny that he better not find him drinking up there.

Manny may not have minded the graveyard shift, but he minded graveyards, real graveyards. That was one thing Manny was afraid of. Like a kid, he'd spook himself about graveyards, and I liked to tease him on this—just to goad him a little, since he always thought he was such a man—and told him graveyard stories just so he wouldn't look me in the eye. When I was a kid, right after we moved to the reservation, I was on the bluffs with some others and we found this old graveyard and went in. We were walking around in there and my foot fell in. The ground was rotten, and my foot fell in one of the graves. I told Manny this story and pretended that my foot actually touched a casket. Then I asked him if he wanted to see where that graveyard was, and I was surprised, because he said he did.

It was pretty run down and fenced off, but you could lift the barbed wire and climb in. It was cold that day—November, I think—and the sand was blowing, that fine grit that gets between your teeth. The Navajo graveyards are unkempt places, full of tumbleweed. There were no headstones but wooden crosses here and there, and in two or three places plastic flowers. I didn't think anybody was buried there anymore. You couldn't tell who had been buried there, because there were no names on the crosses. When we were kids, we joked about robbing those graves—we played cops and robbers on the bluffs—and we believed that if anyone actually did rob an Indian grave he would get something. They usually buried people with all their wealth—jewelry and blankets, and so on. But stepping in that one grave really did scare me. "I thought I touched bone," I told Manny the day we went up there. I hadn't been up there since I was thirteen.

"You could have broken a leg," he said.

"I know it."

"You ever see those old Navajo women that limp around?" he said. "My grandmother limps. Some say it's because they used to break a girl's hip when she was a baby so that no one could sell her as a servant to the Spanish later on."

"That's cruel, that they could break a baby's hip," I said.

"It was cruel," he said. "I don't know who came up with that idea. I hate it that they broke my grandmother's hip. But I would break yours."

"Sure."

"Why don't you run across that graveyard for me?"

"You're crazy," I said.

Manny put his boot on one strand of the barbed-wire fence. He pulled another up with his hands, making a gap big enough for a person to enter.

"You want to," he said. Manny wasn't teasing. He was like that. One minute he was joking around, the next this stranger. His face was pasty, almost white, like he had painted it.

"I don't want to," I said.

He said, "Run across the fucking graveyard, or I'll break your fucking hip."

You know, there's no place else to go, really, up there. It's just a row of bluffs, sand pile after sand pile, maybe a child on a horse and the child's sheepdogs, which will tear you limb from limb. Up on the bluffs there's no place, really, to go.

"It's just a game," he said, and didn't care that I didn't want to but pushed me through the barbed wire, and a barb ripped my arm.

Once, when we were making love, Manny stopped and said, "You know, I could take your clothes and put you outside, and then everybody would see you. You want everybody to see you?"

I felt so cold when he said that. I didn't want him to touch me anymore, and I pushed him away and said I didn't want to finish it. Manny thought this was hilarious. He lay on his back and laughed at the ceiling until I tried to choke him, and he thought that was even funnier, and I laughed right back until I was almost dead with screaming at him.

That day on the bluffs I felt as though he'd put me naked on the other side of the door. I was afraid of him that day, so all I wanted to do was turn around, walk through the barbed wire, through him, through the whole damn reservation, but he twisted me around and whispered, "Run or I'll break your fucking hip."

I walked. Manny yelled, "Do I have to come in there?" and then I couldn't move. Manny yelled, "Jump." I'm standing in the middle of this graveyard. My husband is telling me to jump up and down. He says he wants to see if I'll fall through.

I sat down, right there in the middle of that graveyard. I knew that he wouldn't come in after me. I knew that Manny was too afraid of something in there to come after me. I thought I was safe sitting on those Indian graves.

He hated to be alone, so the graveyard shift was a bad idea. I guess he was spoiled in that way. He needed a lot of attention. There was nobody to perform for up there at the mill, in the middle of the night—just the yellowcake roasters, usually, and Manny. He got a little crazy when he had to be alone. Like, he came home from work one morning, put both hands on my face, and said, "Brenda, do you think you're flesh and blood?" I could smell he had been drinking.

I said, "My dad'll fire you if he catches you drinking on the job."

"What do you think is flesh and blood if not you, Brenda?"

I told him I thought he should get a day job. That he wasn't around people enough, the way he had to sleep during the days and didn't talk to anybody at night.

"Oh, I talk," he said. "You know what uranium is?"

I knew what uranium was.

"There's a thousand little bombs going off in those furnaces every night and we have us some discussions. We talk about you, sweetheart. You're the main thing on my mind, you know that?" He hadn't just been drinking, he was drunk. "Of course, they don't listen. Here's how it is." He pulls out a kitchen chair and straddles it. "This is me," he says. He points at himself. "This is Furnace One." He points at his right leg. "Imagine it's a metal box with uranium inside, and the fire's going sixteen hundred degrees," he says. He starts stomping with the foot. "This is Furnace Two." He points at the left leg. "Imagine it's a metal box." He starts stomping with that foot. He's got both feet hammering against the kitchen floor, making a racket. Then he starts speaking in Navajo, looking at the ceiling. There's a lot of noise in that kitchen.

"I listen to you," I yell at him. "Who else am I going to listen to? You want all the goddam attention."

He said, "Let's go to bed."

I told him I didn't want to.

He told me a man needed sex. But I didn't want to.

He got like that. But, too, he was a charmer. You have to love a man like that and mostly not mind his moods. When we were still kids, just married, Manny came home from work one morning with a pink bird under his arm—one of those plastic things you see in people's yards—and I had seen this particular plastic bird in the high-school principal's yard forever. Manny had stolen it on his way home from work. He put it in the middle of the kitchen table, and the bird had breakfast with us. Manny said, "Baby, I brought you the stork."

I said, "Manny, that's a pelican."

He said, "It is? I thought it was a stork."

I said, "You better get off this reservation so you can figure out the difference between a pelican and a stork. You better got to a zoo somewhere."

He said, "How are we going to have a baby if this is a pelican?"

I said, "You're my entertainment committee, you know that?"

He said, "Brenda, this is a flamingo."

Well, as soon as he said it I knew that's what it was, and felt a little stupid, and mad at him—at how he was always just playing me—and wouldn't have talked to him all the rest of that morning, but then he comes over and squats in front of me. He puts his elbows on his knees and holds his face like a little boy. He says that maybe we should pawn that flamingo and get a stork, so we could have a baby, and I said, "O.K. by me."

Except when he was drinking, just about anything Manny said was O.K. by me. Not that I'd let him know this. I'm not just a go-along sort of person. What I believe in is timing. I mean, you keep a guy guessing, but the timing has got to be right. This once—we'd been on the reservation a year or so and I thought Manny was starting to like me. I decided to test him. I was supposed to meet him in my front yard, and we were going to get up a game of softball. He was late. I knew he'd expect me to be waiting. What I did was just put the ball in the yard, then I ran in the house. This was so I could see his face when he came to meet me. You know if you're getting to a guy depending on how his face looks when he's expecting to find you someplace but you're not there. I hid behind the curtains in our front room, and after a while Manny shows up. The ball is in the middle of the front lawn. He stands over that ball, then stoops down, picks it up, starts tossing it up, catching it. And he walks off. Like he's found a prize, like that ball was all he was after in the first place. He never glanced at the house.

I figured my timing was off. He didn't like me well enough yet to miss me. And after he left me for good, I figured my timing had been off the whole time I knew Manny and maybe there wasn't such a thing as timing at all.

Manny came home one morning carrying a foreman's white hard hat under his arm. I said, "You get a promotion?"

He said my dad had been for a 3 A.M. visit to the roaster room at the mill and forgot his hat when he left. Manny also said that he thought a man should spend a lot of time with his wife, and from here on we would be spending a lot of time together. Then he went and hung the hard hat on a peg in the living room.

Manny stayed home nights after my dad caught him drinking at the mill. He didn't sleep. He said he couldn't shake that nightshift habit, but I think it was the liquor, the way it keeps you awake. He'd want me to stay up with him to keep him company. "We'll sleep during the day," he'd say. I tried to, but I'm a night sleeper, and anyway Manny didn't sleep day or night. He didn't sleep. I told him I needed to sleep. "Then fucking sleep!" he'd yell, and he'd leave, sometimes for weeks. I'd have nightmares of him splattered on some highway, drunk in front of some off-reservation bar.

One night, I woke up and Manny was sitting by the side of my bed. He'd been gone maybe a month, and at first I was glad to see him, but then I notice he's weird. He's talking to me about the Navajos in the Second World War, how they used Navajo for a code language, and after a while he isn't making any sense. "And Brenda, them Nazis couldn't break it, because it wasn't written—how about that? We never thought to write it down, and my cousin Mae went to Deermont and she said there were no boys—how about that—but she liked it anyway and never came home to the reservation. She went to Paris or Spain drinking tequila—Indians shouldn't drink, Brenda, like your dad says, because we have type-A blood and you have type B. . . ."

I mean, it was weird waking up to his talk, and his eyes were dead—they didn't see me. I didn't think he knew me. I screamed over his gibberish, "Manny, Manny, Manny—Manuelito!"

"Was a drunk," he said. He laughed.

I said, "Manny, why do you drink?"

He said, "To get drunk."

I left the bedroom. He yelled after me, "And I don't want to be talked out of it."

I went to the kitchen to make coffee. In the kitchen I found a puddle on the floor. It was urine. Manny came into the kitchen. He stared at the puddle on the floor, and then at me, foolishly, with a little smile. He said, "I don't think I'm responsible for that."

My heart was cold. You don't ever really know a person, and maybe it's just those childhood games that make you think you do—you try to remember how he used to look, but all you know is how he looks when he drinks. It's not like a country song. It's not the good and then the bad, and how it gives you a reason to sing. It's that you don't know a person. He was a goddam drunk and I was a goddam drunk's wife and it was just piss on the floor.

• • •

He left that night for good, and good riddance is what I said to him. But he was in my head. Like a bad dream, but worse, because I was nothing but scared most of the time living with Manny. Still, after he left I didn't think about how scared he could make me. I'd just think about him—how he stole the stork that time, how he could make me laugh. And that's a bad dream, when you know good and well somebody's a drunk. I guess I never thought Manny would leave me for good. I'd watch for him sometimes, at night when I couldn't sleep. I'd go sit with the plastic pink stork that I kept in the living room, just like it was a live thing. Funny, huh? With all the lights off, me and this bird; maybe we were watching for a face in the window. Manny said that if a Navajo witch comes for you, you'll see a painted white face in the window; then he said I didn't have to worry, since I wasn't Navajo. Still, I'd watch that window and think how a Navajo skinwalker *could* witch a white. How things get in your head and you can't get them out. You can't sleep for thinking about something.

Then, a couple of days ago, they called me from a detoxification center eighty miles north of the reservation and said the police had picked up Manny. He had to detox for a few days, then he could go, but they wouldn't let him go on his own recognizance, because he was a danger to himself. I said to tell him I wasn't his wife anymore. Then I said never mind, I would do it myself.

There is a women's ward and a men's ward in the center. The walls of both are painted green. The whole place smells of vomit. In each ward there are rows of cots lined up against the walls, and in most beds lumps that are people sleeping, although some of the people are sitting in bed smoking and others are walking around. There is a young, black-haired woman who lies flat on her back and yells to the ceiling, "Put the music on!"

I hear Manny before I see him. When I turn the corner from the women's ward into the men's, he's right there on the cot closest to me, next to the wall. His hair is long, he wears a red bandanna around his forehead, and his pajamas are paisley. He doesn't sound drunk. I can't see his face. He's sitting on his bed, talking to the man next to him. The man is asleep.

Manny is saying, "So they took me to this center for detoxification, and I told them I'm no ordinary drunk Indian. I'm Todacheene, man. Bitterwater. And that don't mean whiskey, neither. Manuelito was Bitterwater. So, first thing, they took my clothes, gave me pajamas with feet. Like kids wear—pajamas with feet, man. And the next thing, they processed me. That girl said, 'First thing, we have to sober you up, boss.' Chester, I was twenty-four hours dead drunk. That girl said I was being processed on the second day because I was dead drunk on the first. And she asked me, 'How old are you?' and I said, 'Old enough to know better.' What do you think of that, hey, Chester? And she asked me, 'When did you start to drink?' I told her, 'About two days ago.' I told her I am a social drinker, that I only drink socially. Chester, she's a slick chick. She said, 'Quit fooling around.' "

Manny leans closer to Chester. "So I asked her, 'Who put feet in my pajamas?' She said, 'That's so you won't run away.' And I told her, 'Man, I can run with feet in my pajamas.' And she said, 'Yeah, but you'd look a little silly, don't you think?' What do you think of that, man?

"Hey, look here, Chester—it's my wife."

"I'm not your wife anymore, Manny."

Manny scoots back on the bed. He says, "That's O.K." He pats the mattress beside him. He says, "Have a sit-down."

From his bunk we can see the glassed-in nurses' station and two Navajo nurses are watching us. There is also a white man. Manny says he drives the drunkmobile. Manny introduces me to Chester.

I say, "Manny, he's drunk. He's passed out and can't hear you."

Manny stares at his hands in his lap. He says quietly, "I know that." We both stare at his long fingers; the skin is peeling around the nails. "I'm just trying to make it interesting for him." The fingernails are white and look cold. His hands look very cold. He yells, so everybody in the room can hear, "I'm just trying to make things interesting for my bedmate here." The Navajo nurses squint at us.

I take Manny's left hand and put it between my hands, but they are too small, so I put it under my thigh to warm it.

Manny is staring at his feet. He says, "You know, these pajamas didn't always have feet. Somebody sewed them there. Who do you think is responsible for that?"

"I don't know."

He says, "If you were still my wife, I'd ask you to do something."

"What?"

"Cut the feet out of these pajamas."

"You'd just go get drunk again."

Manny leans his head back against the wall and closes his eyes. He says, "Maybe." He sticks his right hand under his own thigh to warm it. He says, "Maybe not."

COWBOYS

Up and over Strang Knob, west from Kentucky, Ravenel Masterson drives the family gift horse, a 1964 Rambler Rebel with scarlet bucket seats, a black vinyl roof, Flash-o-matic floor shift and an affection for running hot. Riding in the passenger seat is Willy, a middle-aged German hitchhiker whom Ravenel picked up west of St. Louis, to help with driving and gas. Willy is too old to be hitchhiking, when the gas bill arrives he always manages to be in the bathroom, but Ravenel is too exhilarated to care. He has never driven cross-country, he knows nothing of cars, but for the first time he is driving his own car, with a red-haired radical European riding shotgun. Together they are discovering America, easy riders in the family sedan.

Across hours of Missouri Willy complains of the new morality. "In the sixties we took to the streets to fight for the right to express our love freely. Now you are getting married, having children." Willy sniffs. "Was it for this that we fought the tear gas and dogs?"

"Tear gas?" Ravenel is puzzled. "Are you talking about Vietnam? Or getting married?"

"I am talking about the free expression of love," Willy says. "Between men and women, or women and women. Or men and men." He touches Ravenel's shoulder lightly. "But perhaps I offend. Perhaps you are married."

"Oh, no," Ravenel says. "I'm only twenty-one."

"Or engaged."

"No, no."

Ravenel wonders at the drift of this conversation, and its uneasy progression from marriage to sex to himself. He pushes his suspicions from his mind. He is on his way to California, where he has determined he will meet and fall in love with a girl, probably Californian, preferably blonde. Elated at the thought he grins, raising his fist to the roof. "To the new morality!" he cries. "In defeat of ourselves!"

Willy nods. "I will tell my friends of this," he says. "They visit New York, they see men in shirts from Italy and think they have seen America." He pats Ravenel's shoulder. "*I* have set out to see the true America. And *you* are my first true American."

"Don't call me American," Ravenel says. "Just because I was born here. I haven't been to church since I was eighteen. I'm driving a twenty-year-old car, built in Detroit. I'm not even registered for the draft."

"What could be more American?" Willy answers his own question. "There are cowboys, of course. I am interested in cowboys. Are there cowboys in Missouri?"

Ravenel turns to the window to hide his smirk. "There aren't any cowboys at all. Not anymore."

"But I've seen them, on television. I learned English from them, in the movies. 'Do not forsake me, oh, my darling.'" Willy sings, Gary Cooper with a German accent. "I saw cowboys, in Chicago. Wearing pointed boots. Big white hats."

"Some people still wear cowboy *clothes,* yes," Ravenel says. "But they aren't real cowboys. The railroads fenced in the West a hundred years ago."

"And Indians, with their beautiful hair, I saw them in the streets, like Sicilians, or Turks. Dirty, poor, drunk at noon."

"Now *they're* your true Americans," Ravenel said. "And you see what America did to them."

"At the hands of the cowboys, yes. Whom we will meet. Although—" here Willy's hand makes an end run around the Flash-o-matic, rising to stroke Ravenel's hair—"*your* hair, it is as nice."

Ravenel shifts in his seat. A chill seizes up his shoulders. He jerks up his arm as if fending off a blow, but Willy's hand is gone, leaving Ravenel waving his own hand above his head and feeling foolish, while Willy plants a crescent fingernail on the map, tracing their route west.

They stop for the night at the Wigwam Village, a bungalow motel outside Emporia, Kansas. The bungalows are built to resemble teepees, reinforced concrete over a tent of rusting I-beams. They range in a circle around a cracked and empty swimming pool. The pop and click of a red neon sign *(OTEL—OTEL—OTEL)* is the only sound.

Willy emerges from the office, holding a key high. "We are in number nine," he says, and sets about scanning numbers over teepee doors.

The motel manager—big-busted, black-haired, with pink curlers—props herself against the office door jamb, holding a shoulder bag. "Kind of young to be traveling alone," she says to Ravenel.

"I'm not that young," Ravenel says. "And I'm not alone."

She saunters to Ravenel's side. He stuffs his hands in the back pockets of his jeans, and scuffs a toe at the rich Kansas loam. "Relatives don't count," she says.

Ravenel frowns. "Relatives?"

"Your brother."

"Brother?"

The manager's eyes drift shut. "Figures," she says, in a long, tired voice. "Whoever he is, he left his purse." She drops the bag. From instinct Ravenel lurches to snatch it up.

"A picture!" Willy beckons from the wigwam door, waving an Instamatic. "We must have a picture. But where did the manager go? You must ask if she will take it."

"No pictures with me," Ravenel says. "No way."

Willy points to the wigwams. "But this is America."

"*Your* America, maybe," Ravenel says. "Not mine." He retrieves his shaving kit from the car. On his way to the room, he drops Willy's bag to the pavement.

Number nine has only one bed, a small double. At the sight a small, terrified fist lodges itself in Ravenel's stomach. "I have a girlfriend," he blurts out.

Willy is unfazed. "Of course," he says, tucking the camera in his bag. "You are a child of the eighties. You will meet your girlfriend in California, where you will marry by the ocean and have children." He rests his hand on Ravenel's shoulder.

"Sure," Ravenel says. "*Many* children."

Willy laughs, stretching his hands over his head, popping his knuckles. "Yes, this is so! This is how it must be." He squeezes Ravenel's shoulder, ruffles his hair.

"I have to be in California in three days," Ravenel says carefully. "I'm meeting my girlfriend in San Francisco on Thursday. I'm not stopping except to sleep." He takes a deep breath, then delivers the punch. "Maybe I should take you to some likely-looking place and let you out. You could get a ride with somebody who's taking time to see the country."

Willy cocks his head. "Your car is not healthy?"

"The understatement of the year."

"You are in luck. I am a mechanic." Willy pulls a film can and a pipe from his shoulder bag. "You would like to get high?"

Ravenel hesitates. To accept this hospitality is to choose to allow Willy to continue on. But hey, Ravenel tells himself. Who is he to leave a mechanic by the wayside? "What the hell," he says, and helps himself to Willy's pipe.

"That woman, with the pink things in her hair," Willy says. "She insulted my accent. I have no accent."

"Mmm," Ravenel says, smoke leaking from his lips.

"A *bitch,*" Willy says, with feeling.

For the first time in his life Ravenel finds himself siding with the curler-headed motel and greasy spoon owners of the hinterlands. "A Kansan," he says. "An American. What do you expect."

"Cowboys," Willy says promptly. "At least, that is what I look for. But we are not far enough west."

Willy strips and climbs into bed. Ravenel retreats to the bathroom. Lingering over his toothbrush, he leans his forehead against the mirror, staring down his reflection. Why has he encouraged Willy's talk of free morals, free love, free sex? Why has he allowed him to stay?

Leaving the bathroom, Ravenel crawls under the covers, still wearing his underwear, his T-shirt, his socks. He is still settling himself when Willy flings an arm over his shoulder, carelessly, as if Ravenel's back were the most convenient armrest.

The mattress sags, hopelessly. Ravenel clings to its edge to keep from sliding downhill, into the hollow created by Willy's weight. He lies on his stomach, crushing his arm to pins and needles, until long after Willy's feigned snores have given way to shallow breathing.

His nails dug into the mattress, Willy's hand dangling before his eyes, Ravenel falls into a place between waking and sleep. Behind his eyelids the road unrolls endlessly. At his side sits his San Francisco girlfriend, blonde and tanned—but Ravenel turns, and it is red-headed Willy, in a Stetson hat and a pearl-buttoned shirt.

Ravenel wakes. Overhead, nesting in the wigwam peak, sparrows chatter. The paper blinds blink: gray with dawn; lurid with neon light. In his half-sleep, he has turned over, slid down into the bed's hollow, cuddled into Willy's arms. Willy's hand is working its way downward.

Ravenel lies stiff, frozen, clammy with sweat. He tells himself that this is not happening; he is not here. He wants nothing more than to be in California, where he will find love, straight and true. He wants nothing more than to get where he is going.

He rises abruptly. Willy's hand flops against the bedclothes. Ravenel heads to the shower, where he stays until he is certain that the hot water has run out, and that Willy's shower will be cold.

Desire, the parish priest told the boys in Ravenel's eighth-grade class, is a many-pointed star, turning and pricking in the heart. Their consolation was to know that with age, its points are worn smooth, even if its turnings never cease. Tailgating farmers across the flattening plains, Ravenel thinks of Willy, warm and hard against his buttocks. He rearranges himself inside his pants and wonders how long he will need to wear down his points.

Kansas drowns in rain. Ravenel considers putting Willy out, but argues himself into letting him stay. The Rambler's temperature gauge continues to rise, and Willy is a mechanic. Ravenel points out to himself that in the crunch, he did not give in to the prickings of desire. He is still in control. Over the cheerful slap of the windshield wipers, he makes small talk.

They approach Dodge City. There is a bypass. Willy, who is driving, ignores the sign. "We want the bypass," Ravenel says.

"You will pass by Dodge City?" Willy is incredulous.

"Dodge City is a tourist trap."

"There will be cowboys in Dodge City."

"There will be Americans in Dodge City. *True* Americans. Fat housewives and used-car salesmen driving

Winnebagos." The bypass signs loom, green and white. "We're taking the bypass. I *have* to be in California by day after tomorrow."

"Just for lunch," Willy says. He digs a finger into Ravenel's side. "Maybe *you* will find your*self* a cowboy."

The bypass is upon them. "Willy, it's my car and my trip and my gas. If you want to walk, get out and walk. Otherwise, take the goddam bypass."

Willy wrenches the car into the right lane. Oblivious to oncoming traffic, he cranes his neck to cast a straining, wistful glance south, over the flat brown plains. Ravenel folds his arms and stares out the window. They are in Colorado before he unclenches his teeth.

Near sunset, they approach the mountains. They stop outside Las Animas. Willy is in the motel office before Ravenel can step from the car.

Again Willy rents a room with only one double bed. His neck aching from the day's strain, Ravenel flops down. Willy sits on the foot of the bed. Ravenel hears one shoe drop. When the second drops, he promises himself, he will sit up and insist they switch to a room with two beds.

The bed lurches. Willy's elbow brushes Ravenel's foot. "Touch me and I'll break your neck," Ravenel says, shocking himself.

Willy scoots over, reties his shoe. "I am going," he says. "I will walk." He picks up his shoulder bag and his suitcase.

"Get some cowboy to give you a ride," Ravenel says, turning his back. He hears Willy open the door, and the thrumming of the rain on the pavement. Willy's footsteps click away, crossing the asphalt.

Ravenel lunges across the bed to peer through the curtains. Willy stands in the rain, staring up at the sky. He turns and retraces his steps.

His heart pounding, Ravenel dives under the covers, feigning sleep, one eye cracked. Willy tiptoes in, undresses and climbs into bed, his underwear ghostly pale in the room's dim light.

The next day, Ravenel and Willy climb the high passes of the Sangre de Cristo. They drive fifty miles, stop to let the car cool, drive another fifty miles. At each stop Willy listens to the engine. Once he opens the hood. "A-OK," he says, making a circle with his thumb and forefinger. Throughout that day they say nothing more.

It is dark when they descend from the mountains above Salt Lake. The city is awash with orange sodium-vapor light, extending exactly as far as its water lines. Beyond the sharp line defined by that limit, there is no light, no scattered farms or small towns, only darkness, reaching to the massive black shapes of the mountains to the west.

Ravenel stops for gas. Willy heads for the bathroom. Ravenel fills the tank and moves the car forward from the pump. He sits for a single moment, his forefinger tracing the Flash-o-matic's luminescent dial; then he leaps from the car. He pulls Willy's suitcase and shoulder bag from the trunk, sets them by the pumps. As he drives off, he avoids looking in the rearview mirror.

He barrels out of the city, ignoring the speed limit, driving into the blackness of the mountains and the lake. He tries to conjure his vision of the woman who waits for him in California, tall and blonde and full of love. Instead he thinks only of Willy, abandoned on the neon-washed apron of some Union 76. Ravenel rubs each eye with the heel of his palm. Is he so transparent, is his desire written across his forehead, that Willy so quickly sought it out? The thought wrenches knots in Ravenel's gut. He turns on the radio, sings along.

He exits and turns back.

Willy is at the gas station, sitting on his suitcase. Ravenel stops and rests his forehead on the steering wheel.

The roar of the trailer trucks along I-80 mixes in his ears with the car's lingering whine. Amid this din, Willy gently deposits his bags in the back seat and climbs in. "You have come back."

"Shut up," Ravenel says. "Shut up, shut up, shut up." He floors the gas and peels from the station.

They stop that night in Salt Lake. While Willy rents their room, Ravenel paws through his bag, until he finds Willy's hashish. With deep-sucking breaths he lights the pipe, then knocks its ashes into the gutter. He hides the pipe in Willy's bag, tries to still his racing heart against what he is about to do, follows Willy inside; into a room with two single beds. Ravenel sits on the nearest, high beyond words, hiding his humiliation.

Willy pulls on a fresh shirt. "I know this town," he says. "Near here the Golden Spike was driven. I saw it in a movie, with Barbara Stanwyck and Joel McCrea." He peers into the mirror, humming snatches of some tune, combing his red hair. "You need not worry that I will touch you. I am going out. I will be back late."

"Looking for a cowboy?" Ravenel says, his voice heavy with sarcasm.

"Perhaps I will get lucky. Should I return with one, or two?"

"You don't understand," Ravenel says, but Willy is gone.

Ravenel wakes the next morning to Willy bustling about the room, peering in drawers, opening cabinets. He turns up a Gideon Bible. "What are you looking for?" Ravenel asks.

"Oh, nothing." Willy turns. Above his left eye a black-and-purple cauliflower blooms, flecked with dried blood. Ravenel props himself on his elbows. "My God, Willy. What did you do to your head?"

Willy shrugs. "I went to a bar. I was watching. I asked for a cigarette. Then they turned on me, a foreigner, they said. A queer. I knew this anger and I left." He touches his bruise. "I did not leave fast enough."

Ravenel turns to the wall. "You should put some ice on it. There's a machine in the hall. It's free."

"It is nothing. You will see as much, in your time." Willy roots through scattered clothes. "I am not complaining. My cowboy followed me out. He took me to his place, to feed me drinks and nurse my wounds."

"So where is this cowboy," Ravenel says to the wall. He hears the door open. "Taking your time in here," a voice says, in a flat western twang. Ravenel flips over. A tall, thin blond in glove-tight jeans and a pearl-buttoned shirt lounges in the doorway, smoking a cigarette. He wears boots studded with turquoise and tipped at their toes with silver. With the cigarette between his thumb and forefinger he inhales a last drag, then flicks the butt into a puddle outside the motel door. On its quick hiss Ravenel's heart sinks.

"I beg your pardon," the blond says. He winks at Ravenel. "I had no idea." He turns his back.

"Wait," Ravenel says. "You don't understand."

Willy bends to the foot of the bed. "Good. It is found." He stands, clutching his shoulder bag to his chest. From the bag he pulls a patterned, lidded tin. He opens it and removes several bills. The blond takes the money, then shies from Willy's hug. Ravenel watches him climb into a late-model Corvette. He guns the engine and rumbles from the parking lot.

Ravenel leaps from the bed and slams the door shut. "Asshole. You told me you were broke."

"So I keep a little reserve, for emergencies," Willy says. "Is this so terrible for a stranger in a foreign country?"

"That was no cowboy," Ravenel says. "That was a goddam whore. And you let yourself be hustled."

"Call him what you like. He helped me when I needed help."

"Much like myself," Ravenel says. "Only *he* had the sense to get paid." He throws himself around the room, tossing aside Willy's clothes, pulling on his own jeans. "Well, I'm happy you found your cowboy. Or maybe I should say he found you. The guy who knocked you up side the head. *He* was the real cowboy."

"The man who hit me was *not* a cowboy. He wore a white shirt and brown pants."

"The only kind left," Ravenel says. He strikes his knee against the half-open drawer and he kicks it shut, savagely. "Welcome to America."

They enter Nevada and fences drop away. Signs crop up along the interstate: "Open Range," "Cattle Crossing." Every few miles fake cattle guards are painted across the pavement, to fool the cows from wandering. Yet they see no cows, no water, little wildlife, only endless sagebrush, with an occasional raven circling overhead or a black-and-white chukar winging up from the shoulder.

Traffic is light; Willy drives. Ravenel has nothing to do but nurse his anger. "You will see as much," Willy said to him, only that morning. Ravenel leans back, closing his eyes against the notion, to be confronted with a picture of himself, standing on street corners, provoking brawls in redneck bars, hiding wounds from a suspicious wife.

Climbing Battle Mountain, the Rambler boils over. They stop, let the engine cool, start again, but the grade is steep and the car rebels after a few miles. Ravenel cannot remember the last service station. He has no credit cards, little money. A few cars and trucks speed by, their drivers hardly glancing in the Rambler's direction.

He turns to Willy. "OK, so earn your keep."

Willy smiles, rolls his eyes. "My keep? I do not understand."

"You're the mechanic. What do we do now? Let it cool? Push it over the mountain?"

Unbelievably, Willy's eyes fill with tears. In the roadside's parched glare, his fingers resting on the lump above his eye, he looks older, *old.* "I am no mechanic," he says. "I bought a used car in Canada. I was to drive it to California. I was to stop in Dodge City, in the Monument Valley where the movies are made, in the Death Valley with its twenty mules. Then I broke down, in St. Louis. I had been standing by the road for hours. I looked at you. I liked you. I wanted to give you a good reason to keep me along. Everything else I have said is true. Only there did I not speak right."

Furious, Ravenel climbs from the car. He raises the hood, to be confronted with a hot maze of wires and plugs and blades, all mysterious and to his eyes potentially lethal.

Willy stands beside him. "Perhaps if we let it cool—"

"You lied!" Ravenel, who has never raised his voice to an older man, is yelling. "I could have left you sitting in Salt Lake. But *no-o,* I go back, looking for a mechanic. And what do I get. A liar. A fag."

Willy sets his chin, plants his feet. "That is enough. You turned back for me. You are old enough to face this."

"I turned back for a mechanic."

"You turned back for love."

"Love," Ravenel says. His voice shakes with contempt. "What do you know about love?"

Willy sits on the fender, crosses his knees, rests his chin on his fist. "Please," he says.

"Please what."

Willy waves his hand, an angry flick. "Please continue. I am waiting to have it explained."

Ravenel crouches by the open hood, numbed from himself. He rests his chin on his hands, watching the radiator cap bubble and seep.

Willy touches his shoulder, and Ravenel is so tired and angry that he does not shy away. Willy points to the north. The sky is searingly blue, but nearby a mustard-colored cloud boils upward. As they watch, it grows closer, until its mass of dust separates into tens, hundreds of cows. Within minutes, they take refuge in their car from a slow-moving river of bellowing, stinking, long-horned cattle.

Ravenel looks back. Down the road men have blocked traffic. They must be yelling to drivers, but Ravenel can hear nothing over the noise of the herd. To the front his view is blocked by the raised hood. He does not see the horse or its rider until he is looking at spurs, glinting at eye level from a battered, square-toed boot.

"What the hell are you doing here," the voice comes from above. Willy is out of the car before Ravenel can answer. "Stuck!" Willy cries. "Overheated!" Ravenel pokes his head from the window.

The cowboy rides a gray-flecked quarter horse. Erect in his saddle, he wears faded jeans, a ten-gallon hat, a bandana around his sunburned neck. He swings a tight-muscled leg over the saddle horn, tosses the reins to Willy, pokes around in the engine. "Fan belt," he announces. "Loose."

"You will be able to help us?" Willy asks shamelessly.

"Maybe. With the right tools."

"There's a toolbox in the trunk," Ravenel says. "There's a couple of wrenches." He climbs from the car and retrieves the tools.

Standing in the spring sun, watching the cowboy tinker with the engine, Ravenel finds himself acutely aware of his world, in a way he has never before allowed himself to know: the warm tan of the cowboy's boots against the asphalt; the leathery copper of his skin against the mud-spattered blue of his jeans; the heat of Ravenel's own palms, burning to touch this brown-eyed handsome man.

Ravenel forces himself to look away. He closes his eyes, trying for the last time to conjure a vision of the woman, any woman, who must be waiting, in California . . . no luck. He has lost the art of outwitting himself, to the cowboy on the roan horse; to Willy, standing at his side.

The cowboy returns the tools to Ravenel. "That should get you up and over the pass," he says. "But you need a new fan belt. Stop in Winnemucca at the Texaco on the east side of town, ask for Sonny Devine. I expect he won't charge you more than twenty bucks all told."

"Thanks for stopping," Ravenel says. He would like to say more, but he has lost his voice, to the heady smell of saddle soap and horse hair.

"A cowboy," Willy says, awestruck. "An *American* cowboy." His hand slips from the bridle to the horse's neck. He fingers the saddle's worn leather. "A picture," he says. "Please wait, only a moment. I must have a photograph." He dives into the Rambler and retrieves his Instamatic. He hands it to Ravenel. The cattle press too close to the car to allow Ravenel to step back, so he climbs to the car's hood. He snaps Willy and the cowboy, standing beside the horse.

"You'll want one of the two of you," the cowboy says. "For the folks at home." He scrambles atop the Rambler before Ravenel can object.

Ravenel stands next to Willy, while the cowboy fits his eye to the viewfinder. "Closer," the cowboy says, waving them together. "I want to get the mountain." Willy does not budge. Ravenel hesitates, then steps to Willy's side, to droop his arm around Willy's shoulder, casually, as if it might have dropped from the cloudless Nevada sky. "Say horseshit," the cowboy says, and snaps the picture: Willy and Ravenel, grinning, Ravenel's arm around Willy's shoulder, while behind them the long-horned cattle moil and balk, under the glistening, snow-capped peak of Battle Mountain.

The cowboy returns the camera to Willy, mounts his horse and wheels around. *"Hasta luego,"* he says, and clops through the herd and across the highway, towards the rolling plain to the south.

Willy crows with laughter, clapping his hands and dancing around the car in little skips. "For this only, I would have come across the world!" he cries. He dances up to Ravenel, takes his shoulders in his hands. "My thanks to you, and your wonderful car!"

Ravenel jerks back from Willy's hug. "We'd have been in California two days ago if it had been left up to me."

"But you see, it is not left up to you," Willy says. He executes a small bow. "These are the workings of love."

Ravenel slams the hood and climbs into the car.

The herd clears the highway. In minutes Ravenel and Willy are over the pass. Ravenel puts the Flash-o-matic in neutral for the long downgrade. The pavement clicks by. The sun sinks. He lowers the visor against its brightness. Willy tilts back the passenger seat, closing his eyes.

Ravenel steals a sideways glance. Above Willy's eye the lump swells, but a smile wrinkles the corners of his lips. The sun glints from his red hair. He hums a little song. Ravenel fights the tune, but it sticks in his head, leading him on, to the place where he is going.

AH LOVE, REMEMBER FELIS

When a woman wears a hat it is assumed, quite rightly, that she has a destination or a project in the head under the hat. One might guess the kind by observing the nature of the hat. So Beth Gilman thought, lifting hers from a shelf in her closet. It was a classic, low-crowned, broad-brimmed, of natural straw, quite unadorned. No ribbon or flower distracted it from its function. It stayed on in the wind and shaded her eyes. Suitable for a female of seven or seventy, for before the age of coyness or after. Admirable. Unadmired. Cherished. Like a long-accustomed wife.

She put it on her head and went out of her house and got into her car. She had already kissed her husband goodbye. If she were a different kind of woman she would put an artificial rose on the brim, or tie a scarf around the crown. If she were a different woman she wouldn't be going on this trip today. The thought occupied her for several miles until she turned up a canyon road. By this time she had finished with the hat. It rested on her head as easily as it had thirty years before when her hair was brown.

As the road up the canyon grew steeper, Beth thrust the car smoothly down into second gear. There was a time when the old sedan took these curves with never a gasp or wheeze. It ran swiftly past anything she wanted to pass. Now its age was showing. Hers too. The hands on the steering wheel were misshapen. There were brown spots on the backs, small marks of mileage like the dents on the car's fenders. However—she shifted back to third—they were both still going. With the thought came a warm wave of affection for the car, her servant and companion all these years. Her feeling for it had been aroused first by the word horsepower, which she took literally, and saw hooves and a white mane. Under the white hood was an animal sensibility. She said that there was an empathy between them. Well, there had been Bucephalus. And Pegasus. She did not mind a slightly imperfect analogy.

Her husband had laughed at all that. In the days when he laughed much. This September morning Bart was at home in his wheelchair. The practical nurse would know what to do for a stroke victim. Beth thought of other strokes, of intuition or good luck. The word was far-ranging, but for her it would always mean first a jab of evil now.

Still, he was alive, if unable to take this anniversary trip with her. She had not told him about it. If he did not understand, there would be no point. If he did, he might be saddened. She turned off the main canyon road into a flat place full of bright aspens and dark conifers. She did not have to think of where she was going. The car probably knew which parking place to go to. This had been a family joke and source of laughter too. So much of family life was silliness, which had a strength to support that one wouldn't believe, in one's unobservant youth.

The desired familiar spot was empty, a good omen, as if she were expected, would have been missed if she hadn't come. Not that she had to justify the trip. It was no rendezvous with a conspirator or lover. In fact, it was almost a pilgrimage, a journey one made for one's salvation. For absolution. For redemption. She shook her head. For a pagan, this was presumptuous. Highfalutin. All she had come for was to pick some berries.

She locked the car and carrying her basket walked down a narrow path toward the plunging stream. The gold and glisten of autumn shone on mountain slopes and granite outcrops. The path was dusty with the feet of summer. It led to a campsite on a small cliff above the water. She put her basket on a table by a chokecherry bush and sat on the bench to look around. It was the first time she had ever been here alone.

She and Bart had camped at this spot long ago on a day like this. After picking the service berries that hung dark purple on high bushes along the stream, they pitched a small tent, and cooked supper on a hot fire of squaw wood, the dead or downed branches of old trees. Even though they had collected it together, she had felt the term to be somewhat demeaning—wood that a squaw would pick up, not what a brave would chop with great brawny arms. She had not known, then, how strong a squaw could be.

Her awareness, her resentment, of the vulgar put-downs of gender no longer bothered her. This was a relief, like ceasing to ovulate. She had more important things to think about than why the sun was he, the moon was she. She was concerned now with the earth and its survival. The sensible part of her brain gave a twitch and reminded her that she always thought of Mother Nature, or Mother Earth. If she ever thought of him, it was of Father Nature off somewhere flexing his muscles, planning earthquakes and other rapes of the land. A squirrel had climbed a pine tree and sat protesting something. Her perhaps. He was probably not commenting on the tall monolith across the stream, which antedated Freud and all passing nomenclature. Small private joke, for the moment unsharable. Ah well.

She looked around to where their tent had been, a low shelter beside aspens. There had been a storm in the night, quite unforeseeable, which woke them with a gigantic bang. Then there was lightning, flickers and slashes, mumblings and growlings, and reverberations that circled the canyon walls. There was no escape, the car was too far away. For distraction, for comic relief in the drama, they spoke of Zeus commanding his full orchestra, exhorting the timpani to greater efforts. This made him less ferocious, funnier. But the lightning was a real hazard, and when the sky lit up around them as if to reveal the explosion of the world, they drew together. Surrounded by the inhuman threat of thunder, the almost-human groaning of wind in the pines, they had mingled fears and bodies.

Sitting in the lonely sunshine she thought of that night of noise and mingling. If Zeus was directing this small human scene in the intervals of thunderclaps, the scenario was quite to be expected. The great Thunderer was also the great Philanderer, lover of whatever his hot eye fell upon. A role model for mankind.

No bolt had struck them and when the rain stopped they slept. Next morning they spread things to dry on bushes, and walked in a freshened world. On two logs they crossed the stream, a precarious trip for her, but he had held her hand. They went into a meadow of yellowing grass and purple asters and then to a bare place under pines. When she looked down she saw big pawprints in the still wet ground. More than big—enormous. What dog was this, she said. Bart bent down too, and then they looked at each other. The pawmarks had no claws.

Had he been holed up somewhere, not too far away, during the storm, and come out when the rain had stopped, to prowl under the now bright stars? Felis concolor he was. Older and more formidable than Zeus. Even now she sometimes looked down for pawprints on the dampened earth.

She tucked two paper sacks in her pants pockets and carrying a third walked along a path above the stream. There were a few bushes with berries but the crop was poor. She knew a better place and went on, through a tangle of stalks and vines, the dogwood's useless white berries, a few late pink roses, crimson rowan berries. An unknown fragrance came to her at times, one she had never been able to identify, to attach to anything. It hung in the air like a teasing promise, coy and tantalizing, like youth's hope that the world would be full of riches. The scent was delicious and frustrating. She liked to have a name for things.

When she reached a great granite boulder by the stream she looked around. At the top of the rock, rooted in the steep cliff above the water, was a spreading bush with a wealth of purple berries. At its base were a few new plants with a scanty crop. She considered, but no, she could not crawl up the rock to reach the bounty at the peak.

"Damn," she said aloud. "Triple damn." Silently she cursed her knees and indifferent fate. Another stroke of bad luck. Once Bart would have made a run and leaped up, and then pulled her to the top. They would have filled their bags, eating a few squashed berries that tasted a little like strange raisins, winelike. Now, thwarted, grounded, she started picking what was within reach. There would be a few. She felt no resignation in her.

While she searched she heard footsteps, human of course, and a male voice said, "Hi!" The universal greeting.

"Hi!" she said, not looking around.

"What are you picking?" It was a frequent question. Her answer depended on how she was feeling. To children she usually said, "Service berries," and smiled, unless they had been chasing around whacking the heads from the monkshoods. If she was really irked, had seen them throwing cans in the stream, she sometimes growled,

"Death berries," and waved her blue fingers at them. She hoped they thought her a witch as they retreated, a crone gathering something poisonous for a darksome brew. Sometimes she was bored with herself. Once she had been tempted to direct a tobacco-chewing pair with tattoos on their chests to the shiny white dogwood berries. "Moon berries," she wanted to hiss. "They will make you more than a man." She would leer and cackle. But she couldn't quite manage it. It remained a phantasy for the future. Bart would have been shocked. There are things a wife can't do. There are a lot of things she can't tell a husband.

Today she said, "Service berries." The young man had curly hair. No beard, thank God. She was tired of beards that made them all look alike. Jeans and a T-shirt of course. He had a big backpack. After a few minutes he put it down.

"There are a lot up there," he said, pointing.

"I know," she said, answering his silly statement politely.

"What do you do with them?"

"I make jelly."

She could see him walk back a few feet, crouch slightly, spring up the rock, and then crawl to the top. How easy it looked. If one had the knees of twenty summers. She went on gleaning. He took off his T-shirt and tied the bottom in a knot and started picking. His bare back and arms moved fluently as he reached. She felt a stab of envy and then a hot flash of anger. He was a trespasser, a competitor, an enemy. This was her land, her harvest, by reason of seniority. He intruded on a private act. Arrogant and careless youth. A creature of flowing muscles and endless breath. He had no idea what it was like to live in a wheelchair.

Once she would have been up there, hot in the sunshine, her fingers blue and sticky, laughing. Part of the unhappiness of being alone was that there was no one to laugh with. Only witches laugh to themselves, eerily, evilly.

She had finished gleaning but her sack was less than half full. She would have to search somewhere else. She looked up at the young man. His arms were busy, holding down a branch and stripping the fruit. And her anger was stopped by admiration, for efficiency had always pleased her. There was a beauty in it. More than beauty. A rightness. Something lasting. Beauty was transient, like youth. Watching him, her eyes performed a camera trick and sped up his life before her. She saw the lithe arms thinned and stringy, the quick hands slowed, the blond hair whitened. And felt a stroke of grief, for Bart, for herself, and for the boy. Her bag was pitifully light in her hand, but she did not begrudge him his picking. This was his time to collect the fruits of the world, while he could. She had had hers.

She was turning away when he slid down the boulder, holding his shirt in a bunch in one fist. It was stained and bulging. "Gee," he said, smiling, "I got quite a lot. What'll we do with them?"

"We?" she asked.

"Well sure. They're for you. For your jelly."

She remembered how she had accused him of theft, in her selfish mind, before she had given them to him as his right. There was a wonderful kind of justice in his giving them back to her now. It was a matter of grace to give and to accept. "Thank you," she said.

"Do you have another sack?"

Carefully they filled two bags. He shook out his shirt and put it on, stained with purple juice.

"Your shirt is ruined," she said. "I'm sorry."

"It doesn't matter. I'm just going up into the wilderness."

"Where?"

"To the top of the canyon. I'm going to stay overnight."

"By yourself?"

"Yes."

"Then first you must share my lunch."

"Thanks." He had the grace to accept. "Thank you very much."

She led him along the narrow path. Why had she made two thick sandwiches, brought a quart of coffee? Partly it was habit, and the poignancy of bringing only one where always there had been two was bitter. And she was a Westerner and never went far from home without provisions. One never knew what might happen outside the providence of the town. A breakdown. A washout. An unexpected guest. Back at the picnic table she said, "This is a chokecherry bush. They make jelly too but I prefer the service berries." He looked up, interested.

"I'm going to tell my wife about them," he said as they sat down across from each other.

"You're married?" It didn't seem possible, he was so young. Perhaps he meant it for the future.

"I'm going to be next week. I'm twenty-four." He must have read her mind.

"I'm very happy for you." She handed him a roast beef sandwich.

"I'm going up the canyon by myself for a last fling with solitude, to sort of think things over and put my life in order. Afterwards, after next week, things won't be the same."

She could have been flippant. You don't know the half of it, Bub. You're telling me? But he wasn't the sort who throws beer cans in the stream.

"No," she said. "It will never be the same again. Life, I mean. Yours and hers. But it will be together. Not just in what people call conjugal bliss. But sharing things like walking and laughing and picking berries." Simple things that seem so everlasting, but are not. She could not tell him that.

"Is your husband alive?" He saw her ring and her wrinkles.

"Yes. He has had a stroke. He lives in a wheelchair."

"I'm sorry." But the idea was not quite credible to him, here in the September sunshine, by the sound of running water. It hardly was to her.

"We used to come here every year. It was a kind of pagan ceremony near the autumn equinox." They sat eating for a time. Elemental food. Bread and meat. "One of the things that keep marriage alive is the little ritual that has meaning for us that we make ourselves."

"I'll remember that. And will you tell Sally how to make the jelly?"

"Gladly." Jelly making was still the female's job. Her province. Her mystery. She filled the enamel cup with coffee for him, and poured hers into the thermos top. "Once several years ago we were sitting here drinking coffee and looking at the stream, and a mink came down on the other bank, very slow, looking around, and stood at the edge of the water. He had a chipmunk in his mouth. He stayed a long time. I always see him here."

"That's great." He turned around, looking at the far bank. She wished she could evoke a dark mink for him. She would have to be more than a witch.

"What will you do after you are married?" She put bananas and pecan cookies on the table.

"Sally teaches in elementary school. I work for the county assessor. Maybe if I get smart enough I'll go into politics."

"And improve the world?"

"I hope so. It's pretty rotten, you know."

"I know." You're telling me?

"But just now I have to think about my own life. Mine and Sally's. How it will be. That's why I'm going up to the mountain. It's kind of frightening, you know, to promise to love, honor, and cherish somebody for the rest of your life. Even if you want to and mean to, how can you be sure? How can you know that what is drawing you together now will keep you together forever?"

"You can't know. You can only try to keep it going." The squirrel was back, scolding. "Shut up, Squirrel! What do you know about forever?" She was stalling for time, waiting for a stroke of knowledge.

"What kept your marriage going?"

What indeed? Habit. Inertia. Memories. Duty. A few small rituals. She could say this to a contemporary, but not to him. Not now. "Perhaps a poet said it best. 'Ah, love, let us be true to one another.' Perhaps he meant let us be true to what we had in the beginning."

"I'll think about that tonight up on the mountain."

It was not enough. She wanted to say more. "Before you go I must tell you about Felis concolor." She told him about the night of the thunder and rain, and of the big cat padding softly, stealthily, alien, unknowable on the margin of their ignorance.

He was quiet for a while and then he said, "That's great. That's really great."

Had she said enough? "If you are not faithful the memory will stalk you always, like a lion in the night."

"We plan to be."

"I know."

He collected the wax paper and banana peels and put them in the litter can. "Now I know Felis concolor's name and I'll watch out for him. But I don't know yours." They wrote their names and addresses on pieces of the paper sacks.

"Beth," he read. "Is it all right if I call you by your first name?"

"Of course, Clark." They bowed very formally, and laughed together. What a pleasant sound it was, in the hot stillness and the little rippling clapping of aspen leaves.

"Thank you for the lunch," he said.

"Thank you for the berries." She watched him slip into his pack.

"Well." Partings were awkward. "Good luck with the jelly."

"I'll send Sally the recipe."

He grinned and took off. After a few steps he turned and waved. "Good-bye, Beth," he called. His curls gleamed gold in a stroke of sunlight before he passed into the shade.

"Good-bye." There was only the sound of stream and aspens. Nothing human but herself, though the initials of other humanoids hoping for more than mortality had been carved in the tree trunks. She took off her hat and sat awhile in the cooling afternoon, and thought of Clark going up the mountain, slowly because of the heavy pack. It would be a clear night. Big stars would shine on his struggle with incertitude. Perhaps a star would fall, an omen, a stroke of inhuman light that would confirm his hope. It was more than she could give him.

She put her admirable and cherished hat back on her head and slowly walked up the steep little path to the parking place. For an instant she had an image of an old horse waiting, head down, patient and reliable, whose power would take her where she needed to go. The sight was a comfort. She unlocked the car and put the basket on the seat. Then she patted the white metal flank before she got inside.

There was no one to see, or wonder, or laugh at her, an old woman, going off with a picking of simples to make a brew that would preserve her from the teeth and claws of time.

RON HANSEN

WICKEDNESS

At the end of the nineteenth century a girl from Delaware got on a milk train in Omaha and took a green wool seat in the second-class car. August was outside the window, and sunlight was a yellow glare on the trees. Up front, a railway conductor in a navy-blue uniform was gingerly backing down the aisle with a heavy package in a gunnysack that a boy was helping him with. They were talking about an agreeable seat away from the hot Nebraska day that was persistent outside, and then they were setting their cargo across the runnered aisle from the girl and tilting it against the shellacked wooden wall of the railway car before walking back up the aisle and elsewhere into August.

She was sixteen years old and an Easterner just recently hired as a county schoolteacher, but she knew enough about prairie farming to think the heavy package was a crank-and-piston washing machine or a boxed plowshare and coulter, something no higher than the bloody stump where the poultry were chopped with a hatchet and then wildly high-stepped around the yard. Soon, however, there was a juggling movement and the gunnysack slipped aside, and she saw an old man sitting there, his limbs hacked away, and dark holes where his ears ought to have been, the skin pursed at his jaw hinge like pink lips in a kiss. The milk train jerked into a roll through the railway yard, and the old man was jounced so that his gray cheek pressed against the hot window glass. Although he didn't complain, it seemed an uneasy position, and the girl wished she had the courage to get up from her seat and tug the jolting body upright. She instead got to her page in *Quo Vadis* and pretended to be so rapt by the book that she didn't look up again until Columbus, where a doctor with liquorice on his breath sat heavily beside her and openly stared over his newspaper before whispering that the poor man was a carpenter in Genoa who'd been caught out in the great blizzard of 1888. Had she heard of that one?

The girl shook her head.

She ought to look out for their winters, the doctor said. Weather in Nebraska could be the wickedest thing she ever saw.

She didn't know what to say, so she said nothing. And at Genoa a young teamster got on in order to carry out the old man, whose half body was heavy enough that the boy had to yank the gunnysack up the aisle like sixty pounds of mail.

In the year 1888, on the twelfth day of January, a pink sun was up just after seven and southeastern zephyrs of such soft temperature were sailing over the Great Plains that squatters walked their properties in high rubber boots and April jackets and some farmhands took off their Civil War greatcoats to rake silage into the cattle troughs. However, sheep that ate whatever they could the night before raised their heads away from food and sniffed the salt tang in the air. And all that morning street-car mules were reported to be acting up, nipping each other, jingling the hitch rings, foolishly waggling their dark manes and necks as though beset by gnats and horseflies.

A Danish cattleman named Axel Hansen later said he was near the Snake River and tipping a teaspoon of saleratus into a yearling's mouth when he heard a faint groaning in the north that was like the noise of a high waterfall at a fair distance. Axel looked toward Dakota, and there half the sky was suddenly gray and black and indigo blue with great storm clouds that were seething up as high as the sun and wrangling toward him at horse speed. Weeds were being uprooted, sapling trees were bullwhipping, and the top inches of snow and prairie soil were being sucked up and stirred like the dirty flour that was called red dog. And then the onslaught hit him hard as furniture, flying him onto his back so that when Axel looked up, he seemed to be deep undersea and in icehouse cold. Eddying snow made it hard to breathe any way but sideways, and getting up to just his knees and hands seemed a great attainment. Although his sod house was but a quarter-mile away, it took Axel four hours to get there. Half his face was frozen gray and hard as weatherboarding so the cattleman was speechless until nightfall and then Axel Hansen simply told his wife, That was not pleasant.

Cow tails stuck out sideways when the wind caught them. Sparrows and crows whumped hard against the windowpanes, their jerking eyes seeking out an escape, their wings fanned out and flattened as though pinned up in an ornithologist's display. Cats died, dogs died, pigeons died. Entire farms of cattle and pigs and geese and chickens were wiped out in a single night. Horizontal snow that was hard and dry as salt dashed and seethed over everything, sloped up like rooftops, tricked its way across creek beds and ditches, milkily purled down city streets, stole shanties and coops and pens from a bleak landscape that was even then called the Great American Desert. Everything about the blizzard seemed to have personality and hateful intention. Especially the cold. At six A.M., the temperature at Valentine, Nebraska, was thirty degrees above zero. Half a day later the temperature was fourteen below, a drop of forty-four degrees and the difference between having toes and not, between staying alive overnight and not, between ordinary concerns and one overriding idea.

Ainslie Classen was hopelessly lost in the whiteness and tilting low under the jamming gale when his right elbow jarred against a joist of his pigsty. He walked around the sty by skating his sore red hands along the upright shiplap and then squeezed inside through the slops trough. The pigs scampered over to him, seeking his protection, and Ainslie put himself among them, getting down in their stink and their body heat, socking them away only when they ganged up or when two or three presumed he was food. Hurt was nailing into his finger joints until he thought to work his hands into the pigs' hot wastes, then smeared some onto his skin. The pigs grunted around him and intelligently snuffled at his body with their pink and tender noses, and Ainslie thought, *You are not me but I am you,* and Ainslie Classen got through the night without shame or injury.

Whereas a Hartington woman took two steps out her door and disappeared until the snow sank away in April and raised her body up from her garden patch.

An Omaha cigar maker got off the Leavenworth Street trolley that night, fifty yards from his own home and five yards from another's. The completeness of the blizzard so puzzled him that the cigar maker tramped up and down the block more than twenty times and then slept against a lamppost and died.

A cattle inspector froze to death getting up on his quarter horse. The next morning he was still tilting the saddle with his upright weight, one cowboy boot just inside the iced stirrup, one bear-paw mitten over the horn and reins. His quarter horse apparently kept waiting for him to complete his mount, and then the quarter horse died too.

A Chicago boy visiting his brother for the holidays was going to a neighbor's farm to borrow a scoop shovel when the night train of blizzard raged in and overwhelmed him. His tracks showed the boy mistakenly slanted past the sod house he'd just come from, and then tilted forward with perhaps the vain hope of running into some shop or shed or railway depot. His body was found four days later and twenty-seven miles from home.

A forty-year-old wife sought out her husband in the open range land near O'Neill and days later was found standing up in her muskrat coat and black bandanna, her scarf-wrapped hands tightly clenching the top strand of rabbit wire that was keeping her upright, her blue eyes still open but cloudily bottled by a half inch of ice, her jaw unhinged as though she'd died yelling out a name.

The one A.M. report from the Chief Signal Officer in Washington, D.C., had said Kansas and Nebraska could expect "fair weather, followed by snow, brisk to high southerly winds gradually diminishing in force, becoming westerly and warmer, followed by colder."

Sin Thomas undertook the job of taking Emily Flint home from their Holt County schoolhouse just before noon. Sin's age was sixteen, and Emily was not only six years younger but also practically kin to him, since her stepfather was Sin's older brother. Sin took the girl's hand and they haltingly tilted against the uprighting gale on their walk to a dark horse, gray-maned and gray-tailed with ice. Sin cracked the reins loose of the crowbar tie-up and helped Emily up onto his horse, jumping up onto the croup from a soapbox and clinging the girl to him as though she were groceries he couldn't let spill.

Everything she knew was no longer there. She was in a book without descriptions. She could put her hand out and her hand would disappear. Although Sin knew the general direction to Emily's house, the geography was so duned and drunk with snow that Sin gave up trying to nudge his horse one way or another and permitted its slight adjustments away from the wind. Hours passed and the horse strayed southeast into Wheeler County, and then in misery and pneumonia it stopped, planting its overworked legs like four parts of an argument and slinging its head away from Sin's yanks and then hanging its nose in anguish. Emily hopped down into the snow and held on to the boy's coat pocket as Sin uncinched the saddle and jerked off a green horse blanket and slapped it against his iron leggings in order to crack the ice from it. And then Sin scooped out a deep nook in a snow slope that was as high and steep as the roof of a New Hampshire house. Emily tightly wrapped herself in the green horse blanket and slumped inside the nook in the snow, and the boy crept on top of her and stayed like that, trying not to press into her.

Emily would never say what was said or was cautiously not said that night. She may have been hysterical. In spite of the fact that Emily was out of the wind, she later said that the January night's temperature was like wire-cutting pliers that snipped at her ears and toes and fingertips until the horrible pain became only a nettling and then a kind of sleep and her feet seemed as dead as her shoes. Emily wept, but her tears froze cold as penny nails and her upper lip seemed candlewaxed by her nose and she couldn't stop herself from feeling the difference in the body on top of her. She thought Sin Thomas was responsible, that the night suited his secret purpose, and she so complained of the bitter cold that Sin finally took off his Newmarket overcoat and tailored it around the girl; but sixty years later, when Emily wrote her own account of the ordeal, she forgot to say anything about him giving her his overcoat and only said in an ordinary way that they spent the night inside a snowdrift and that "by morning the storm had subsided."

With daybreak Sin told Emily to stay there and, with or without his Newmarket overcoat, the boy walked away with the forlorn hope of chancing upon his horse. Winds were still high, the temperature was thirty-five degrees below zero, and the snow was deep enough that Sin pulled lopsidedly with every step and then toppled over just a few yards away. And then it was impossible for him to get to his knees, and Sin only sank deeper when he attempted to swim up into the high wave of snow hanging over him. Sin told himself that he would try again to get out, but first he'd build up his strength by napping for just a little while. He arranged his body in the snow gully so that the sunlight angled onto it, and then Sin Thomas gave in to sleep and within twenty minutes died.

His body was discovered at noon by a Wheeler County search party, and shortly after that they came upon Emily. She was carried to a nearby house where she slumped in a kitchen chair while girls her own age dipped Emily's hands and feet into pans of ice water. She could look up over a windowsill and see Sin Thomas's body standing upright on the porch, his hands woodenly crossed at his chest, so Emily kept her brown eyes on the pinewood floor and slept that night with jars of hot water against her skin. She could not walk for two months. Even scissoring tired her hands. She took a cashier's job with the Nebraska Farm Implements Company and kept it for forty-five years, staying all her life in Holt County. She died in a wheelchair on a hospital porch in the month of April. She was wearing a glamorous sable coat. She never married.

The T. E. D. Schusters' only child was a seven-year-old boy named Cleo who rode his Shetland pony to the

Westpoint school that day and had not shown up on the doorstep by two P.M., when Mr. Schuster went down into the root cellar, dumped purple sugar beets onto the earthen floor, and upended the bushel basket over his head as he slung himself against the onslaught in his second try for Westpoint. Hours later Mrs. Schuster was tapping powdered salt onto the night candles in order to preserve the wax when the door abruptly blew open and Mr. Schuster stood there without Cleo and utterly white and petrified with cold. She warmed him up with okra soup and tenderly wrapped his frozen feet and hands in strips of gauze that she'd dipped in kerosene, and they were sitting on milking stools by a red-hot stove, their ankles just touching, only the usual sentiments being expressed, when they heard a clopping on the wooden stoop and looked out to see the dark Shetland pony turned gray and shaggy-bearded with ice, his legs as wobbly as if he'd just been born. Jammed under the saddle skirt was a damp, rolled-up note from the Scottish schoolteacher that said, Cleo is safe. The Schusters invited the pony into the house and bewildered him with praises as Cleo's mother scraped ice from the pony's shag with her own ivory comb, and Cleo's father gave him sugar from the Dresden bowl as steam rose up from the pony's back.

Even at six o'clock that evening, there was no heat in Mathias Aachen's house, and the seven Aachen children were in whatever stockings and clothing they owned as they put their hands on a Hay-burner stove that was no warmer than soap. When a jar of apricots burst open that night and the iced orange syrup did not ooze out, Aachen's wife told the children, You ought now to get under your covers. While the seven were crying and crowding onto their dirty floor mattresses, she rang the green tent cloth along the iron wire dividing the house and slid underneath horse blankets in Mathias Aachen's gray wool trousers and her own gray dress and a ghastly muskrat coat that in hot weather gave birth to insects.

Aachen said, Every one of us will be dying of cold before morning. Freezing here. In Nebraska.

His wife just lay there, saying nothing.

Aachen later said he sat up bodingly until shortly after one A.M., when the house temperature was so exceedingly cold that a gray suede of ice was on the teapot and his pretty girls were whimpering in their sleep. You are not meant to stay here, Aachen thought, and tilted hot candle wax into his right ear and then his left, until he could only hear his body drumming blood. And then Aachen got his Navy Colt and kissed his wife and killed her. And then walked under the green tent cloth and killed his seven children, stopping twice to capture a scuttling boy and stopping once more to reload.

Hattie Benedict was in her Antelope County schoolyard overseeing the noon recess in a black cardigan sweater and gray wool dress when the January blizzard caught her unaware. She had been impatiently watching four girls in flying coats playing Ante I Over by tossing a spindle of chartreuse yarn over the one-room schoolhouse, and then a sharp cold petted her neck and Hattie turned toward the open fields of hoarfrosted scraggle and yellow grass. Just a half mile away was a gray blur of snow underneath a dark sky that was all hurry and calamity, like a nighttime city of sin-black buildings and havoc in the streets. Wind tortured a creekside cottonwood until it cracked apart. A tin water pail rang in a skipping roll to the horse path. One quarter of the tar-paper roof was torn from the schoolhouse and sailed southeast forty feet. And only then did Hattie yell for the older boys with their cigarettes and clay pipes to hurry in from the prairie twenty rods away, and she was hustling a dallying girl inside just as the snowstorm socked into her Antelope County schoolhouse, shipping the building awry off its timber skids so that the southwest side heavily dropped six inches and the oak-plank floor became a slope that Hattie ascended unsteadily while ordering the children to open their *Webster Franklin Fourth Reader* to the Lord's Prayer in verse and to say it aloud. And then Hattie stood by her desk with her pink hands held theatrically to her cheeks as she looked up at the walking noise of bricks being jarred from the chimney and down the roof. Every window view was as white as if butchers' paper had been tacked up. Winds pounded into the windowpanes and dry window putty trickled onto the unpainted sills. Even the slough grass fire in the Hay-burner stove was sucked high into the tin stack pipe so that the soot on it reddened and snapped. Hattie could only stare. Four of the boys were just about Hattie's age, so she didn't say anything when they ignored the reading assignment and earnestly got up from the wooden benches in order to argue *oughts* and *ought nots* in the cloakroom. She heard the girls saying Amen and then she saw Janusz Vasko, who was fifteen years old and had grown up in Nebraska weather, gravely exiting the cloakroom with a cigarette behind one ear and his right hand raised high overhead. Hattie called on him, and Janusz said the older boys agreed that they could get the littler ones home, but only if they went out right away. And before she could even give it thought, Janusz tied his red handkerchief over his nose and mouth and jabbed his orange corduroy trousers inside his antelope boots with a pencil.

Yes, Hattie said, please go, and Janusz got the boys and girls to link themselves together with jump ropes and twine and piano wire, and twelve of Hattie Benedict's pupils walked out into a nothingness that the boys knew from their shoes up and dully worked their way across as though each crooked stump and tilted fence post was a word they could spell in a plain-spoken sentence in a book of practical knowledge. Hours later the children showed up at their homes, aching and crying in raw pain. Each was given cocoa or the green tea of the elder flower and hot bricks were put next to their feet while they napped and newspapers printed their names incorrectly. And then, one by one, the children disappeared from history.

Except for Johan and Alma Lindquist, aged nine and six, who stayed behind in the schoolhouse, owing to the greater distance to their ranch. Hattie opened a week-old Omaha newspaper on her desktop and with caution peeled a spotted yellow apple on it, eating tan slices from her scissor blade as she peered out at children who seemed irritatingly sad and pathetic. She said, You wish you were home.

The Lindquists stared.

Me too, she said. She dropped the apple core onto the newspaper page and watched it ripple with the juice stain. Have you any idea where Pennsylvania is?

East, the boy said. Johan was eating pepper cheese and day-old rye bread from a tin lunch box that sparked with electricity whenever he touched it. And his sister nudged him to show how her yellow hair was beguiled toward her green rubber comb whenever she brought it near.

Hattie was talking in such quick English that she could tell the Lindquists couldn't quite understand it. She kept hearing the snow pinging and pattering against the windowpanes, and the storm howling like clarinets down the stack pipe, but she perceived the increasing cold in the room only when she looked to the Lindquists and saw their Danish sentences grayly blossoming as they spoke. Hattie went into the cloakroom and skidded out the poorhouse box, rummaging from it a Scotch plaid scarf that she wrapped twice around her skull and ears just as a squaw would, and snipping off the fingertips of some red knitted gloves that were only slightly too small. She put them on and then she got into her secondhand coat and Alma whispered to her brother but Hattie said she'd have no whispering, she hated that, she couldn't wait for their kin to show up for them, she had too many responsibilities, and nothing interesting ever happened in the country. Everything was stupid. Everything was work. She didn't even have a girlfriend. She said she'd once been sick for four days, and two by two practically every woman in Neligh mistrustfully visited her rooming house to squint at Hattie and palm her forehead and talk about her symptoms. And then they'd snail out into the hallway and prattle and whisper in the hawk and spit of the German language.

Alma looked at Johan with misunderstanding and terror, and Hattie told them to get out paper and pencils; she was going to say some necessary things and the children were going to write them down. She slowly paced as she constructed a paragraph, one knuckle darkly striping the blackboard, but she couldn't properly express herself. She had forgotten herself so absolutely that she thought forgetting was a yeast in the air; or that the onslaught's only point was to say over and over again that she was next to nothing. Easily bewildered. Easily dismayed. The Lindquists were shying from the crazy woman and concentrating their shame on a nickel pad of Wisconsin paper. And Hattie thought, *You'll give me an ugly name and there will be cartoons and snickering and the older girls will idly slay me with jokes and imitation.*

She explained she was taking them to her rooming house, and she strode purposefully out into the great blizzard as if she were going out to a garden to fetch some strawberries, and Johan dutifully followed, but Alma stayed inside the schoolhouse with her purple scarf up over her mouth and nose and her own dark sandwich of pepper cheese and rye bread clutched to her breast like a prayer book. And then Johan stepped out of the utter whiteness to say Alma had to hurry up, that Miss Benedict was angrily asking him if his sister had forgotten how to use her legs. So Alma stepped out of the one-room schoolhouse, sinking deep in the snow and sloshing ahead in it as she would in a pond until she caught up with Hattie Benedict, who took the Lindquists' hands in her own and walked them into the utter whiteness and night of the afternoon. Seeking to blindly go north to her rooming house, Hattie put her high button shoes in the deep tracks that Janusz and the schoolchildren had made, but she misstepped twice, and that was enough to get her on a screw-tape path over snow humps and hillocks that took her south and west and very nearly into a great wilderness that was like a sea in high gale.

Hattie imagined herself reaching the Elkhorn River and discovering her rooming house standing high and honorable under the sky's insanity. And then she and the Lindquist children would duck over their teaspoons of tomato soup and soda crackers as the town's brooms and scarecrows teetered over them, hooking their green hands on the boy and girl and saying, Tell us about it. She therefore created a heroine's part for herself and tried to keep to it as she floundered through drifts as high as a four-poster bed in a white room of piety and weeping. Hattie pretended gaiety by saying once, See how it swirls! but she saw that the Lindquists were tucking deep inside themselves as they trudged forward and fell and got up again, the wind drawing tears from their squinting eyes, the hard, dry snow hitting their skin like wildly flying pencils. Hours passed as Hattie tipped away from the press of the wind into country that was a puzzle to her, but she kept saying, Just a little farther, until she saw Alma playing Gretel by secretly trailing her right hand along a wave of snow in order to secretly let go yet another crumb of her rye bread. And then, just ahead of her, she saw some pepper cheese that the girl dropped some time ago. Hissing spindrifts tore away from the snow swells and spiked her face like sharp pins, but then a door seemed to inch ajar and Hattie saw the slight, dark change of a haystack and she cut toward it, announcing that they'd stay there for the night.

She slashed away an access into the haystack and ordered Alma to crawl inside, but the girl hesitated as if she were still thinking of the gingerbread house and the witch's oven, and Hattie acidly whispered, You'll be a dainty mouthful. She meant it as a joke but her green eyes must have seemed crazy, because the little girl was crying when Hattie got inside the haystack next to her, and then Johan was crying, too, and Hattie hugged the Lindquists to her body and tried to shush them with a hymn by Dr. Watts, gently singing, Hush, my dears, lie still and slumber. She couldn't get her feet inside the haystack, but she couldn't feel them anyway just then, and the haystack was making everything else seem right and possible. She talked to the children about hot pastries and taffy and Christmas presents, and that night she made up a story about the horrible storm being a wicked old man whose only thought was to eat them up, but he couldn't find them in the haystack even though he looked and looked. The old man was howling, she said, because he was so hungry.

At daybreak a party of farmers from Neligh rode out on their high plowhorses to the Antelope County schoolhouse in order to get Hattie and the Lindquist children, but the room was empty and the bluetick hound that was with them kept scratching up rye bread until the party walked along behind it on footpaths that wreathed around the schoolyard and into a haystack twenty rods away where the older boys smoked and spit tobacco juice at recess. The Lindquist girl and the boy were killed by the cold, but Hattie Benedict had stayed alive inside the hay, and she wouldn't come out again until the party of men yanked her by the ankles. Even then she kept the girl's body hugged against one side and the boy's body hugged to the other, and when she was put up on one horse, she stared down at them with green eyes that were empty of thought or understanding and inquired if they'd be okay. Yes, one man said. You took good care of them.

Bent Lindquist ripped down his kitchen cupboards and carpentered his own triangular caskets, blacking them with shoe polish, and then swaddled Alma and Johan in black alpaca that was kindly provided by an elder in the Church of Jesus Christ of Latter-Day Saints. And all that night Danish women sat up with the bodies, sopping the Lindquists' skin with vinegar so as to impede putrefaction.

Hattie Benedict woke up in a Lincoln hospital with sweet oil of spermaceti on her hands and lips, and weeks later a Kansas City surgeon amputated her feet with a polished silver hacksaw in the presence of his anatomy class. She was walking again by June, but she was attached to cork-and-iron shoes and she sighed and grunted with every step. Within a year she grew so overweight that she gave up her crutches for a wicker-backed wheelchair and stayed in Antelope County on a pension of forty dollars per month, letting her dark hair grow dirty and leafy, reading one popular romance per day. And yet she complained so much about her helplessness, especially in winter, that the Protestant churches took up a collection and Hattie Benedict was shipped by train to Oakland, California, whence she sent postcards saying she'd married a trolley repairman and she hated Nebraska, hated their horrible weather, hated their petty lives.

On Friday the thirteenth some pioneers went to the upper stories of their houses to jack up the windows and crawl out onto snow that was like a jeweled ceiling over their properties. Everything was sloped and planed and caped and whitely furbelowed. One man couldn't get over his boyish delight in tramping about on deer-hide snowshoes at the height of his roof gutters, or that his dogwood tree was forgotten but for twigs sticking out of the snow like a skeleton's fingers. His name was Eldad Alderman, and he jabbed a bamboo fishing pole in four likely spots a couple of feet below his snowshoes before the bamboo finally thumped against the plank roof of his chicken coop. He spent two hours spading down to the coop and then squeezed in through the one window in order to walk among the fowl and count up. Half his sixty hens were alive; the other half were still nesting, their orange beaks lying against their white hackles, sitting there like a dress shop's hats, their pure white eggs not yet cold underneath them. In gratitude to those thirty chickens that withstood the ordeal, Eldad gave them Dutch whey and curds and eventually wrote a letter praising their constitutions in the *American Poultry Yard.*

Anna Shevschenko managed to get oxen inside a shelter sturdily constructed of oak scantling and a high stack of barley straw, but the snow powder was so fine and fiercely penetrating that it sifted through and slowly accumulated on the floor. The oxen tamped it down and inchingly rose toward the oak scantling rafters, where they were stopped as the snow flooded up, and by daybreak were overcome and finally asphyxiated. Widow Shevschenko decided then that an old woman could not keep a Nebraska farm alone, and she left for the East in February.

One man lost three hundred Rhode Island Red chickens; another lost two hundred sixty Hereford cattle and sold their hides for two dollars apiece. Hours after the Hubenka boy permitted twenty-one hogs to get out of the snowstorm and join their forty Holsteins in the upper barn, the planked floor in the cattle linter collapsed under the extra weight and the livestock perished. Since even coal picks could no more than chip the earth, the iron-hard bodies were hauled aside until they could be put underground in April, and just about then some Pawnee Indians showed up outside David City. Knowing their manner of living, Mr. Hubenka told them where the carcasses were rotting in the sea wrack of weed tangles and thaw-water jetsam, and the Pawnee rode their ponies onto the property one night and hauled the carrion away.

And there were stories about a Union Pacific train being arrested by snow on a railway siding near Lincoln, and the merchandisers in the smoking car playing euchre, high five, and flinch until sunup; about cowboys staying inside a Hazard bunkhouse for three days and getting bellyaches from eating so many tins of anchovies and saltine crackers; about the Omaha YMCA where shop clerks paged through inspirational pamphlets or played checkers and cribbage or napped in green leather Chesterfield chairs until the great blizzard petered out.

Half a century later, in Atkinson, there was a cranky talker named Bates, who maintained he was the fellow who first thought of attaching the word *blizzard* to the onslaught of high winds and slashing dry snow and ought to be given credit for it. And later, too, a Lincoln woman remembered herself as a little girl peering out through yellowed window paper at a yard and countryside that were as white as the first day of God's creation. And then a great white Brahma bull with street-wide horns trotted up to the house, the night's snow puffing up from his heavy footsteps like soap flakes, gray tunnels of air flaring from his nostrils and wisping away in the horrible cold. With a tilt of his head the great bull sought out the hiding girl under a Chesterfield table and, having seen her, sighed and trotted back toward Oklahoma.

Wild turkey were sighted over the next few weeks, their wattled heads and necks just above the snow like dark sticks, some of them petrified that way but others simply waiting for happier times to come. The onslaught also killed prairie dogs, jackrabbits, and crows, and the coyotes that relied upon them for food got so hungry that skulks of them would loiter like juveniles in the yards at night and yearn for scraps and castaways in old songs of agony that were always misunderstood.

Addie Dillingham was seventeen and irresistible that January day of the great blizzard, a beautiful English girl in an hourglass dress and an ankle-length otter-skin coat that was sculpted brazenly to display a womanly bosom and bustle. She had gently agreed to join an upperclassman at the Nebraska School of Medicine on a journey across the green ice of the Missouri River to Iowa, where there was a party at the Masonic Temple in order to celebrate the final linking of Omaha and Council Bluffs. The medical student was Repler Hitchcock of Council Bluffs—a good companion, a Republican, and an Episcopalian—who yearned to practice electro-therapeutics in Cuernavaca, Mexico. He paid for their three-course luncheon at the Paxton Hotel and then the couple strolled down Douglas Street with four hundred other partygoers, who got into cutters and one-horse open sleighs just underneath the iron legs and girders of what would eventually be called the Ak-Sar-Ben Bridge. At a cap-pistol shot the party jerked away from Nebraska and there were champagne toasts and cheers and yahooing, but gradually the party scattered and Addie could only hear the iron shoes of the plowhorse and the racing sleigh hushing across the shaded window glass of river, like those tropical flowers shaped like saucers and cups that slide across the green silk of a pond of their own accord.

At the Masonic Temple there were coconut macaroons and hot syllabub made with cider and brandy, and quadrille dancing on a puncheon floor to songs like the

"Butterfly Whirl" and "Cheater Swing" and "The Girl I Left Behind Me." Although the day was getting dark and there was talk about a great snowstorm roistering outside, Addie insisted on staying out on the dance floor until only twenty people remained and the quadrille caller had put away his violin and his sister's cello. Addie smiled and said, Oh what fun! as Repler tidily helped her into her mother's otter-skin coat and then escorted her out into a grand empire of snow that Addie thought was thrilling. And then, although the world by then was wrathfully meaning everything it said, she walked alone to the railroad depot at Ninth and Broadway so she could take the one-stop train called The Dummy across to Omaha.

Addie sipped hot cocoa as she passed sixty minutes up close to the railroad depot's coal stoker oven and some other partygoers sang of Good King Wenceslaus over a parlor organ. And then an old yardman who was sheeped in snow trudged through the high drifts by the door and announced that no more trains would be going out until morning.

Half the couples stranded there had family in Council Bluffs and decided to stay overnight, but the idea of traipsing back to Repler's house and sleeping in his sister's trundle bed seemed squalid to Addie, and she decided to walk the iron railway trestle across to Omaha.

Addie was a half hour away from the Iowa railway yard and up on the tracks over the great Missouri before she had second thoughts. White hatchings and tracings of snow flew at her horizontally. Wind had rippled snow up against the southern girders so that the high white skin was pleated and patterned like oyster shell. Every creosote tie was tented with snow that angled down into dark troughs that Addie could fit a leg through. Everything else was night sky and mystery, and the world she knew had disappeared. And yet she walked out onto the trestle, teetering over to a catwalk and sidestepping along it in high-button shoes, forty feet above the ice, her left hand taking the yield from one guy wire as her right hand sought out another. Yelling winds were yanking at her, and the iron trestle was swaying enough to tilt her over into nothingness, as though Addie Dillingham were a playground game it was just inventing. Halfway across, her gray tam-o'-shanter was snagged out just far enough into space that she could follow its spider-drop into the night, but she only stared at the great river that was lying there moon-white with snow and intractable. Wishing for her jump.

Years later Addie thought that she got to Nebraska and did not give up and was not overfrightened because she was seventeen and could do no wrong, and accidents and dying seemed a government you could vote against, a mother you could ignore. She said she panicked at one jolt of wind and sank down to her knees up there and briefly touched her forehead to iron that hurt her skin like teeth, but when she got up again, she could see the ink-black stitching of the woods just east of Omaha and the shanties on timber piers just above the Missouri River's jagged stocks of ice. And she grinned as she thought how she would look to a vagrant down there plying his way along a rope in order to assay his trotlines for gar and catfish and then, perhaps, appraising the night as if he'd heard a crazy woman screaming in a faraway hospital room. And she'd be jauntily up there on the iron trestle like a new star you could wish on, and as joyous as the last high notes of "The Girl I Left Behind Me."

DAVID HORGAN

THE GOLDEN WEST TRIO PLUS ONE

"Most people think Buck Owens has a harelip," the woman is saying, "but that's no harelip, it's a scar, and Lyle here is the one who gave it to him. The jerk made a pass at me, and Lyle hit him right here and caught him with his high school ring." She taps just below her nose.

I had said Buck Owens off the top of my head, when she asked me what country singers I liked. Ever since I'm sleeping alone again, I've been keeping my clock radio tuned to this one station up in Oakland that plays country oldies from nine to noon every morning. Today I happened to wake up to Buck Owens and His Buckeroos doing "Act Naturally." If I'd really thought about it, I'd have said somebody else. Merle Haggard, maybe.

The woman, Kay, is on the couch across from me. Lyle is on the other side of the room, bent forward in a wooden chair with his fiddle in his lap, wiping down the strings with a white towel. Lyle has hardly said a word since I came in the house. He doesn't even look up when she says that about Buck Owens.

I'm there answering an ad for a guitar player that they posted at the music store. On the phone Kay had said it was a steady weekend job for good money, but they needed to hear me play first. My guitar case is right here next to my chair, I've been sitting around for twenty minutes, but so far nobody has said another word about the gig.

For such a small person, the woman has a powerful voice.

"This was up in Reno, a good twenty-five years ago," she says. "You see him now, the big star of *Hee-Haw* with his red-white-and-blue guitar, you think he's just a good old boy with a good old-fashioned American harelip. Well, back then he was nothing but a two-bit hick who needed to learn his manners the hard way." She holds out the bag of potato chips she's had gripped between her knees. "Here, take a few. You look like you need some carbohydrates."

"No thanks," I say, but when she frowns and shakes the bag at me I take it anyway. I pull out one chip and pass the bag over to the daughter, Little Kay, who is at the other end of the couch watching some game show with the sound turned off. She looks to me to be about sixteen. Her legs are folded up beneath her, and she's wearing a red T-shirt pulled down over her knees. She takes the potato chips, reaches in for a fistful, and passes the bag to her mother, all without taking her eyes off the TV screen.

I lean forward in my chair, with the idea of bringing up the subject of why I'm here, when suddenly Kay is pointing her finger at me. Her eyes are deep and black, and there are dark crescent-shaped creases in her cheeks.

"I know what to expect from guitar players. Every yokel who knows two chords thinks he's the next Casanova." She gives me a sharp stare. "We were working the old Riverside Hotel, alternating shows with Mr. Big Shot Buck Owens, and one night he sneaks up to me backstage and starts putting on the moves. So there I am, fighting him off and trying not to get my makeup all smeared, when along comes Lyle and *pow*"—she slaps her hand with her fist—"right in the kisser."

I hear a throat clearing close by on my right. I turn and there's Lyle, who has scooted his chair right up next to me. He has thick bi-focal glasses, and he's wearing a fake-looking hairpiece that isn't a very good match with the gray hair around his ears and at the back of his neck.

"Well," he says, in a gentle voice. "What'd you say your name was?"

"His name is Carl, and he's been waiting half the night for you, Lyle, and so have the rest of us." Kay uses a tone of voice that makes me grab the arms of my chair.

Lyle doesn't act as if he has heard her. He gives me a little smile.

"The thing is, Carl, Kay and I want to get the trio back together again. Not to go on the road or anything like that." He chuckles to himself. "Just as a family thing. Kay's been teaching Little Kay some songs, and we thought it might be fun to go out and play somewhere. It's sure been a long time. I don't get much chance anymore, on account of my striping business."

"Striping?" I say. I realize I'm still gripping the arms of my chair.

Lyle makes a stroke across the carpet with his fiddle bow. "I paint stripes on parking lots. There's pretty good money in it."

"Oh, for God's sake, Lyle, he doesn't want to hear about *that.*" Kay jumps up from the couch. "Let's get down to business before we bore him to death. I'll be right back. You guys get yourselves tuned up." She's walking out of the room as she talks.

I start to unpack my guitar, glad to finally have something to do, and while I'm getting it out Lyle leans over and winks at me. "Don't let her scare you," he says. "She's not as mean as she looks."

Over on the couch Little Kay gives a snicker. Then she turns her head for the first time. She's got the same dark eyes as her mother. "If you want to know," she says, "the whole idea here is to keep me out of trouble." She turns right back to the TV without waiting for a response.

Lyle is still smiling at me. "Play me a G chord there, Carl." I play him the chord, and he pulls his fiddle up to his chin and strokes a beautiful little lick, very bluesy. And right away I start to feel better about all this. He lifts his bow off the strings. "Sounds like we're in pretty good tune to me," he says, and I'm about to agree with him when Kay comes back into the room. She's carrying a full-sized standup bass, gripping it around the middle with both arms. She stops in the center of the room, next to me, and sets it down with a grunt.

"God," she says, "this thing's heavier than it used to be." Then to me: "What are you staring at? You never saw a lady with a doghouse bass before? Come on, give some notes so I can tune up."

The three of us do a version of "Hey Good Lookin'." Kay plays bass in the old slap-rhythm style, whacking her hand against the fingerboard on the upbeats between each note. She closes her eyes and keeps her head tilted back, and considering the size of their living room she sings a lot louder than she needs to. She's got that shrill Kitty Wells sound, the kind of voice you don't hear much anymore. After the second verse, she looks over her shoulder and without missing a beat shouts, "Get over here, Little Kay!"

Little Kay unfolds herself from the couch and comes over. With the bag of potato chips in her hand she sings along on the bridge, trying to do a high harmony with her mother, but she isn't really in tune. Not even close. Then Lyle and I each take a little solo break. His playing is loose, but it's easy to hear that he must have been a fine fiddle player when his chops were in shape.

When we finish Lyle says, "Say, that was a sweet break you did there, Carl. Not too psychedelic if you know what I mean. A lot of guys these days, they act like they're getting paid by the note."

"Thanks," I say. "You played some nice stuff too, Lyle."

Little Kay goes back to the couch, and Kay stands with the bass leaning against her hip, looking back and forth at Lyle and me.

"When you two are done complimenting each other, maybe we can get around to talking business." She reaches over and pokes me in the shoulder. "We told you we had work, and that was no baloney. Go on, Lyle, tell him about it."

"Well," says Lyle, scratching the top of his hairpiece. "I've got this friend who owns one of those Straw Hat pizza parlors, up the road here in San Jose. I did his parking lot for him last year. He wants some live music for the weekends, something for a family-type crowd. Not too loud, not too weird." There's a snort from over on the couch, but Lyle hardly even blinks. "We need a guy who can play nice tasty guitar on these old tunes. Sixty bucks a night and free beer. What do you say?"

I feel another jab on my shoulder. "You got a white shirt, with pearl snaps?"

"Yeah, I do," I say.

"And some dark slacks, nice and conservative?"

I look over at Lyle. "What are you going to call the group?" I'm not really dying to know. I'm just stalling for a little time.

Lyle and Kay exchange a glance.

"The Golden West Trio," he says, smiling again. "It's the name we always used in the old days."

Something—call it common sense—tells me to stay clear of this. But I can sure use the money. For weeks all I've done is sit around the house playing along with records.

Kay looks over her shoulder at Little Kay. When she turns back to me her eyes have that same fierce look as when she first handed me the potato chips.

"The Golden West Trio plus One," she says. "So, are you in or out?"

The pizza parlor is a long narrow room with about twenty wooden tables set in two rows, and a stage at one end. The waitresses are wearing red and white striped outfits and little flat hats made of styrofoam instead of straw. A movie screen is on one of the long side walls, and they show old silent movies continuously, even while we're on the bandstand.

It's our first break of the night and I'm having a beer. Little Kay is across the table from me, sitting sideways on the bench. She and her mother are wearing identical outfits—short turquoise skirts with fringe, white blouses with puffy sleeves, and white boots almost up to their knees. Kay made the skirts and blouses herself, along with the turquoise vests Lyle and I are wearing with our white shirts and bolo ties.

The first set seemed to go fine. Kay and Lyle know every old waltz and country-western tearjerker—Hank Williams, Ernest Tubb, Patsy Cline. They hardly bother with anything written after about 1965. On every tune Lyle does a snappy fiddle intro that clues me into the tempo, while Kay does her standard walk-in lick on the bass. I try to play something compatible underneath Lyle for a few bars, and then Kay rears back and belts out the song. They keep the tunes flowing without even looking at each other. Little Kay has sung on only one tune so far, which is fine with me.

She turns toward me. She's drinking Diet Coke, and all I can see of her face are her eyes above the lip of her quart-sized paper cup. Suddenly she slaps the cup on the table, bouncing out a couple of ice cubes.

"This is a total *drag,* don't you think?"

I look around the room. There are about twenty people at the tables, mostly families with kids, and everybody is eating pizza and watching the movies.

"Oh, I don't know," I say. "It'll probably pick up later."

"No, it won't. Nobody comes in here. I wouldn't be caught dead in here."

She has a way of looking at you—just like her mother—that makes you think twice before you say anything.

"How can you stand to play this stupid corny music? I mean, you're a *guitar* player."

"I don't really mind it," I say. "I kind of like it. Your dad's a damn good musician, you know."

"Oh, come off it. How old are you anyway, Carl? Thirty? Forty?" She starts to laugh. "Fifty?"

I try to stare back at her. But I know I can't keep it up for long. "I'm thirty-four." I reach for my beer.

"How come you don't have your own band?"

"I used to." I might as well answer her next question in advance. "I got a little sick of travelling."

She raises her eyebrows. "What kind of band? A rock band? You don't look like the type to me."

Now it's my turn to laugh. Her idea of a rock band is probably four twelve-year-olds with filed teeth. "Sort of. Rock and roll, anyway. And rhythm and blues."

"Hey, you mean like B. B. King? He's pretty cool for an old guy."

I shrug. "Yeah, that's the idea."

She tilts her head sideways. "So, are you married, or what?" She starts chewing on the lip of her cup.

"I used to be." I try for a tone of voice that'll cut the subject short.

"Divorced, huh? How long ago? Was it before your band split up?"

I take a gulp of my beer. It's starting to go flat.

"Come on, Carl. It's good for you to talk about it. What was her name?"

I take another drink, then have a nice long look at my watch.

"Okay, be that way," she says. I'm thinking maybe she's about to get up and leave, but suddenly she smiles. "Alright, I'm being nosy. I'm sorry."

She pours a few ice cubes into her mouth, slurps them around for awhile, and spits a couple of them back into her cup. She looks at me again.

"You *know* why they're doing this to me, don't you?"

It seems like another good time to not say anything.

"Well, I'll tell you why. They're doing this to keep me out of trouble." She leans closer. "They're doing this to keep me off the streets." She's speaking in an exaggerated whisper. "I'm a *very bad girl.*"

Her head snaps back as she bursts out giggling. She has to grab the edge of the table to keep from slipping off the bench.

"They think I'm a juvenile delinquent," she says. "I have boy friends, and I ride around in cars and smoke pot. I've been kicked out of school once already. So they got this idea for a family band. The trouble is I don't have a microgram of talent. The other trouble is this band stuff starts reminding them how wild and stupid they were when *they* were young. And that makes them even more paranoid about me."

She stares at me again. I have the feeling she's waiting to see whose side I'm on.

"Her name was Rhonda," I say. This even takes me by surprise—not that the thought came up, but that I suddenly decided to tell her.

She gives me another smile. Then she winks. It's the first thing she's done that reminds me of Lyle. "Rhonda, huh? What a crazy name. So who left who?"

I could very easily keep my mouth shut again. I'm not sure why I don't.

"She met somebody while I was on the road. That's all there is to it, really."

"Oh, *sure* it is."

Her eyes shift. She's looking past me, over my shoulder. "Here comes Mom to get you," she says. "She really likes you, you know. You think she's a total ogre, but believe me, to her you shy types are the best thing since sliced bread."

She leans in close again. "She'd never let me sit and talk to you this long if she didn't like you a lot. You just wait. Next thing you know, she'll be inviting you to dinner. You better be prepared." She taps me on the arm. "Sorry about Rhonda," she whispers, and then she lifts her cup and tosses her head back.

I feel a hand on my shoulder.

"Time to hit it again, Carl," Kay says. Then to Little Kay, with a rise in her voice: "We're going to try that one we practiced, the Loretta Lynn one." They look at each other with their dark eyes. Little Kay bites down on an ice cube and breaks it with a loud crack. "Sure thing, Mom," she says. "Your wish is my command."

I step over the bench fast and head for the bandstand. It suddenly seems like it's been a long fifteen minutes. Lyle is already up there, plucking his fiddle with his thumb and humming to himself. After I climb up and put on my guitar he says, "Hey, Carl, you know a silly old Joe Venuti tune called 'Hot Canary'?" Already I can feel myself snapping into a better mood.

"Never heard of it," I say. "But I'll be glad to fake the chords underneath you."

He beams at me. "That's what I like to hear. Let's give it a go. I'll hack at it for awhile and you'll get the idea. You catch that, Kay? We're starting with 'Hot Canary.' Key of D, as in Dreadful."

Kay has climbed up behind me and picked her bass up off the floor. "Oh, Jesus," she says. "That stupid old thing?"

She takes a minute to adjust the height of her microphone and tug at something underneath the back of her skirt. Then she steps up to the mike and switches it on. Her voice comes booming back to us as it bounces off the far wall: "Now here's one for all you fans of the good old fiddle tunes, a novelty number from way back called 'Hot Canary.' We hope you like it as much as we do—take it away, boys!"

Lyle taps out a quick bar with his foot, does a variation of his standard intro, and we're in.

The photography studio is in a converted gas station and is run by a woman named Inez Hooker. Kay said she was an old friend, and she probably gave them a good deal, but anybody can see it isn't the most professional operation in the world.

When I first got here, Lyle said hi to me and winked and shook my hand the way he always does. Kay and Little Kay were having some trouble, and weren't talking to anybody. It turns out Little Kay isn't too pleased at the idea of being photographed in her performing outfit. While I was cinching up my bolo tie in front of the mirror in the hallway I heard them going at it on the other side of the door behind me. They were in a closet that served as a storage and dressing room. Little Kay was crying and carrying on about having to dress up like a drum majorette, and how it didn't matter in a pizza parlor where nobody in their right mind would go anyway, but getting her picture taken for an ad in the paper that would be seen by half the people in northern California was another story. She went on like that for awhile, and then Kay spoke in a couple of quick bursts at low volume. I couldn't quite make out what she said, but whatever it was, a minute later Kay came out alone and we are now proceeding with the photo session.

We're posing in front of the camera—Lyle, Kay, and me. Little Kay still hasn't emerged from the closet. Inez Hooker is standing on a little step ladder, peering down into the lens of her camera which is mounted on a high tripod. She is a thin woman in yellow slacks and a black T-shirt that says SMILE! in big pink letters across her chest. Lights with umbrella reflectors are positioned on both sides of us. One of these has already fallen over. The bulb shattered, and it took some time to sweep it up and reposition the light and comb our hair again, but now we're finally ready to go once more. We all have our instruments, and we're supposed to be holding a pose that looks like we're playing. I'm between Kay and Lyle, holding a C-seventh chord and trying not to blink.

Inez looks up.

"Guitar player. I'm getting a bad reflection off your glasses."

"No problem, I'll take them off," I say, and I put them in my pocket.

"What about Lyle's glasses, Inez?" says Kay. "Are they reflecting too? They're so damn thick."

"His are okay I think, as long as his face is pointing down. Just don't look up from your violin, Lyle, whatever you do."

She adjusts the camera some more. "I think we're all set here." Then she suddenly snaps her fingers. "I've got a great idea. I'll take a quick Polaroid, to give you an idea how you really look. Don't move, it'll only take a sec." She jumps off the ladder and runs out and comes back with a Polaroid camera. Back up the ladder, she points it at us and says, "Come on now, smile everybody!" She snaps, the picture slides out the front, and Inez hops down and trots over with it.

Kay holds the snapshot in her hand as it fades into view. There we are all right, a perfect likeness. Kay in her fresh beehive hairdo, Lyle with his wig on straight, and me in my vest and bolo tie. I make a mental note to stop squinting.

"Oh my God," Kay says. "I look awful."

"No, you don't, dear," says Lyle. "You look very nice."

"I don't either look nice, I look horrible. I look like a fat broad hugging a fat bass fiddle." She holds the picture closer. "It just isn't ladylike."

We stand there for a minute, all of us just looking at the picture. I consider putting my glasses back on, but then think better of it. I don't want anyone to think I'm ready to give an opinion. It isn't until I hear Little Kay's voice behind me that I realize she has finally come out to join us.

"Listen, Mom, I've got an idea." She reaches over and takes the snapshot out of Kay's hand. "You know that old picture you showed me the other day, of you and Dad when you were on that radio show? Where you were sitting right on the bass—sort of sexy. Remember?"

Kay snatches the picture back and looks at it even more intently than before, as if expecting a new image to materialize. If she's wondering at all about her daughter's sudden change of attitude, she doesn't show it. I tell myself not to, but I can't help catching Little Kay's eye. She winks at me. Even without my glasses, I see it clearly.

"Okay, let's try it," Kay says. And without another word she puts the bass down on its side, steps around in front of it, and with one hand holding her turquoise skirt against her rump she slowly lowers herself backwards, so that she sits on the bass where the body curves inward, opposite the f-hole. Then she leans over sideways and rests her elbow on the fat part of the bass. She smooths down her skirt in front with her other hand.

"There," she says. "What do you think?"

We all step around to where we can see her better. Now I do put my glasses back on. Inez takes a few steps back with her hand on her chin. "Hmm," she says. "Very interesting."

Kay crosses her legs. "Is that any better?"

Her legs, especially above the knees, are thick and muscular-looking and kind of purplish in places. Her white boots are tight around her calves, and something about the position she is in seems to draw your attention to her kneecaps, which look heftier and knobbier than when she's standing up. It's a type of pose that might make sense for someone young and long and lean. And maybe not even then.

"Not bad," Inez says. "Not bad at all. Why don't you two fellas step back in there, just the way you were before. Let's see what we've got." She goes back to her ladder and climbs up. Lyle and I step around and face the camera again. I take my glasses off. "A little closer in, fellas." Inez is peering into her lens again. "I think we may just have it."

Little Kay has gone back to stand next to the ladder. "Oh, yeah," she calls out. "That's it, all right. That's absolutely beautiful." Then she suddenly marches toward us and comes all the way around to stand between Lyle and me. "How does this look, Inez, if I squeeze in right here?"

"Well, well," says Kay from down in front. "Miss Primadonna wants her picture taken after all."

I notice Little Kay is being careful to keep most of herself hidden behind her mother and the bass. "I can change my mind, can't I? Otherwise who's ever going to believe this?"

"It looks great, everybody," says Inez. "It really does. I think we can shoot this one for real."

I steal a quick glance at Lyle. As usual, his face doesn't give you a clue. His fiddle is in position under his chin with the bow on the strings and his elbow up high in the air. He's wearing a nice big smile. He looks like he's right in the middle of "Orange Blossom Special."

"Here we go!" says Inez. "Look happy everybody. Very good!" And she starts snapping away. From up on her ladder she keeps saying, "Oh, that's nice, that's just a beauty. We'll be out of here in no time at all." And before long, we are.

Saturday night, our third weekend on the job, and we still aren't playing to more than twenty or thirty people at a time. Of these, it's clear most of them are coming in for beer and pizza and silent movies, not to listen to heartbreak ballads and fiddle tunes.

Still, I'm enjoying certain things about the gig. Lyle's good for a few surprises every night. The more he plays, the more tunes he remembers. He's starting to throw quotes from things like "Take The 'A' Train" into the middle of two-chord waltzes. If I pick up on it and quote it back to him later in the tune, he'll double over as if he's about to burst out laughing—but this turns out to be a trick to get me to laugh first. Sooner or later Kay starts to slap the bass extra hard or sing a couple of lines extra loud, which is our signal to quit horsing around. In terms of complaining about what we play, that's about as far as she usually goes, as long as the tunes begin and end together and we stay out of her way while she's singing.

Little Kay is up to two or three songs per set, usually just singing backup lines to her mother. Sometimes it sounds all right, but most of the time it doesn't, and then Kay has to sing even harder to drown her out. This often causes people sitting up front to gather up their pizza platters and their pitchers of beer and move to a table further back. When Little Kay's numbers are done, she moves over to the side of the stage to play tambourine and practice dance moves she's picked up from MTV. Eventually Kay gives her the signal to go sit back down.

Now I'm outside on my break, around the corner from the front door, leaning against the building and finishing a beer. It's a nice warm night, with a light breeze blowing in off the Bay. I guess I've had my eyes closed or something, because when I hear her voice it takes me by surprise.

"Hi."

I turn my head fast.

She's right next to me, about a foot away. She's leaning against the wall with one shoulder, her outside hand on her hip. She's looking at me.

"Little Kay," I say. "Where'd you come from?"

"Oh, I just parachuted in. Airlifted by the Libyans. I came from inside, birdbrain, where else?" Her eyes get wider. "I followed you out here. I snuck up on you, while you were lost in thought."

"Is it time to go inside?" My voice has an edgy sound to it. You might even say nervous.

"No, there's loads of time still. Ten minutes, at least. Aren't you so goddamn bored you could just scream?"

Our heads are very close together. I hadn't realized until now that Little Kay and I are just about the same height. The sensible thing for me to do is take a couple of steps sideways. Instead, I lift my cup and go through the motions of taking a drink, which only makes me feel sillier, since I finished off my beer a couple of minutes ago.

"I hear you're coming to dinner tomorrow night," she says. "What'd I tell you?"

"Yeah, I guess I am. Your dad's the one who asked me."

"She told him to, though. She makes these decisions, in case you haven't noticed."

I look straight ahead again, out toward the Bay. I want to say something to her, something about Lyle's integrity that I don't think she understands, but before I can say it she has stepped around fast and put both hands on the back of my neck. Then she falls forward against me, pushing me against the wall. Her face comes in fast and she kisses me hard on the mouth—a real grown-up kiss. I can feel the pressure of the cinderblock against the back of my head.

It doesn't last long. She steps away from me, dropping her hands, and as she moves back my arms fall away from her waist. I don't have any idea what happened to my cup. It's a curious thing: in the two or three seconds it takes her to back away some fast impressions replay in my mind—the lightness of her body up against me, the feeling of her mouth rubbing against mine, even the sweet, soapy smell of her hair—but for the life of me, I can't remember reaching around and taking hold of her. Maybe I was just trying to keep my balance. My cup, I can see now, is lying on the ground next to her foot.

She puts both hands on her hips and stands there smiling.

"Jesus Christ," I say.

She giggles. "My curiosity was killing me. You're the first guy I've ever liked that my mother approved of. I wanted to know how it would feel."

Then she starts walking away. After a few steps she turns and looks back. "It was nice, don't you think?" Without waiting for an answer, she goes ahead on inside.

I stay out there as long as I can, trying to relax, trying to remember that I came outside to take in the fresh breeze. But finally I realize that if I've got to go back in there and get up on the bandstand and play through the rest of the night, what I really need fast is another beer. At least.

"Have some more, Carl. There's plenty of white meat still. There's a whole leg left there too. Take as much as you want."

Lyle's holding out the platter, so I take it from him even though I don't want any. I pass it over to Kay sitting at my left. I still have plenty of everything—turkey, stuffing, peas and carrots, both kinds of cranberry sauce. It's a regular Christmas dinner at grandma's house. All afternoon I kept thinking that the smart thing to do was call them up and say I couldn't make it. And here I am anyway. I'm not even hungry.

Little Kay is sitting across from me. She's wearing a pink tank top and a pair of earrings that are miniature globes, with tiny oceans and continents. So far I've avoided looking her in the eye. On the wall above her is a large framed photograph, about three feet square—an aerial view of a baseball stadium.

"You're not too crazy about my cooking, I can see that." Kay pops a forkful of mashed potatoes into her mouth.

"Oh, no," I say. "I'm just not a big eater, is all." This is far from the truth, under normal circumstances.

"It figures. You guitar players are all like that. I don't know where you get your protein from. Drugs and alcohol, I guess, same as always."

I'm looking down, spearing a couple of peas with my fork, so I don't see who it is—one of them, Lyle or Little Kay, must have given her the eye.

"I was only kidding, for God's sake," Kay says. "Let's not be so touchy around here. Carl's practically one of the family, anyhow."

Little Kay flops against the back of her chair and looks at the ceiling. "Mother, I don't *believe* you sometimes."

On my right Lyle clears his throat, nice and loud, and I'm glad to have the chance to turn his way.

"Candlestick Park," he says. He's pointing at the photograph on the wall. "That picture was taken from a helicopter. Thirty-seven thousand parking spaces. Thirty-seven thousand two hundred and fourteen, to be exact."

The photograph is in sharp focus. The pitcher's mound and base-paths are easy to see. So are the white lines criss-crossing the huge expanse of parking lots.

"It took us sixteen weeks to do the job. Biggest contract I've ever had. Just me and my partner, working seven days a week for four months. That's what made the down payment on this house." With Lyle you can never tell for sure, but it sounds like real pride in his voice. Then he reaches over and puts his hand on my arm. His grip is surprisingly tight. He's wearing his same old smile. "But I'll tell you something, Carl," he says. His voice just got a lot softer. "It's the most boring God-awful work you ever imagined in your life. I wouldn't recommend it to a dog."

I pull my arm away. My stomach just took a jump, like being in an airplane when it hits an air pocket and drops. Maybe that's just the effect Lyle was trying for. A little kick in the pants to get me to use my head.

"Listen," I say. It comes out so loud and firm, I don't even sound like myself. Before I say anything else, I meet Little Kay's eye. She's staring hard at me, her mouth drawn up tight. Her forehead and cheeks are giving off a soft pink glow. She's a beautiful girl, really. That's not such a tough thing to admit at all.

"So out with it, Carl," says Kay. She's tapping the tablecloth with the handle of her spoon. "We haven't got all night. There's dessert coming, you know."

I carefully put my fork down next to my plate, and then I say, "I'm afraid I have to quit the band."

There's a moment of silence.

Kay's fist comes down on the table hard. My glass and silverware and plate all jump. "What did you say?" Her voice sounds pinched, up out of its normal range.

I should have had a nice tidy explanation ready to go. Now all I do is sit there staring at the picture of Candlestick Park. Behind the stadium on the right field side, you can see the waves of San Francisco Bay breaking onto the landfill shore. And I start thinking about how Candlestick Park is built on a gigantic pile of garbage, thousands of tons of fish heads and coffee grounds and old tires, paved over to look like solid ground.

"Mother," says Little Kay, "are you deaf, or what?"

My eyes move down. Little Kay is wearing just a trace of a smile now. "Carl just said he had to quit the band." She's speaking in the calmest tone I've heard her use yet. "He's quitting because he got an offer from another band. It's a rock band, and they're going on the road, and they're really good. And not only that, his new girlfriend is in the band. Her name's Rhonda, and she's a singer. They're crazy about each other, and this is their chance to be together all the time. Carl told me so last night. He was going to let you know then, but I told him it would be easier for you if he waited till today."

She faces me again, with that same little half-smile. I could get mad and throw my plate of food at her. Or I could answer her dare, and play right along with this cockeyed story. I hesitate, but only for a second.

"That's right," I say, turning to Kay. Her hand is still clenched where it landed on the table. Her eyes are wide and her mouth is clamped in a frown. I'm surprised at how easy it is to look her square in the eye. "It's a pretty hot band, and they've got a lot of work lined up. I just can't turn it down. They've got great gigs, Tahoe and things like that." It's coming nice and easy now. I look over at Lyle. "I'm sorry about it, Lyle. You guys have been nice to work for. But you can see how it is."

Lyle's expression doesn't change, and he doesn't say a word. He just keeps right on smiling. I can't see his eyes too well because of the light bouncing off his glasses. I could be imagining things, but I think I might have seen him wink.

"Oh, we can see how it is, all right." Kay has stood up and now she's leaning over toward me with both hands gripping the edge of the table. "You're no different from all the rest. You take the best offer of the week. You chase after anything in skirts. You don't care who you're letting down. You don't care who's counting on you." Her voice keeps rising in pitch, like a tape being sped up. "What about the money we spent on those goddamn glossy photos? What about the audience we were beginning to build up? What about that, Mr. Big Shot Guitar Player?"

Now the rest of us are standing up too. In a couple of minutes, I think to myself, this whole crazy scene will be over, I'll be outside getting in my car and going back to my radio and my record player.

"You'll find another guitar player, Kay," I say. "There's a million guitar players."

"Oh, don't I know it!" She's shouting now. "You're a dime a dozen. I don't need you to tell me that. I don't need you to walk in my house and sit down at my table and make eyes at my baby daughter and then tell me there's a million guitar players in the world." She's starting to cry, but it doesn't affect the power of her voice. "Why don't you just get the hell out of here? Why don't you take your polite ass and get the hell out of my house?"

She's pointing a beefy outstretched arm at the front door. It doesn't take me long to get my jacket off the back of the chair in the living room, put it on, open the door, and step out into the Sunday night air.

There's a cool breeze. Lyle follows me outside and then walks beside me to the car without a word. We stand there quietly for a minute. Finally he says, "She didn't mean it like that, Carl. She never really means to be that way."

"It's okay, Lyle. I'm sorry about all this. I truly am."

I'm thinking that I ought to shake his hand, or something, when the front door of the house opens again. Little Kay steps out onto the porch and closes the door behind her. She has on a sweater that's way too big for her. It must be one of Lyle's. She comes up and stands close to him.

"She's going to be fine," Little Kay says. "I told her to go lie down, and she did."

She links her arm through Lyle's. She's looking at me, but it's hard to see her face in the dark. "So anyway, Carl, good luck with your new band. I bet you'll make it big someday." She runs a hand through her hair. "Stay in touch, huh?" She still sounds so cool and collected. I'd even say sincere, if I didn't know better. It could fool anybody. It's a talent that seems to run in this little family.

"That's right," Lyle says. "Best of luck to you, Carl. You're a good guitar man. Maybe we'll see you on TV or something."

"Thanks for everything, Lyle," I say. But now I'm suddenly thinking of something else. It must have been what he said about seeing me on TV. Maybe I ought to leave it alone, but I don't know when I'll ever see him again.

"Lyle, can I ask you something? About that business with Buck Owens. You know—his scar, or harelip, or whatever it is. Did you really hit him the way Kay said? Is that whole story true?"

Lyle starts to laugh, and so does Little Kay.

"Is it true?" he says. "Well, no, not exactly. Though it might as well be, when you get right down to it." He laughs softly to himself again. "What I mean is, it works just as good as the truth. Or maybe even better."

In spite of the darkness, I can tell by the sound of his voice exactly the look Lyle's giving me. I feel like I'm beginning to catch on about this knack for sticking to a story. Maybe it's what in the end counts the most. Maybe it's the thing that can hold a family together. All of a sudden I feel very sure of this.

"Yeah," I say, and now for some reason I'm laughing too. "I think I see what you mean, Lyle. Forget I asked."

So I finally do shake his hand, and we say good night all around and then I turn around and get in my car. Once I have the keys out and the motor started, I look up and see Lyle and Little Kay one last time, arm in arm, standing on their front porch. As I drive away, they both wave with their free hands.

LOUISE ERDRICH

MATCHIMANITO

from *Tracks*

We started dying before the snow, and, like the snow, we continued to fall. We were surprised that so many of us were left to die. For those who survived the spotted sickness from the south and our long fight west to Dakota land, where we signed the treaty, and then a wind from the east, bringing exile in a storm of government papers, what descended from the north in 1914 seemed terrible, and unjust.

By then we thought disaster must surely have spent its force, that disease must have claimed all of the Anishinabe that the earth could hold and bury.

But along with the first bitter punishments of early winter a new sickness swept down. The consumption, it was called by young Father Damien, who came in that year to replace the priest who had succumbed to the same devastation as his flock. This disease was different from the pox and fever, for it came on slowly. The outcome, however, was just as certain. Whole families of Anishinabe lay ill and helpless in its breath. On the reservation, where we were forced close together, the clans dwindled. Our tribe unraveled like a coarse rope, frayed at either end as the old and new among us were taken. My own family was wiped out one by one. I was the only Nanapush who lived. And after, although I had seen no more than fifty winters, I was considered an old man.

I guided the last buffalo hunt. I saw the last bear shot. I trapped the last beaver with a pelt of more than two years' growth. I spoke aloud the words of the government treaty and refused to sign the settlement papers that would take away our woods and lake. I axed the last birch that was older than I, and I saved the last of the Pillager family.

Fleur.

We found her on a cold afternoon in late winter, out in her family's cabin near Matchimanito Lake, where my companion, Edgar Pukwan, of the tribal police, was afraid to go. The water there was surrounded by the highest oaks, by woods inhabited by ghosts and roamed by Pillagers, who knew the secret ways to cure or kill, until their art deserted them. Dragging our sled into the clearing, we saw two things: the smokeless tin chimney spout jutting from the roof, and the empty hole in the door where the string was drawn inside. Pukwan did not want to enter, fearing that the unburied Pillager spirits might seize him by the throat and turn him windigo. So I was the one who broke the thin-scraped hide that made a window. I was the one who lowered himself into the stinking silence, onto the floor. I was also the one to find the old man and woman, the little brother and two sisters, stone cold and wrapped in gray horse blankets, their faces turned to the west.

Afraid as I was, stilled by their quiet forms, I touched each bundle in the gloom of the cabin, and wished each spirit a good journey on the three-day road, the old-time road, so well trampled by our people this deadly season. Then something in the corner knocked. I flung the door wide. It was the eldest daughter, Fleur, so feverish that she'd thrown off her covers. She huddled against the cold wood range, staring and shaking. She was wild as a filthy wolf, a big bony girl whose sudden bursts of strength and snarling cries terrified the listening Pukwan. I was the one who struggled to lash her to the sacks of supplies and to the boards of the sled. I wrapped blankets over her and tied them down as well.

Pukwan kept us back, convinced that he should carry out the agency's instructions to the letter: he carefully nailed up the official quarantine sign, and then, without removing the bodies, he tried to burn down the house. But though he threw kerosene repeatedly against the logs and even started a blaze with birch bark and chips of wood, the flames narrowed and shrank, went out in puffs of smoke. Pukwan cursed and looked desperate, caught between his official duties and his fear of Pillagers. The fear won out. He finally dropped the tinders and helped me drag Fleur along the trail.

And so we left five dead at Matchimanito, frozen behind their cabin door.

Some say that Pukwan and I should have done right and buried the Pillagers first thing. They say the unrest and curse of trouble that struck our people in the years that followed was the doing of dissatisfied spirits. I know what's fact, and have never been afraid of talking. Our trouble came from the living, from liquor and the dollar bill. We stumbled toward the government bait, never looking down, never noticing how the land was snatched from under us at every step.

When Edgar Pukwan's turn came to draw the sled, he took off like devils chased him, bounced Fleur over potholes as if she were a log, and tipped her twice into the snow. I followed the sled, encouraged Fleur with songs, cried at Pukwan to watch for hidden branches and deceptive drops, and finally got her to my cabin, a small, tightly tamped box overlooking the crossroads.

"Help me," I cried, cutting at the ropes, not even bothering with knots. Fleur closed her eyes, panted, and tossed her head from side to side. Her chest rattled as she strained for air; she grabbed me around the neck. Still weak from my own bout with the sickness, I staggered, fell, lurched into my cabin, wrestling the strong girl inside with me. I had no wind left over to curse Pukwan, who watched but refused to touch her, turned away, and vanished with the whole sled of supplies. I was neither surprised nor caused enduring sorrow later when Pukwan's son, also named Edgar and also of the tribal police, told me that his father came home, crawled into bed, and took no food from that moment until his last breath passed.

As for Fleur, each day she improved in small changes. First her gaze focused, and the next night her skin was cool and damp. She was clearheaded, and after a week she remembered what had befallen her family, how they had taken sick so suddenly, gone under. With her memory mine came back, only too sharply. I was not prepared to think of the people I had lost, or to speak of them, although we did, carefully, without letting their names loose in the wind that would reach their ears.

We feared that they would hear us and never rest, come back out of pity for the loneliness we felt. They would sit in the snow outside the door waiting until from longing we joined them. We would all be together on the journey then, our destination the village at the end of the road, where people gamble day and night but never lose their money, eat but never fill their stomachs, drink but never leave their minds.

The snow receded enough for us to dig the ground with picks. As a tribal policeman, Pukwan's son was forced by regulation to help bury the dead. So again we took the dark road to Matchimanito, the son leading rather than the father. We spent the day chipping at the earth until we had a hole long and deep enough to lay the Pillagers shoulder to shoulder. We covered them and built five small board houses. I scratched out their clan markers, four crosshatched bears and a marten; then Pukwan Junior shouldered the government's tools and took off down the path. I settled myself near the graves.

I asked those Pillagers, as I had asked my own children and wives, to leave us now and never come back. I offered tobacco, smoked a pipe of red willow for the old man. I told them not to pester their daughter just because she had survived, or to blame me for finding them, or Pukwan Junior for leaving too soon. I told them that I was sorry they must abandon us. I insisted. But the Pillagers were as stubborn as the Nanapush clan and would not leave my thoughts. I think they followed me home. All the way down the trail, just beyond the edges of my sight, they flickered, thin as needles, shadows piercing shadows.

The sun had set by the time I got back, but Fleur was awake, sitting in the dark as if she knew. She never moved to build up the fire, never asked where I had been. I never told her about it either, and as the days passed we spoke rarely, always with roundabout caution. We felt the spirits of the dead so near that at length we just stopped talking.

This made it worse.

Their names grew within us, swelled to the brink of our lips, forced our eyes open in the middle of the night. We were filled with the water of the drowned, cold and black—airless water that lapped against the seal of our tongues or leaked slowly from the corners of our eyes. Within us, like ice shards, their names bobbed and shifted. Then the slivers of ice began to collect and cover us. We became so heavy, weighted down with the lead-gray frost, that we could not move. Our hands lay on the table like cloudy blocks. The blood within us grew thick. We needed no food. And little warmth. Days passed, weeks, and we didn't leave the cabin for fear we'd crack our cold and fragile bodies. We had gone half windigo. I learned later that this was common, that many of our people died in this manner, of the invisible sickness. Some could not swallow another bite of food because the names of their dead thickened on their tongues. Some let their blood stop, took the road west after all.

One day the new priest—just a boy, really—opened our door. A dazzling and painful light flooded through and surrounded Fleur and me. Numb, stupid as bears in a winter den, we blinked at the priest's slight silhouette. Our lips were parched, stuck together. We could hardly utter a greeting, but we were saved by one thought: a guest must eat. Fleur gave Father Damien her chair and put wood on the gray coals. She found flour for gaulette. I went to fetch snow to boil for tea water, but to my amazement the ground was bare. I was so surprised that I bent over and touched the soft, wet earth.

My voice rasped at first when I tried to speak, but then, oiled by strong tea, lard, and bread, I was off and talking. You could not stop me with a sledgehammer once I started. Father Damien looked astonished, and then wary, as I began to creak and roll. I gathered speed. I talked both languages in streams that ran alongside each other, over every rock, around every obstacle. The sound of my voice convinced me I was alive. I kept Father Damien listening all night, his green eyes round, his thin face straining to understand, his odd brown hair in curls and clipped knots. Occasionally he took in air, as if to add observations of his own, but I pushed him under with my words.

I don't know when Fleur slipped out.

She was too young and had no stories or depth of life to rely upon. All she had was raw power, and the names of the dead that filled her. I can speak them now. They have no more interest in any of us. Old Pillager. Ogimaakwe, Boss Woman, his wife. Asasaweminikwesens, Chokecherry Girl. Bineshii, Small Bird, also known as Josette. And the last, the boy Ombaashi, He Is Lifted by Wind.

They are gone, but sometimes I don't know where they are anymore—this place of reservation surveys or the other place, boundless, where the dead sit talking, see too much, and regard the living as fools.

And we were. Starvation makes fools of anyone. In the past some had sold their allotment land for a hundred pound weight of flour. Others, who were desperate to hold on, now urged that we get together and buy back our land, or at least pay a tax and refuse the settlement money that would sweep the marks of our boundaries off the map like a pattern of straws. Many were determined not to allow the hired surveyors, or even our own people, to enter the deepest bush.

But that spring outsiders went in as before, permitted by the agent, a short round man with hair blond as chaff. The purpose of these people was to measure the lake. Only now they walked upon the fresh graves of Pillagers, crossed death roads to plot out the deepest water where the lake monster, Misshepeshu, hid and waited.

"Stay here with me," I said to Fleur when she came to visit.

She refused.

"The land will go," I told her. "The land will be sold and measured."

But she tossed back her hair and walked off, down the path, with nothing to eat till thaw but a bag of my onions and a sack of oats.

Who knows what happened? She returned to Matchimanito and stayed there alone in the cabin that even fire did not want. A young girl had never done such a thing before. I heard that in those months she was asked for fee money for the land. The agent went out there and got lost, spent a whole night following the moving lights and lamps of people who would not answer him but talked and laughed among themselves. They let him go, at dawn, only because he was so stupid. Yet he went out there to ask Fleur for money again, and the next thing we heard he was living in the woods and eating roots, gambling with ghosts.

Some had ideas. You know how old chickens scratch and gabble. That's how the tales started, all the gossip, the wondering, all the things people said without knowing and then believed, since they heard it with their own ears, from their own lips, each word.

I am not one to take notice of the talk of those who fatten in the shade of the new agent's storehouse. But I watched the old agent, the one who was never found, take the rutted turnoff to Matchimanito. He was replaced by a darker man who spoke long and hard with many of our own about a money settlement. But nothing changed my mind. I've seen too much go by—unturned grass below my feet, and overhead the great white cranes flung south forever.

I am a holdout, like the Pillagers, and I told the agent, in good English, what I thought of his treaty paper. I could have written my name, and much more too, in script. I had a Jesuit education in the halls of Saint John before I ran back to the woods and forgot all my prayers.

Since I had saved Fleur from the sickness, I was entangled with her. Not that I knew it at first. Only when I look back do I see a pattern. I was the vine of a wild grape that twined the timbers and drew them close. I was a branch that lived long enough to touch the next tree over, which was Pillagers. The story, like all stories, is never visible while it is happening. Only after, when an old man sits dreaming and talking in his chair, does the design spring clear.

There was so much I saw, and never knew.

When Fleur came down onto the reservation, walking right through town, no one guessed what she hid in that green rag of a dress. I do remember that it was too small, split down the back and strained across the front. That's what I noticed when I greeted her. Not whether she had money in the dress, or a child.

Other people speculated. They added up the money she used now to buy supplies and how the agent disappeared from his post, and came out betting she would have a baby. He could have paid cash to Fleur and then run off in shame. She could even have stolen cash from him, cursed him dead, and hidden his remains. Everybody would have known, they thought, in nine months or less, if young Eli Kashpaw hadn't gone out and muddied the waters.

This Eli never cared to figure out business, politics, or church. He never applied for a chunk of land or registered himself. Eli hid from authorities, never saw the inside of a classroom, and although his mother, Margaret, got baptized in the church and tried to collar him for Mass, the best he could do was sit outside the big pine door and whittle pegs. For money Eli chopped wood, pitched hay, harvested potatoes or cranberry bark. He wanted to be a hunter, though, like me, and he had asked to partner that winter before the sickness.

I think like animals, have perfect understanding for where they hide. I can track a deer back through time and brush and cleared field to the place where it was born. Only one thing is wrong with teaching these things, however. I showed Eli how to hunt and trap from such an early age that he lived too much in the company of trees and wind. At fifteen he was uncomfortable around human beings. Especially women. So I had to help him out some.

I'm a Nanapush, remember. That's as good as saying I knew what interested Eli Kashpaw. He wanted something other than what I could teach him about the woods. He was no longer curious only about where a mink will fish or burrow, or when pike will lie low or bite. He wanted to hear how, in the days before the priest's ban and the sickness, I had satisfied three wives.

"Nanapush," Eli said, appearing at my door one day, "I came to ask you something."

"Come on in here, then," I said. "I won't bite you like the little girls do."

He was steadier, more serious, than he was the winter we went out together on the trapline. I was going to wonder what the different thing about him was when he said, "Fleur Pillager."

"She's no little girl," I answered, motioning toward the table. He told me his story.

It began when Eli got himself good and lost up near Matchimanito. He was hunting a doe in a light rain, having no luck until he rounded a slough and shot badly, which wasn't unusual. She was wounded to death but not crippled. She might walk all day, which shamed him, so he dabbed a bit of her blood on the barrel of his gun, the charm I taught him, and he followed her trail.

He had a time of it. She sawed through the woods, took the worst way, moved into heavy brush like a ghost. For hours Eli blazed his passage with snapped branches and clumps of leaves, scuffed the ground, or left a bootprint. But the trail and the day wore on, and for some reason that he did not understand, he gave up and quit leaving sign.

"That was when you should have turned back," I told him. "You should have known. It's no accident people don't like to go there. Those trees are too big, thick, and twisted at the top like bent arms. In the wind their limbs cast, creak against each other, snap. The leaves speak a cold language that overfills your brain. You want to lie down. You want never to get up. You hunger. You rake black chokecherries off their stems and stuff them down, and then you shit like a bird. Your blood thins. You're too close to where the Lake Man lives. And you're too close to where I buried the Pillagers during the long sickness that claimed them like it claimed the Nanapush clan."

I said this to Eli Kashpaw: "I understand Fleur. I am alone in this. I know that was no ordinary doe drawing you out there."

But the doe was real enough, he told me, and it was gunshot and weakening. The blood dropped fresher, darker, until he thought he heard her just ahead and bent to the ground, desperate to see in the falling dusk, and looked ahead to catch a glimpse, and instead saw the glow of fire. He started toward it, then stopped just outside the circle of light. The deer hung, already split, turning back and forth on a rope. When he saw the woman, gutting with long quick movements, her arms bloody and bare, he stepped into the clearing.

"That's mine," he said.

I hid my face, shook my head.

"You should have turned back," I told him. "Stupid! You should have left it."

But he was stubborn, a vein of Kashpaw that held out for what it had coming. He couldn't have taken the carcass home anyway, couldn't have lugged it back, even if he had known his direction. Yet he stood his ground with the woman and said he'd tracked that deer too far to let it go. She did not respond. "Or maybe half," he thought, studying her back, uncomfortable. Even so, that was as generous as he could get.

She kept working. Never noticed him. He was so ignorant that he reached out and tapped her on the shoulder. She never even twitched. He walked around her, watched the knife cut, trespassed into her line of vision.

At last she saw him, he said, but then scorned him as though he were nothing.

"Little fly"—she straightened her back, the knife loose and casual in her hand—"quit buzzing."

Eli said she looked so wild her beauty didn't throw him, and I leaned closer, worried as he said this, worried as he reported how her hair was clumped with dirt, her face thin as a bony bitch's, her dress a rag that hung, and no curve to her except her breasts.

He noticed some things.

"No curve?" I said, thinking of the rumors.

He shook his head, impatient to continue his story. He felt sorry for her, he said. I told him the last man who was interested in Fleur Pillager had vanished, never to be found. She made us all uneasy, out there so alone. I was a friend to the Pillagers before they died off, I said, and I was safe from Fleur because the two of us had mourned the dead together. She was almost a relative. But that wasn't the case with him.

Eli looked at me with an unbelieving frown. Then he said he didn't see where she was so dangerous. After a while he had recognized her manner as exhaustion more than anger. She made no protest when he took out his own knife and helped her work. Halfway through the job she allowed him to finish, and then Eli hoisted most of the meat into the tree. He took the choice parts into the cabin. She let him in, hardly noticed him, and he helped her start the small range and even took it on himself to melt lard. She ate the whole heart, fell on it like a starved animal, and then her eyes shut.

From the way he described her actions, I was sure she was pregnant. I'm familiar with the signs, and I can talk about this since I'm an old man, far past anything a woman can do to weaken me. I was more certain still when Eli said that he took her in his arms, helped her to a pile of blankets on a willow bed. And then—hard to believe, even though it was, for the first time, the right thing to do—Eli rolled up in a coat on the other side of the cabin floor and lay there all night, and slept alone.

• • •

"So," I said, "Why have you come to me now? You got away, you survived, she even let you find your way home. You learned your lesson and none the worse."

"I want her," Eli said.

I could not believe that I heard right, but we were sitting by the stove, face to face, so there was no doubt. I rose and turned away. Maybe I was less than generous, having lost my own girls. Maybe I wanted to keep Fleur as my daughter, who would visit me, joke with me, beat me at cards. But I believe it was only for Eli's own good that I was harsh.

"Forget that thing so heavy in your pocket," I said, "or put it somewhere else. Go town way and find yourself a tamer woman."

He brooded at my tabletop and then spoke. "I want know-how, not warnings, not my mother's caution."

"You don't want instruction!" I was pushed too far. "Love medicine is what you're after. A Nanapush never needed any, but Old Lady Aintapi or the Pillagers, they sell it. Go ask Moses for a medicine and pay your price."

"I don't want anything that can wear off," the boy said. He was determined. Maybe his new, steady coolness was the thing that turned my mind, the quiet of him. He was different, sitting there so still. It struck me that he had come into his growth, and who was I to hold him back from going to a Pillager, since someone had to, since the whole tribe had got to thinking that she couldn't be left alone out there, a girl ready to go wild, a woman whose family would not leave her, even dead, but stayed close to her, whispered, passed on their power. People said that she had to be harnessed. Maybe, I thought, Eli was the young man to do it, even though he couldn't rub two words together and get a spark.

So I gave in. I told him what he wanted to know. He asked me the old-time way to make a woman love him, and I went into detail so that he would make no disgraceful error. I told him about the first woman who had given herself to me. Sanawashonekek, her name was, The Lying-Down Grass, for the place where a deer has spent the night. I described the finicky taste of Omiimii, The Dove, and the trials I'd gone through to keep my second wife pleasured. Zezikaaikwe, The Unexpected, was a woman whose name was the exact prediction of her desires. I gave him a few things from the French trunk my third wife left—a white woman's fan, bead leggings, a little girl's soft doll made of fawn skin.

When Eli Kashpaw stroked their beauty and asked where these things had come from, I remembered the old days, opened my mouth.

Talk is an old man's last vice.

I wore out the boy's ears, but that is not my fault. I shouldn't have been caused to live so long, been shown so much of death, had to squeeze so many stories into the corners of my brain. They're all attached, and once I start, the telling doesn't end, because they're hooked from one side to the other, mouth to tail.

During the year of sickness, when I was the last one left, I saved myself by starting a story. One night I was ready to bring to the other side the fawn-skin doll I now gave Eli. My wife had sewn it together after our daughter died, and I held it in my hands when I fainted, lost breath so that I could hardly keep moving my lips. But I did continue and recovered. I got well by talking. Death could not get a word in edgewise, grew discouraged, and traveled on.

Eli returned to Fleur, and stopped badgering me, which I took as a sign she liked the fan, the bead leggings, and maybe the rest of Eli, the part where he was on his own.

The thing I've found about women is that you must use every instinct to confuse.

"Look here," I told Eli, before he went out my door. "It's like you're a log in a stream. Along comes this bear. She jumps on. Don't let her dig in her claws."

So keeping Fleur off balance was what I presumed Eli was doing. But, as I learned in time, he was further along than that, way off and running beyond the reach of anything I said.

His mother was the one who gave me the news.

Margaret Kashpaw was a woman who had sunk her claws in the log and peeled it to a toothpick, and she wasn't going to let any man forget it. Especially me, her dead husband's partner in some youthful pursuits.

"Aneesh," she said, slamming my door shut. Margaret never knocked, because with warning you might get your breath, or escape. She was headlong, bossy, scared of nobody, and full of vinegar. She was a little woman, but so blinded by irritation that she'd take on anyone. She was thin on the top and plump as a turnip below, with a face like a round molasses cake. On each side of it gray plaits hung. With age her part had widened down the middle so that it looked as though the braids were slipping off her head. Her eyes were harsh, bright, and her tongue was honed keen. She sat right down.

"Would you care to know what you have my son doing?"

I mumbled, kept reading by the window, tucked my spectacles from Father Damien more comfortably around my ears. My newspaper came from Grand Forks once a week, and I wasn't about to let Margaret spoil my pleasure or get past my hiding place.

"Sah!" She swiped at the sheets with her hand, grazed the print, but never quite dared to flip it aside. This was not for any fear of me, however. She didn't want the tracks rubbing off on her skin. She never learned to read, and the mystery troubled her.

I took advantage of that, snapped the paper in front of my face and sat for a moment. But she won, of course, because she knew I'd get curious. I felt her eyes glittering beyond the paper, and when I put the pages down, she continued.

"Who learned my Eli to make love standing up? Who learned him to have a woman against a tree in clear daylight? Who learned him to . . ."

"Wait," I said. "How'd you get to know this?"

She shrugged it off, and said in a smaller voice, "Boy Lazarre."

And I, who knew that the dirty Lazarres don't spy for nothing, just smiled.

"How much did you pay the fat-bellied dog?"

"The Lazarres are like animals in their season! No sense of shame!" But the wind was out of her. "Against the wall of the cabin," she said. "Down beside it. In grass and up in trees. Who'd he learn that from?"

"Maybe my late partner Kashpaw."

She puffed her cheeks out, fumed. "Not from him!"

"Not that you knew." I put my spectacles carefully upon the windowsill. Her hand could snake out quickly.

She hissed. The words flew like razor grass between her teeth. "Old man," she said with scorn. "Two wrinkled berries and a twig."

"A twig can grow," I offered.

"But only in the spring."

Then she was gone, out the door, leaving my tongue tingling for the last word, and still ignorant of the full effect of my advice. I didn't wonder until later if it didn't go both ways, though—if Fleur had wound her private hairs around the buttons of Eli's shirt, if she had stirred smoky powders or crushed snakeroot into his tea. Perhaps she had bitten his nails in sleep and swallowed the ends, snipped threads from his clothing and made a doll of them to wear between her legs. For they got bolder, until the whole reservation gossiped.

Then one day the big, unsteady Lazarre, an Indian on whose birth certificate was recorded simply "Boy," returned from the woods talking backwards, garbled, mixing his words. At first people thought the sights of passion had cleft his mind. Then they figured otherwise, imagined that Fleur had caught Lazarre watching and tied him up, cut his tongue out, and sewn it in reversed.

The same day I heard this, Margaret burst into my house a second time. "Take me out to their place, you four-eyes," she said. "And be ready with the boat tomorrow, sunup!"

She stamped through the door and vanished, leaving me with hardly any time enough to patch the seams and holes of the old-time boat I kept, dragged up in a brush shelter on the quieter inlet, the south end of the lake. I took some boiled pine gum to the seams that afternoon, and did my best. I was drawn to the situation, curious myself, and though I didn't want to spy either on the girl whose life I'd saved or on the boy I'd advised on courting, I was down by the water with the paddles at dawn.

The light was chill and green, the waves on the lake were small, confused ripples, and no steady wind had gathered. The water could be deceptive, set snares for the careless young or for withered-up and eager fools like ourselves. I put my hand in the current.

"Margaret," I said, "the lake's too cold. I never could swim, either, not that well."

But Margaret had set her mind, and made her peace, too.

"If he wants me"—she was talking about the lake spirit but out of caution, using no names—"I'll give him good as I get."

"Oh," I said, "has it been that long, Margaret?"

Her eyes lit and I wished I had kept my mouth shut. But she only commented, later, after we had launched, "Not so long that I would consider the dregs."

I handed her the lard can I kept my bait in. "You better take this, Margaret. You better bail."

So at least on that long trip across I had the satisfaction of seeing her bend to the dipping and pouring with a sour but desperate will. We rode low. The water covered our ankles by the time we beached on shore, but Margaret was forced to shut her mouth in a firm line. The whole idea had been hers. She was so relieved to stand finally upon solid ground that she helped me haul the boat and wedge it in a pile of mangled roots. She wrung her skirt and sat beside me, panting. She shared some dried meat from the pocket of her dress, tore at it like a young snapping turtle. How I envied her sharp, strong teeth.

"Go on, eat," she said, "or I'll take an insult."

I put the jerky into my mouth.

"That's right," she sneered. "Suck long enough and it will soften."

I had no choice. I could think of no other way to get any of it down.

"Go now," I said, after a while. "I was thinking. I had this old barren she-dog once. She'd back up to anything. But the only satisfaction she could get was from watching the young."

Margaret jumped to her feet, skirts flapping. I had said too much. Her claws gave my ears two fast, furious jerks that set me whirling, sickening me so that I couldn't balance or even keep track of time. She took herself up the bank and into the Pillager woods, but I don't know when she went there or how long she stayed, and I had barely set myself to rights before she returned.

By then the sky had gone dead gray, the waves rolled white and fitful. Margaret took tobacco from a pouch in her pocket, threw it on the water, and said a few distracted, imploring words. We jumped into the boat, which leaked worse than ever, and pushed off. The wind blew harsh, in heavy circular gusts, and I was hard put. I never saw the bailing can move so fast, before or since. The old woman made it flash and dip, and hardly even broke the rhythm when, halfway across, she reached into her pocket again and this time dumped the whole pouch into the pounding waves. From then on she alternated between working her arms and addressing different Manitous along with the Blessed Virgin and Her heart, the sacred bloody lump that the blue-robed woman held in the awful picture Margaret kept nailed to her wall. We made it back by the time rain poured down, and hoisted ourselves over the edge of the boat. When we got back to my house, after she'd swallowed some warm broth and her clothes had begun to steam dry upon her, Margaret told me what she had seen with her own eyes.

Fleur Pillager was pregnant, going to have a child in spring. At least that's what Margaret had decided with her measuring gaze. I stirred the fire with my walking stick. Maybe I had a shiver, a feeling, a worry. I was close as a relative, closer perhaps. Maybe I knew already that when spring did come, the ice milky, porous, and broken, Margaret and I were the ones who would have to save Fleur a second time.

Margaret, however, had no such premonition. The child would turn out fork-footed, she predicted, with straw for hair, yellow as the agent's. Its eyes would glow blue, its skin shine white. As she sipped from her cup, Margaret's memory of the agent made a monster, and she savored the variations the child might reveal: red, flapping ears, a strange birthmark, chicken lips, an extra finger, by which the taint of its conception would be certain and people convinced, at last, that it did not belong to her son.

The morning we got word, the water had just opened for a boat, if you dared to travel that way so early in spring. Fleur was in trouble with her baby. That's all I heard, as the women kept the particulars to themselves.

Out of desperation Eli had run to Margaret on the way to the midwife's. He wanted us to take the shortcut and stay with Fleur until he brought back the woman whose hands held the wisdom, who wore the dried caul of a rabbit in a little belt around her waist.

Margaret was puffed up, full of satisfaction, until she saw the boat, leaking even more than usual after another winter of neglect. On the ride, bailing for her life, Margaret raged at me between her prayers and muttered strict assurances that her reasons for helping in this matter were not ties of kinship. Her presence did not count as acknowledgment, she said. It was her duty to see the evidence, whatever that turned out to be—the hair gold as straw, the blazing eyes.

But the child had none of those markings.

She was born on the day we shot the last bear, drunk, on the reservation. The midwife was the one who shot it, and the bear was drunk, not her. That she-bear had broken into the trader's wine I had brought across the lake beneath my jacket and then stowed in a rotten stump off in the woods behind the house. She bit the cork and emptied the white clay jug. Then she lost her mind and stumbled into the beaten grass of Fleur's yard.

By then we were a day in the waiting. In all that time we heard not a sound from Fleur's cabin, just crushing silence, like the inside of a drum before the stick drops. Eli and I slumped against the woodpile. We made a fire, swaddled ourselves in blankets. My stomach creaked with the lack of food, for Eli was starving himself from worry and I hated to eat in front of him. His eyes were rimmed with blood as he moaned and talked and prayed beneath the burden, which grew heavier.

On the second day we leaned to the fire, strained for the sound of the cry a baby makes. Our ears picked up everything in the woods, the rustle of birds, the crack of dead spring leaves and twigs. Our hearing had by then grown so keen that we heard the muffled sounds the women made inside the house. Now we heard other activity, which gave us hope. The stove lid clanked, pans rang together. Margaret came to the door and we heard the tear of water splashing on the ground. Eli moved then, fetched more. But not until the afternoon of that second day did the stillness finally break, and then the Manitous all through the woods seemed to speak through Fleur, loose, arguing. I recognized them. Turtle's quavering scratch, Eagle's high shriek, Loon's crazy bitterness, Otter, the howl of Wolf, Bear's low rasp.

Perhaps the bear heard Fleur calling, and answered.

I was alone when it happened, because Eli had broken when the silence shattered, slashed his arm with his hunting knife, and run out of the clearing, straight north. I sat quietly after he was gone, and sampled the food that he had refused. I drew close to the fire, settled my back against the split logs, and was just about to have a second helping when the drunk bear rambled past. She sniffed the ground, rolled over in an odor that pleased her, drew up and sat, addled, on her haunches like a dog. I jumped straight onto the top of the woodpile—I don't know how, since my limbs were so stiff from the wet cold. I crouched, yelled at the house, screamed for the gun, but only attracted the bear. She dragged herself over, gave a drawn-out whine, a cough, and fixed me with a long patient stare.

Margaret flung the door open. "Shoot it, you old fool," she hollered. But I was empty-handed. Margaret was irritated with this trifle, put out that I had not obeyed her, anxious to get rid of the nuisance and go back to Fleur. She marched straight toward us. Her face was pinched with exhaustion, her pace furious. Her arms moved like pistons, and she came so fast that she and the bear were face to face before she realized that she had nothing with which to attack. She was sensible, Margaret

Kashpaw, and turned straight around. Fleur kept her gun above the flour cupboard in a rack of antlers. The bear followed, heeling Margaret like a puppy, and at the door to the house, when Margaret turned, arms spread to bar the way, it swatted her aside with one sharp, dreamy blow. Then it ambled in and reared on its hind legs.

I am a man, so I don't know exactly what happened when the bear came into the birth house, but they talk among themselves, the women, and sometimes they forget I'm listening. So I know that when Fleur saw the bear in the house she was filled with such fear and power that she raised herself on the mound of blankets and gave birth. Then the midwife took down the gun and shot point-blank, filling the bear's heart. She says so, anyway. But Margaret says that the lead only gave the bear strength, and I'll support that. For I heard the gun go off and then saw the creature whirl and roar from the house. It barreled past me, crashed through the brush into the woods, and was not seen after. It left no trail, either, so it could have been a spirit bear. I don't know. I was still on the woodpile.

I took the precaution of finishing my meal there. From what I overheard later, they were sure Fleur was dead, she was so cold and still after giving birth. But then the baby cried. That I heard with my own ears. At that sound, they say, Fleur opened her eyes and breathed. That was when the women went to work and saved her, packed moss between her legs, wrapped her in blankets heated with stones, kneaded Fleur's stomach and forced her to drink cup after cup of boiled raspberry leaf, until at last Fleur groaned, drew the baby against her breast, and lived.

JOHN BENNION

DUST

B*itter Springs, Utah*: My Father's Property. Since morning, perhaps because today marks the second anniversary of my removal to the desert, my eye has inclined toward the junction of my lane and the gravel road between Salt Lake and Ely. I'm expecting no one in particular, but between me and the road lies three miles of wavering, ground-heated air, giving the alkali flat the appearance of movement, as if a cloud of white dust billows from its surface. Such a cloud signifies either an approaching vehicle or a misdirected shell, a gift from the chemical weapons testing grounds north of here. My polygamist neighbors to the south might read the coil of dust as a sign of the apocalypse. Leaving my window, I walk to the butte, three hundred steps above and behind my cabin. Like the pale and arid flat below, the butte presents a mingled aspect: breast-shaped but with a column of lava on top, an igneous plug which my eye reads variously: sometimes as the thick phallus of the volcano's last thrust, sometimes as a hardened black nipple. From this vantage I inspect for any change in the size or direction of the potential cloud. The white blotch shimmers in the heat, dust motes whirling, as real as the pillar of fire in Cecil B. De Mille's *Ten Commandments.*

Blackwood, Utah: forty miles northeast. From my position I can see the range of mountains around my former home. My wife, Sylvia, and our five children—Benjamin, Abigail, Joshua, Ruth and Heather—live there with my mother in the town named after my violent great-grandfather, James Darren Blackwood, who was once a body-guard to the prophet Joseph Smith. Anti-Mormon historians claim that Great-grandpa shot the mayor of Carthage, Illinois, Frederick Diggs, because Diggs harassed the People of God. Grandpa J. D.'s violence is genetic: my brother poisoned his boss after being fired, and I experienced a sigh of religious fulfillment after completing the chemical blueprint for the nerve gas that killed the sheep.

In Blackwood, when I changed my daughter's diapers, she raised her arms above her head so I could tickle her. "Doat," she said. "Doat, Daddy." Her laugh comes from her belly, a gurgle of mirth. The faces of my son and wife were identically solemn when I left them two years ago.

Alone on my inherited section of desert, I try to isolate my fear of the apocalypse (as predicted by the Book of Revelations, Jeanne Dixon, and anti-nuclear activists), but the core of my fear is as various as the cloud of dust.

Skull Valley Testing Grounds: The Limits of Nonradioactive Gas. Formerly I worked thirty miles to the northwest of here, where the government designs, tests, and stores lesser tools of the apocalypse. To approach my bunker I passed through three barriers—woven wire, chain link, brick—presenting my I.D. to three sets of guards. My fingerprints were taken daily, to insure that the guards, who saw me daily, hadn't mistaken my face.

As head chemist my duties were to create equations on a blackboard. Two second-level chemists transferred the numbers and letters to paper, a committee ordered the batch, and technicians, dozens of them, manipulated the stuff with long-armed machinery from behind thick glass windows. Working over my abstractions, I was elevated to a pure sphere, like a high priest delineating the mind of God.

Once, on my way home from work, a great ball of orange gas flung outward from one of the army's testing bunkers, boiling toward my car past the boundary fence. I shit myself, understanding that the mind of God held subtleties I hadn't yet grasped. I didn't breathe while I bounced across the desert road for three miles. Behind me the wind gathered the potent molecules, dissipating them upward toward the bench land of the nearby mountains.

The newspapers soon discovered that five thousand head of Hyrum Jorgenson's sheep had died. Government veterinarians explained that the animals were undernourished and had eaten loco weed. Within a year two movies were made about the event: *Rage,* starring George C. Scott, whose son was killed by the descending gas, and *Whiffs,* a spoof which showed tendrils of white drifting through nearby Tooele, Utah. The excitement of seeing their children as extras caused all my friends to forget the dead sheep. After viewing both movies, I had the recurring dream that a technician found a way to disseminate my gas using an atomic warhead.

The summer of our first wedding anniversary, my water turn came between one and three in the morning. Several times Sylvia crept down through the cedars above our horse pasture, wrapped only in a blanket, and seduced me before I could remove my irrigation boots.

Lot's Wife: Does Flesh Turn to Sodium Inside Ground Zero? The morning after my bolt of terror, a Saturday, Sylvia and I lay in bed late. The children played in the next room, waiting for breakfast. "That's Daddy's briefcase," Benjamin said. "He won't like you playing with it."

"He won't mind," Ruth said. "He won't mind at all."

"He will."

"Daddy, Daddy, Daddy," the baby said into the shut door. Sylvia smiled but I couldn't: the word didn't seem to apply to me. We heard struggling and a shower of papers. Then I smiled. I didn't go to work the next week.

After the third month without a paycheck, Sylvia began to think my fears were silly. "You've got to face it that accidents happen." She shouted arguments at me. I shouted my fear back. Abigail started taking long walks. The baby crawled into our bed every night, unable to sleep alone. Finally, insecure myself, I spanked her to make her stay in her own bed. Joshua wet his pants three days out of five at school. "I try to make it to the toilet but I can't get there in time," he said. Their troubles, poignant as they were, had little to do with me. I told Sylvia I was going to live on my father's property in the desert.

"Dramatic," she said. "It's really just Andrea, isn't it? You're going to pretend you're pioneering with her." My father had homesteaded the property, finally abandoning my mother, who wouldn't leave Salt Lake City to live in the desert with him. I couldn't understand either my father's motivating dream or the adulterous one Sylvia supplied for me.

When she plays the guitar, Sylvia sits in her rocking chair, eyes closed. Her fingers ripple on the strings, moving according to laws of clarity, grace, and intuition, marked by the rhythm of the moving chair.

An Acolyte's Guide to Androgynous Thinking: On this, the second anniversary of leaving my job, my family, and my town, I don't trust my eye's interest in the junction. My mental/emotional apparatus will take any non-event today and say, "This is what you were waiting for. The reverberation of the coming event impinged on your neurons, causing the condition you call anticipation." I say to my neurons, "Parascience." I deny that my brain picks up invisible signals, creating an impossible tension between me and some other object in time or space.

Despite my lack of faith in my own nervous system, my flesh still organizes itself for someone's possible arrival. And I'm double-minded again, split between rationality and mysticism, unable to be either a scientist or a saint, as if the bolt of fear at the swarming gas traumatized my corpus callosum, the bridge in my brain.

Coriantumr, Utah: Five miles south of my cabin lives a community of apostates from the Mormon Church, two hundred strong, who have returned to the practices of the nineteenth-century pioneers—living in polygamy with all things in common. In preparation for the last day, they have hoarded wheat, honey, and rifles. To satisfy present needs they have a Montessori school and a dairy. They sent a group of their brethren to Switzerland to purchase a strain of bacteria for culturing milk into cheese which they trade in Paradise, Utah, farther south. They want to pipe the water from my spring to their alfalfa fields so they can grow feed for another fifty cows, but they never mention that. A hundred miles west of them lies Ely, Nevada, where madams and casino owners also live with everything in common.

A Star Named Kolob: My father, the former owner of this property, is in Heaven, which the polygamists have determined to be on a planet near Kolob, a hundred trillion miles past our sun. God lives there, they believe, with all the spirits who are waiting to come to earth. My sixth through twelfth children are presently on Kolob also, they say. I doubt that my wife's rhythm and my own will coincide seven more times, but that doesn't concern the polygamists.

A Six-by-Four Patch of Floor Under My Chalkboard: Vive Vas Deferens: During lunch in my bunker at Skull Valley Testing Grounds, I ate tomato sandwiches, the juice running down my fingers onto the floor. My cochemist, Andrea Armstrong, looked at me across my red and dripping hands. Suddenly we were tumbling on the floor in the chalk dust and sandwich remains. Upon confessing this to my Mormon bishop, I was disfellowshipped from the Church. My lack of guilt disgusted him. My emotional incontinence worried me.

Salt Lake City, Utah: a hundred miles northeast of Blackwood. On the highest spire of the temple the gold statue of Moroni, his horn to his lips, prepares to signal the rolling together of the scroll. Sometimes in my dreams I hear his trump then sense the stealthy movement of the quivering gas.

My Journal: The Tao of Listing. Like Robinson Crusoe, I have a "certain Stupidity of Soul," and like him I trust lists, not of provisions, but of anchors in space and time. Lists are beautiful—they don't whine. They require no explanation, are non-ardent, noncausal, calm, static, unpretentious, a periodic table of my own elements. However I'm wary of listing *toward,* as in "Our ship listed toward starboard after it struck the rock" or "Since morning my eye has listed toward the junction."

A selection from Robinson Crusoe's list:

small Ropes and Rope-twine
a Piece of spare Canvass
a barrel of wet Gunpowder
a great Hogshead of Bread
three large Runlets of Rum or Spirits
a Box of Sugar

My list:

the black ridge extending between here and Ely, Nevada, looking like God's darkening brow
the bank of the spring my father cleared out twenty-five years ago
the pattern of tomato seeds on Andrea's back
my son skipping rocks across a green pond
the harmony of equations across the blackboard, the purer image of the orange gas
the Rorschach blots created in a mobile cloud

Andrea, Kolob, and I: The Physics of Attraction Between Bodies. Sitting on the butte with the border of Nevada a wall behind me, I can sense the faint reverberations of these places and events. Closing my eyes, I sense here the salt sea, here the mounds of stored bombs and gasses, here my wife and children, my friends, Kolob, the potential cloud, the polygamists. I feel the lines of tension—physical, disinterested—between myself and them.

The Angle of the Cloud: Playing the Futures. If the dust arrives from the north today, it may be Sergeant Mertzke, Recreation Administrator for the Officers' Club at Skull Valley Testing Grounds. We were once hunting buddies, but when I see his dust, I'll compose myself, adopting a persona which will fit into his consciousness—the calculating but cautious land holder.

"Have they left?" he says, referring to the deer he wants to shoot by spotlight from the back of his jeep.

"A five-point, three two-point, six doe." I count on my fingers.

"Where're you going to get a better offer?" And he explains again the idea of the R&R Area. He looks over this desert property, barren except for the fifty square yards around the spring, and sees officers and women of the New Army frolicking through the sagebrush.

"I don't know," I say. "Land's stable, money is mobile."

"But gauge the possibilities."

I won't disturb his vision of my father's property, but before he gets to the part about the raw hunters returning to the tents of their women, I will recast myself as the religious ascetic—a desert saint. I motion for silence, bowing my head. "I will ask." Holding him with my silence for five, maybe ten minutes. "No. My father on Kolob says no. He warns you that God is as displeased with you as he was with the people of Sodom and Gomorrah. His wrath is kindled."

"The hell it is," he says. He comes in the evening anyway, the fever for killing heavy in him. I flash the light on this doe, that buck. He shoots and I hear the thud as his hollow-points hit muscle and bone. Even the shower of blood creates no motion inside of me. I could be butcher, conservationist, harvester, accomplice. Any of these could explain my relationship to the event: the spurting blood. Nothing moves.

On winter mornings my son built elaborate houses out of chairs, blankets, boards, and cushions. Once he and his siblings decided that the structure was a houseboat and that I was the shark. My baby lifted her body onto her toes, pumping her legs in place as she tried to escape. I ate her squealing body four times.

The Ark: How Many Roentgens Will Kill a Dove? If the dust arrives from the south, it will come slowly: three of the brethren from the polygamous camp navigating the ruts and rocks in their decrepit pickup.

"Brother Blackwood," the Elders say. "Toward the end of the world, wars and pestilence will be poured out upon the land. The moon will turn red like blood, and lightning will flash from east to west as the Son of Man approaches. Only the righteous—those who have entered the new order—will be spared."

I lead them along. "Vanity, vanity," I say. "The work of man's own hands will destroy the world. The only thing that will spare any of us is your buried vault."

"The mind of God moves in mysterious ways."

They have a stainless steel and cement ark buried fifty feet under the desert. Its walls are six feet thick. They plan to go down there and emerge two by two, or rather one by seven, into the millennium. I could believe their myth that the Pentagon, public education, and the mind of Satan move in collusion toward the apocalypse, but I don't let myself trust major abstractions anymore. At this point I profane the name of their God and deny their pragmatic mysticism. "I am a rational, enlightened humanist," I say. "A member of a powerful conspiracy." And they leave saddened because I can't comprehend their God or their milk barn.

Masters and Johnson on Solitude: Why Crusoe Kept Goats. Through a pleasant inversion of perspective, for a moment the potential dust is my own as I drive my white Ford Fairlane southward to Ely for the weekly venting of my seminal vesicles. In the back are stacks of *Chemical Review,* a weight which keeps me from getting stuck when it's winter. As I drive, I call myself adulterer, hedonist, lecher, fallen saint: but all the fragments crumble before I can build them into a consistent foundation. I drive quickly past the polygamist community, made of two-story houses large as dormitories. Beyond their establishment is a black volcanic ridge, the extension of my butte, connecting me with Ely.

I park my car in the city and shuffle toward a casino under the swirl of lights. For the girls and the card dealers, I am the rich and eccentric desert rat, dusty, hunch-shouldered. I engage the first prostitute I see, a sad-eyed woman with long black hair. In our room she takes off her clothes slowly, teasing my expectation. The absurdity of our puny climax drains the life from my penis, and I feel disconnected from it. However, she is an efficient woman, improvising with clever lips and tongue, and she makes my body perform. I spend the rest of the evening flipping the lever of a slot machine, anticipating a windfall.

The Prodigal Father: A northern originating dust could also signify my friend, Jonathon Boone, driving from Blackwood. "Howard, your wife is pining," he says. "She's got no more money. She's had to get her food and clothing from the Bishop's Storehouse, and that makes her ashamed. What can I tell her? What are you doing? Is it worth the problems you're causing your friends?"

"I'm making no stand," I say to him.

"You're not changing anything. Why do you stay here?"

"I've got no reform in mind," I say.

"Why don't you just come back with me?"

"Please don't talk anymore," I ask him. He doesn't understand the ways his questions strain my introspective faculty. For an hour we walk in the cool of the evening. The breeze has died, and, bending low, we smell the mint growing on the banks of my spring.

Options on My Father's Property: Usually if I wait long enough, my back against the butte, someone comes. Last week a friend who was a Democratic Socialist in college drove through. Still an idealist after twenty years, he looked around and his vision was powerful enough to transform the dead soil.

"This is like Paradise," he said.

"No, that's twenty miles farther on."

"Can you picture a community here, all friends, lovers, family? People who have repudiated hate." His voice nearly revived my own visions of Zion, a place where people live in peace. "We could cast off the dead husk of society," he said, and I understood he wanted to build a nudist retreat.

"I won't sell."

"I don't want you to sell." He was eager, running through the greasewood and shadscale, blinded by his narrow optimism.

For him I was the sharp agribusinessman. "My god, man. This land can produce seven maybe eight tons of prime alfalfa to the acre and you talk to me about a damn spa. That artesian spring brings up two or three second feet of water and all you can think of is some kind of orgy." He left in his jeep, driving with only a centimeter of metal between him and the sky.

The Penultimate Human: Once a man drove through looking for the road to Topaz Mountain. He had his wife and children with him—a family man on an outing. He showed me a sample of geode he'd found. "We cut and polish these nippers. A real fine hobby for the kids, and it teaches them something. Might as well kill two birds with one stone." He laughed, watching for my response. "Every second they're polishing, they're learning geology. And then we sell them. Isn't it something? A real tidy income." The pleasant wife and pleasant children smiled and nodded.

His soft-bellied words irritated me, violated my integrity. I told him the blacktop began twenty miles farther. If the heat is great enough when the lightning flashes from east to west, his stones will melt to glass. For him my eyes became hard and clear, glistening with intensity. "Gog and Magog are gathering for battle: the apocalypse draws near," I said. "I-am-that-I-am says 'Beware the wrath of the Lamb.' " Wide-eyed, he left me alone to ruminate on my father's property.

Personal History: An Escape From My True Self Before God. I can establish no relationship with any point or person secondary to myself in space which is as important as my fear. No end depends from a middle in my life, no new and glorious future which grows organically out of my past, as Aristotle, Alexander Hamilton, Walt Whitman, Brigham Young, Horatio Alger, and Karl Marx promised.

When my son was two, he backed into a kettle we had set for scalding chickens. I tore off his diaper and turned the hose full across him. His back and buttocks peeled white wherever the water touched. Later he clawed the healing skin, biting my hands when I held his. I slapped his mouth, hard, and the print faded slowly.

When he was three, he helped me harvest corn from our garden, pulling the sheath downward from the silk, breaking out the yellow ears. We filled ten buckets with corn for bottling.

When I was four, I walked across this property, following my father as he planned where the fences would go on his new homestead—320 acres of desert land. He irrigated his alfalfa by pumping water from an underground river.

I was six. My father sent me to this cabin from the fields a mile westward, where he was working. "You start dinner," he said. "I'll be along." The road I watched back over became dark through the window. The toads croaking and the coyotes yelping made the loneliest sound I've heard. He didn't come until an hour after the food was cold.

For years from behind our kitchen door in Blackwood, I heard my mother and father arguing religion: evolution, modern revelation, Christ's miracles, Joseph Smith talking to God. "If the prophet in Salt Lake told you to walk off a cliff, you would do it, wouldn't you?" my father said.

"But he wouldn't ask," said my mother.

"But if he did?"

"But he won't."

Once I fell asleep while listening, and my father discovered me, from my snoring he said, and carried me to my bed.

When I was nine, I cut out the heart of a newly dead rattlesnake and watched it beat eighty-three times in the palm of my hand. During my seventeenth summer, as my friend and I irrigated the farm, we grew a potato plant which we watered with only our urine.

When I was twenty-two and Sylvia wouldn't see me any more, my father rode on horseback with me over the mountains surrounding Blackwood and down into the desert toward this homestead. Each night he talked to me about his life, telling me stories, singing songs to me his mother had sung to him—administering to my pain with his voice. Sometimes now I hear him murmuring to me out of the rocks above my cabin.

In 1973 when diesel prices started rising with gasoline prices and he couldn't afford to pump water from the underground river anymore, my father sold the ranch on mortgage and repossessed it four times: from some dairy farmers out of central Utah, from a group of Salt Lake bankers, from a machinist who wanted to live in the desert with his family, and from a sheepman who wanted to build sheds for his herds. None of them could make the property produce.

One year before my father died, the day we finished clearing the hayfields between the cabin and the spring, I drove him to the shack someone built over a mineral pool ten miles west of here. His mind was already partly in the next world, and he howled and swore as I lugged him into the water, which was heavy as amniotic fluid. I guess he thought I would scald him. I only wanted to ease his joints, but I howled with him as we floated.

When I was thirty, my father imagined that the sighing of the wind through the boulders was Marilyn Monroe and her sirens, who had inhabited the butte. He renamed it Whorehouse Rock in her honor. One night he climbed naked through the snow to visit her. When we found him, near where I'm sitting, coyotes had gnawed his nose, ears, and penis.

In the genealogical library in Salt Lake, I tried to trace my ancestry back to Adam. Once I discovered their names and dates of birth, temple officiators could seal each family member to me by ordinance, soul by soul creating an eternal indivisible unity. As I worked I felt a completeness-in-others: I was the epiphany toward which all those souls had been living. In my research, I only made it back to 1698, to a man who had to run away from Wales because he murdered his landlord.

When Abigail was small, she burned her hand with a spot of sauce while eating a Sloppy Joe. I placed a leaf of iceberg lettuce on the burn to draw the heat out. She ate the rest of the meal with one hand, balancing the green leaf on her other fist.

The Broken Flask: I have more fragments of my own history, but if I add them point by point, measuring the degree of gravity between each one, what is their sum?—a minute and irrepressible motion of my chromosomes toward the apocalypse. From whom can I learn how to think about this singular and revolutionary inclination?

Can I sacrifice my wife and children to warn the people as Abraham and Tolstoy did? Can I like Moses carry myself and my children toward a new world after the fire storms and plagues? Like Einstein or Newton can I invent a new mathematics, a tool for analyzing my inscrutable impulse toward destruction? The prophet of the polygamists and a Navajo Indian I once knew both believed that they could make it rain by thinking. Can I like Kierkegaard think hard enough, a Knight of vital Faith, to purge this violence from my blood and make mental impulses become corporeal? I can find no myth, no introspective process, through which I can reconnect myself to my father, to my wife, or my children: a double-minded man is uncertain in all his ways. I am here, not farming my father's property, while my autobiography unravels itself.

On good days, after someone leaves, it is only me independent—no frustrated motion. No pointing finger or angle of apprehension. During those minutes, I float in benevolent stasis, a calm which is always violated by my anticipation. As of this moment, I repudiate the junction from which dust doesn't yet rise. The iron-gray igneous rocks dribbled out over the land in confusion, the ashen alkali desert: these are the emblems of my new world, the world which waits for the cloud.

As I leave the butte behind my cabin, I make an oath that I will hold myself firm against returning to watch again. I will not picture her face and the firm line along her jaw as she drives across the desert—four children in the back of the car, one in the front. The children sit with their hands on their knees, and they say nothing though the air inside the car is stifling.

GORDON WEAVER

THE AMERICAN DREAM: THE BOOK OF BOGGS

In the Oklahoma Panhandle, in the vicinity of the Texas border, lived a man named T. Boone Boggs. And this T. Boone Boggs did prosper mightily, and was wondrously content, and was full of praise and good works for the Lord. And he did bask in the benevolence of the Lord, who watched over him and did guard him against the misfortunes that may befall a man in life.

This T. Boone Boggs, upon arising each morning, did turn to his wife and say, "Praise the Lord, Jeanmarie, ain't this the life though!" And his wife was wont always to reply that it did appear they had been blessed. And after arising from their king-size round bed, and after performing their daily ablutions in the gleaming double bathroom of the master bedroom, T. Boone Boggs and his wife did, each morning, walk through the patio doors that gave entrance to a redwood deck, wherefrom they might look upon the landscape and know the pleasure of all that had come to them in life. And T. Boone Boggs with his wife did look out upon the world and consider what he saw as his reward for his unstinting labor and the righteousness of his ways in the service of the Lord. "Hoo boy!" he was wont to say to his wife, "Jeanmarie, did you ever once think we'd be riding this high on the hog? Praise the Lord, Hon, and thanks to a little help from old Cletus Dalrymple, wherever he is, and the oil depletion laws and my having such good sense for business!"

"I'll confess I never thought you'd become a corporate tycoon, Boone," his wife Jeanmarie was wont to say to him.

Close at hand, they did look upon the ornamental shrubs and the banks of bright flowers blooming in beds cultivated by their full-time Mexican gardener, Patricio Sandoval, already at work, his bare, muscled back gleaming with sweat in the bright sun of morning. And they did look upon the crushed gravel drive that formed a great white arc before the massive Spanish doors of their half-million-dollar split-level home, paid for in cash less than a year before. And they looked upon the broad expanse of their barbered lawn, the rich green of carpet grass dotted here and there with the shapes of live oak, magnolia, cedar, and pine, in the branches of which mockingbirds and cardinals and jays sang in praise of the new day.

And T. Boone Boggs did lift his eyes to look upon the boundaries of his property, marked with a white rail fence, and did lift his eyes yet higher to look into the distance. There he did discern the black shafts of oil rigs alternating with pumpers and storage tanks, and beyond them the misty bulk of Boggs Refinery, Inc., looming like a small mountain on the flatness of the Panhandle, and farther did he look, to the small town of Goshen, Oklahoma, where, above the roofs of the homes of his refinery workers shone the tower of the Crystal Palace of God's People, a bright needle thrust upward through the drifting refinery haze, a great church built by T. Boone Boggs as witness to his love of the Lord.

"Jeanmarie," he did say to his wife, "do you ever think sometimes how mysterious it is we are so blessed? I mean, where did old Cletus Dalrymple run off to just when I struck it rich? What must he be thinking now if he reads about me in *Time* or *U.S. News & World Report* or *Business Week,* or about me building the Crystal Palace and getting Reverend Dr. Vardis Klemp to be its preacher if he reads in *Christianity Today* or one of them others wrote me up? Oh, Jeanmarie, praise to the Lord and hard work is what it is!" he did say to his wife.

And his wife did say, "Boone, did you ever look at that Mexican Patricio when he's working with his shirt off? Lordy, how them muscles is all shiny rippling in his back from sweating!"

And as he broke his fast each morning with fried eggs and whole-hog sausage and Texas toast and strong, black coffee in the breakfast nook of his half-million-dollar house, sitting across from his wife and his daughter Mary Helen, the heart of T. Boone Boggs was yet filled with the rapture of his knowledge of all that had come to him and was his in this life.

And he did consider the facts of his life. He did consider that, though his own mama and daddy were only poor country people from Payne County, Oklahoma, now dead and gone, they had been hard-working, God-fearing folk who suffered and survived the Dust Bowl on a hard-scrabble farm, and had raised him in righteousness and the discipline of hard labor by which to earn his bread. And he did consider his still-lovely wife Jeanmarie, who had placed third-runnerup in the Miss Oklahoma pageant of 1961. And he did consider his beautiful little daughter Mary Helen, who sat across from him in her cheerleader's uniform, and who was active in 4-H and Junior Achievement. And T. Boone Boggs thought of his son, T. Boone Jr., away at the University of Oklahoma to study petroleum engineering, and the heart of T. Boone Boggs was gorged on pride and love for the wonderful family that had come to him in his life.

And there was yet more for the thoughts of T. Boone Boggs to dwell upon as he rose from the breakfast nook to begin his day's work. He thought of all he possessed, of his half-million-dollar home with extensive grounds tended by the full-time Mexican gardener Patricio Sandoval, and of the huge garage in which were parked his vehicles, a matched pair of Cadillacs and a Datsun 280-Z and a gentleman's pickup he drove in memory of his humble beginnings. He thought of his Olympic pool and his sauna and of the tennis courts and the stable where his daughter's horses neighed for their oats. He thought of the walk-in closets that held his wardrobe, and of the closets of his wife and daughter and his absent son. And the thoughts of T. Boone Boggs whirled to a blur of all that he owned that he might reach out and touch at any moment he wished.

And there was yet more. In the bank of Goshen, Oklahoma, in a vault, were stock certificates and promissory notes and government bonds and letters of credit and certificates of option on mineral rights to likely acreage all over America's Southwest, and deeds to land and rent-houses and apartment buildings and nursing homes and motels and supermarkets. And all of these were his, and were managed for him by hosts of shrewd lawyers and accountants. And there was even a leather sack of Krugerrands, purchased more on a whim than as a hedge against unbridled inflation. And there was, of course, much cash in various accounts.

All this he knew, and took great joy of it, and praised the Lord for it, and knew that it was the product of great labor on his part, and perhaps a bit of luck, and did for a moment wonder what had become of Cletus Dalrymple, with whom it all began years ago. And he said to his wife and daughter, "I got to get in to work. The Lord gives us a day and then it's up to us to make the most of it."

And his daughter bade him good day, and so did his wife, and she said further to him, "I got to find that Mexican Patricio and tell him not to work around the house with his body half-naked. It don't look right Mary Helen seeing him that way."

And T. Boone Boggs did set forth in his gentleman's pickup truck in the direction of Goshen, where lay his refinery and his corporate headquarters and the Crystal Palace of God's People, Reverend Dr. Vardis Klemp, Pastor, which church had been built by Boggs to praise the Lord for His benevolence.

And the Lord looked down upon his man T. Boone Boggs there in the Oklahoma Panhandle, and was well pleased with him. And He did say to Satan, "Can I pick 'em or can I pick 'em, Nick? You got to grant Me old Boggs there is going some!"

And Satan said, "Big deal."

"Sour grapes," said the Lord.

And Satan said unto the Lord, "Sure Your boy Boggs does right. And why shouldn't he, what with all You done for him? Didn't you marry him to an ex-beauty queen and give him two picture-book kids? And didn't You send him that angel in the form of an independent oilfield speculator named Cletus Dalrymple who convinced him to drop out of the A & M college at Stillwater and go wildcatting wells out to the Panhandle? Which angel named Cletus Dalrymple then put him onto mineral leases at rock bottom prices and set his rigs up over the biggest pockets of black gold since Teapot Dome and Anadarko Basin, big as Spindletop practically! And then when he was pumping gushers, then what'd You go and do for him?" Satan did ask of the Lord.

"Okay, so I give him a nudge up to start," the Lord said.

"Nudge!" Satan did cry out. "I'd say *nudge*! You went and had them Arabs embargo oil is what You done! You created your Boggs an energy crisis is what You done! You decontrolled well-head prices is all You done for him! You made him an energy tycoon almost overnight is what-all You done!"

"Calm down, Nick," said the Lord. "Okay, so I helped him. But he was a good boy to start with. His old mama and daddy was good country folks from up near to Stillwater, went through My Dust Bowl with nary a whimper, and they raised little T. Boone up righteous. You don't see My system. Folks do good works because they believe in the possible rewards of it. I just give T. Boone some of the fruits coming to him and his folks both."

"Fruits?" said Satan unto the Lord. "I'd call them *fruits* and then some. No wonder he funds half the charities in his part of the Panhandle, giving generously for senior centers and daycare for his refinery people, donated dialysis machines to a mess of hospitals I recollect, sponsors Junior Achievement and 4-H and recreational fast-pitch softball and Good Government Day in Austin and Oklahoma City both, oh, he is a pure-fire monument to faith and works, he is, witnessing at all them chamber of commerce prayer breakfasts too, don't he!"

And the Lord said, "Your trouble is you don't like giving credit for credit due, Nick, You-all are forgetting that chair he endowed at the University of Oklahoma, and the big pledge he just made for a Free Enterprise Center on the Norman campus, and also how about all those under-the-table athletic scholarships? Which is not even to speak of that Crystal Palace of God's People there in Goshen. And how are you liking the success of Reverend Dr. Vardis Klemp now he's getting media attention with his book, *Corporate Capitalism: God's Way?* First one he ever wrote, and it's a big hit! 'Fess up, Nick, you are just plain contrary."

And Satan said, "What I say is, take some of them fruits away from him, see how righteous he stays. You and Your system. It only works when You make it do!"

"Are you daring me, Nick?" asked the Lord.

"I double dare You," Satan said.

"That ties it!" said the Lord, and He was exceeding wroth, and Satan did tremble for fear of the Lord's anger. And then the Lord was calmed, and said unto Satan, "Okay. You go have a crack at T. Boone Boggs there and we'll just see."

"Carte blanche?" asked Satan.

"To a point," answered the Lord. "You can hit him in his bankbook, and you can grieve him through his family, and I don't give a rap for his reputation in Oklahoma or Texas neither one, and you can trouble him some personally, but I don't want to hear about him being no way damaged permanent physically."

"Got You," Satan did say. "I know the ways of it. I will maybe show up Your system for something folks will sour on when they see it go bad on them of a sudden."

"Your trouble, Nick," said the Lord unto Satan, "is you never think big enough. My system works out of its bigness."

"Just watch me do!" said Satan.

"I plan to," said the Lord.

And the decline of the fortunes of T. Boone Boggs was rapid and complete. The Arab oil embargo was lifted, and American industry, its markets shrinking in a world-wide recession, its ability to borrow venture capital inhibited by high interest rates, did sharply reduce the national demand for energy fuels, and the American motoring public did practice fuel conservation. And it came to pass that there was an international oil glut. And so it was that the corporate finances of T. Boone Boggs were found to be vastly overextended, and the consortium of lenders who had assured his line of credit were loath to continue their support of his endeavors, and did, instead, call upon his long and short-term notes, and bankers in Oklahoma and

Texas and Illinois and Pennsylvania were ruined in the debacle. And even, wondrously, such few new holes as T. Boone Boggs did manage to drill were all found to be dusters.

And there came soon the day of reckoning, when all was lost, and his corporation and all its subsidiary companies were declared bankrupt, and what little remained of his life's work was placed in the hands of a federal receivership, and the nation's politicians were called upon to speak soothing words to cushion the shock to the stock market. And the news of this disaster was reported for all to read in the pages of *Time* and *U.S. News & World Report* and *Business Week.*

And T. Boone Boggs did say to his wife Jeanmarie, "I don't understand the first part of it! Ever'thing was going so right, and now look at the pickle I'm in!"

And his wife did say to him, "You got too big for your britches is what you done. Now it's come to me to keep house in a rented trailer like it was twenty years ago, I suppose? Not this gal, Boone!"

And he lost not only his corporate holdings, but also his personal fortune, to include even the sack of Krugerrands, and his half-million-dollar home was taken for sale at public auction, and he and his wife and his daughter went to live in a trailer court on the outskirts of Goshen, Oklahoma, and the name of T. Boone Boggs had become anathema in the land.

And even more did he lose. His daughter Mary Helen was made pregnant with child out of wedlock by the feckless son of an oilfield roustabout, and did flee to live in sin with the boy in Odessa, Texas. And though he did grieve for this shame, his wife was no comfort to him in his misery, saying, "Maybe you should of give her a taste of your belt once in a while instead of being so busy being a tycoon, she might of turned out better."

Nor did he find comfort in his son and namesake, for T. Boone Jr. was dismissed from the University of Oklahoma for selling cannabis and amphetamine tablets on the Norman campus, and his son did flee to a religious commune in Colorado, and did change his name to New Child of Chemical Light, and did refuse all communication with his parents.

And T. Boone Boggs was utterly disconsolate, and did sit, drinking a bottle of Pearl beer, in the rented trailer that was now his home and exile. And he did cry out to his wife, "It ain't any justice to it! That boy has disgraced us! Now they ain't even going to name that endowed chair after me there!" And his wife was no comfort, saying their son's depravity was not worse than his father's failure, and further, what did he think Cletus Dalrymple thought of him now if he read the newspapers or watched television? And T. Boone Boggs did cry in his beer, and said, "If it wasn't for you and the hope I get reading Preacher Vardis Klemp's book, I don't believe I could go on!"

And then his wife Jeanmarie did tell him she was leaving him to go with another man, their former gardener Patricio Sandoval, for life with T. Boone Boggs was too depressing. "It ain't no way fair!" he did cry out.

"We're shooting for a new life, me and Patricio. We're going to California where's he's got relatives own a greenhouse and landscaping business will give us a start. No hard feelings, Boone, but I just believe you are snake-bit."

And so great was the despair of T. Boone Boggs that he knew not where to turn for succor save to the Reverend Dr. Vardis Klemp, Pastor of the Crystal Palace of God's People. And he did go to a pay telephone and called this divine, and did speak with the Reverend Dr.'s executive secretary, who did inform him that the Reverend was unavailable, being out on the road on an extended tour of bookstores and radio and television interviews to promote his new book, *Grace: God's Tax Shelter.*

"Lady," he did say to the executive secretary, "This is T. Boone Boggs speaking. I'm the man kicked in the lion's share to erect that glass church of yours. I'm hurting. My businesses is all bust, my wife's run off to California with a Mexican, my son's a hippie doper in Colorado last I heard of him, and my little girl's knocked up by a no-account and living in Odessa, Texas, on welfare for all I know. And if that ain't enough, I'm suffering attacks of ulcers and hemorrhoids and my hair's took to falling out in clumps all of a sudden!"

"I'm sorry, Mr. Boggs," she did say to him, "but the Reverend's out of touch. Maybe you could catch him on Carson tomorrow night? He talks as much about spiritual things as he does his new book on them shows."

And T. Boone Boggs, in the throes of despairing rage, did shout over the phone, "Then damn you all and damn it all if I ever give a pure damn for anything ever again and damn me for ever taking the advice of the damn Cletus Dalrymple!"

And Satan did say to the Lord, "How You like them apples?"

And the Lord said, "You pushed him pretty hard, Nick."

"You give me leave to," Satan said.

"It's a disappointment," the Lord did say, "but he was speaking in pain and the heat of the moment there. I might could still salvage something good out of him yet."

And Satan did say, "Oh, don't I know it! I suppose now You'll drop some new windfall on him. I can just see it, You'll send him another angel, maybe in the form of a electronics expert with a patent on a new generation mini-computer, make him rich all over again, won't You?"

"That'll do," the Lord said, and Satan was silent, and waited upon the Lord. And then He did say to Satan, "Nick, your trouble is you take the short view every time.

Send down angels? Quick-fix him? Not likely! What it is, is it takes the long haul to know a man's worth or bring it out either one."

"So what do You calculate doing?" Satan asked the Lord.

"Just you watch Me and see," said the Lord.

And T. Boone Boggs did sleep but fitfully in his rented trailer on the outskirts of Goshen, Oklahoma, crying out, *Why me? Why me!* and *Cletus Dalrymple, where are you when I need you!*

And the Lord spoke to T. Boone Boggs in a dream saying:

It ain't for you to question, Boggs. I'll say what's to be. Now hush up and hear Me. First off, you're well shut of that Jeanmarie. Second, your son's confused now, but I aim to send him a revelation soon. Before you know it, he'll be living clean and witnessing for Me, and I may just make him a media evangelist seeing how tacky that Vardis Klemp turned out. And your little Mary Helen's going to get religion too. She'll birth a fine son and name him for you, and that boy'll comfort your old age.

As for you, you just ain't cut out for corporate success nor celebrity neither one. Maybe I should of left you to work your daddy's homestead over to Stillwater all your days. Messing up like you done, it's hurt the whole idea of rewards for faith and works. So what I reckon for you now is just that: faith and work! You'll have a good restful sleep now, and you'll wake up with that faith back strong forever. And then you'll set to work again because you got it back. You'll sweat like a Mexican all your days with a will because you'll believe the rewards are coming your way for it. Oh, you'll make wages, but that's all. The good of it is the example you'll set all those folks got disillusioned when your businesses collapsed so sudden and your reputation turned all sour. This way, folks making wages like you do will get believing again because they see you sweating and still believing. It will keep My system going.

Now stop your fussing, Boggs, and sleep on it. This is how it'll be, and there's an end on it!

And T. Boone Boggs woke refreshed and filled with a great faith in the day and all days to come. And he did live out his days in peace, laboring at such menial tasks as came his way, to include pumping gasoline, cooking short orders, and hiring out in the annual wheat harvests in the Oklahoma Panhandle. And his example was a powerful witness to all about him who dreamed the American Dream of rewards for faith and works. For they said: if T. Boone Boggs, who got rich in the oil business practically overnight and then went broke even faster can sweat for a dollar and never miss church meetings Sundays or Wednesday evenings either one, who are we to say the system can't work for us?

And the life of T. Boone Boggs was counted a great success, and his old age was comforted by the presence of his only grandson, T. Boone III, and by his joy at the success of his son, T. Boone Jr., who became regionally famous for his radio preaching.

"The odds, I grant you," T. Boone Boggs did say to those who came to hear him, "are heavy against it happening twice, but I can tell you I made it fast and fat once, and I do believe in my heart if I stay at the wheel I might could make it again, Lord willing!"

And Satan did say to the Lord, "You got a funny notion of justice."

And the Lord was not moved, and said unto Satan, "It ain't nothing about justice in it, Nick. What it is, is it works for most people as long as they think it does. The main thing is to keep it going, which is what it is with any system. Just look at old Boggs grunting away at it down there if you don't believe Me. And there's an end to it!"

And the Lord looked down upon T. Boone Boggs there in the Panhandle of Oklahoma, and was well pleased with His man.

WILLIAM KITTREDGE

HERMITAGE

I came from sleep, smelled the exhaust fumes and the dusty cushion of the wide rear seat. The motion slowed and changed. I sat up and looked out the bus window while we rolled down the hill of Merrit Street, saw Paiute again in the dead light of a late afternoon between winter and spring.

The Greyhound stopped on the low end of town, in front of the old Bernard Pharmacy, and I swung down and felt the spring wind blowing off the Pine Forest Mountains to the north, hard and cold as ever. I was the only one that got off. The driver unloaded his newspapers and magazines, then pulled the almost empty bus back onto the highway. I was on foot for at least one night in the town where I started.

The wide and dusty street was part of the highway. Cars and pickups were parked at a diagonal in front of the Mercantile and false-fronted commercial buildings, some with soaped windows and others already lighted, were about the same as when I left, nine years before. The bare trees along the side streets were just coming into bud and seemed to show a little green, but the stained white and yellow houses looked dead as ever.

The sun was low over the valley to the west, just above the rim. The sky was clear and swept fine and almost white, the light thin and brilliant. My father's valley was shadowed by the rim, shaded blue and purple.

In the evening, when the light was blue, we would ride back from the working corrals on the far north edge of the valley, the cold numbing our fingers and freezing the fringes of moisture on our faces, the freezing air carrying no sound but that of leather working and horses breathing their mist which mingled with ours and trailed behind. The men would be tired and those on strong horses would gallop a little over the already freezing stubble of last summer's flowing meadow and the others would walk and trot, each man suiting his own horse and pace, and soon we would be a long string of riders going home through the smoke colored dusk, dipping through the sloughs and winding among the willow patches that were the only shelter in the flat.

At camp we unsaddled quickly and dropped the foam covered bits from the horse's mouths and walked stiff-legged toward the low cookhouse that sat with lighted windows and open doorway among high and skeletal Lombardy poplar trees while our horses rolled in the fine dust of the corral and headed for the open meadow outside the pole gate.

Against the light of the open door we would see the old man, my father, stumping on his bad leg and heading in our same direction. Now would come the moist warmth and, after the silent and clinking meal, a shot of whiskey from my father's bottle. Then slow talk of how the cattle worked that day and horses and riders, town and women and things that happened years before. I lay on a cot bed and listened. For that little piece of the evening, with the day finished and among those men, my father would laugh and talk and tell of his youth when he was new out here from the sod house country of Kansas.

I think those were the times when he was as he might have been, without whatever it was that pushed at him. I lay and listened and felt warmth in that room hung with the clean town hats and used extra clothing and personal things of those men. I later thought that room must have been my father's real home.

They were rough, honest men and I learned from them.

Then it would be night and the old man and I would ride to town in his pickup, a creaking vehicle with no heater. He withdrew during those trips. He had no small talk for me. I was growing to be a man, and different, the heir of his possessions. I think he had an idea of what he wanted me to be, but no idea of how to go about creating the ideal.

Now I was home again. I went in the drug store and sat at the marble topped counter and ordered a grilled ham and cheese and coffee, then tried to snap back into myself after three days on the back ends of buses. People came by and did the things they do in drug stores and I figured I should know one or another of them, but they paid no attention. None came to shake my hand or punch me on the shoulder.

"Good to see you," I hoped they'd say. "Good thing you're home." But none did.

The comics and candy counters were the same, but the white, moustached little man that ran the place was gone. I figured he must be dead. Which saddened me.

Coming home had been on my mind for a long time, but I had it figured different. Evenings I'd lie on my tarp and think of coming back in the warmth of early fall when things were slow, see myself walking up Merrit Street and knowing all the people, laughing until morning in some joint, buying drinks for the crowd at my table, letting all the girls I remembered from high school hang over me. We'd hunt and fish in the Pine Forest Mountains, camping and sleeping by the water, listening to the noise it made, seeing thin smoke rise through the trees, catch little trout for breakfast, pack only salt and vinegar and bacon, the way we did.

When we'd been out two or three weeks and had our fill, we'd come in and I'd winter around here and get onto a new feeling about who I was supposed to be.

Around Paiute I was always somebody.

But that didn't work out. I came back ahead of time, traveling light and ready to stand over the old man's grave. I felt he had at least that much good coming.

Ben Jacobs, who ran the law in this town since I can remember, was the one who got hold of me. I guess he figured it was something he owed my old man. The telegram gave me the news and said they would watch the bus and wait.

My father had been, so far as I know, lying six days in the cold storage room at the undertaker's parlor. No matter what our misunderstandings, I felt bad about that. I don't know why things went wrong. Maybe a woman in the house would have made it different. I don't know. I thought at one time he blamed even that on me and I wonder now if it wasn't the center of the trouble. Anyhow, I didn't turn out to be what he thought of as a model son. The only thing I ever did that came up to his standards was bunch my gear and travel.

Things got worse between us for a long time. When I was supposed to be a freshman down at Davis, where he made me go and where they had nothing that was part of my life, I got on a kid drunk and was locked up for resisting. I wired home for money to pay the bail. They kicked me out of school and when I got back to Paiute my stuff was piled on the curb in front of the house, covered with dust and rained on once. I pulled out with no idea of ever coming back, loaded the stuff in an old car I had at the time and drove away. Never looked in the house or went to see the old man, just got the hell out of town quick as I could. My last memory of him is at breakfast in the cook house the morning I left for Davis. He waited until the men were gone, then handed me five hundred dollars in a little roll and went out to look over the cattle.

The evening was getting late and it was almost dark when Old Ben came through the door of the drug store. I'd been about ready to give up waiting and get a room.

"We quit on you yesterday," he said, sliding in to sit beside me at the counter and ordering a cup of coffee.

"How's that?"

He was a big man with a hard gut that hung over his belt and he poured that coffee about half full of sugar and stirred it. "They figured Sam was getting a shade ripe," he said. "So yesterday they planted him. It was a nice funeral."

I told him I thought I'd pull out in the morning.

"You better stick around. It ain't that simple."

He gave up stirring that coffee and looked at me. "His throat was cut. Done in bed with his own knife."

I told him I didn't figure that had anything to do with me, that I was a long way off when it happened.

"I never meant nothing like that," he said.

Somehow it couldn't get me. It wasn't because I didn't care. Rather, it was like some endless thing was finished. The process had gone down to bottom. Ben rubbed his belly like it was bothering his mind. "You better stay," he said. "Your old man left you the works, the ranch and all."

I counted the rose buds on the soda pop sign and watched myself in the mirror behind the counter. Ben was stirring his coffee. There didn't seem much to say, at least not to a man like Ben, who lived believing the same things as my father and was about as close to him as anyone. Not to a man who was ashamed of me, that I turned out so different.

"Get your gear," Ben said finally. "I'll haul you up to the house."

I threw my tin suitcase behind the seat of his car and he drove me up the hill. "Come by the courthouse around noon," he said. "And we'll talk about it."

He handed me the brass key and left me standing on the sidewalk. I thought about going down to the highway and trying to hook a ride. But the wind had turned colder when the sun went down and I figured I'd had enough of that.

The house looked about the same, black and heavy against the stars of the cloudless night. No trees or shrubs to break the outline, no sign a woman had ever been there. My mother planted a lawn and trees the spring they married, but everything died without water during the second summer.

The lock clicked and the door swung easy. The house was built like a machine, the hardware imported from England and the solid wall paneling hand finished and the trim carved by a man brought from Ohio. I wondered if the taste were my mother's, if they talked and agreed on each thing in the house or if he simply built it. It was a time he never spoke of. He in love, she—they were in a time before any I can imagine. I have no conception of the people.

She waited three years to be married so the house could be finished. All that time she lived in the hotel at his expense. He was forty and she a girl from San Francisco and less than twenty-five. It must have been a strange place for her to finish her life.

The entrance was dark and the small illumination of the open door shrank while I searched for a light that worked. I found none and started up the central stairway, remembering the way to my room on the second floor, the only room on that floor ever used. The marble clunked under my heels, a dead and familiar sound from childhood. It seemed the old man must be asleep in the bedroom at the foot of the stairs, the room where my mother died and he always lived.

The last year I came in drunk, sick after my first really bad time with a woman, and fell in the dark and vomited on the stairs. He carried me to his room and rolled me onto his bed and sat reading beside me through the rest of the night. It was his camp bed, rough and narrow, and smelled as he did. In the morning I woke alone and sick, remembering the night.

His room was a storehouse, full of things he used. Books were piled on the floor and the shelves were stacked with more, the walls hung with maps and charts. All I wanted right then was to get out of that room. It was a private place I would never understand, a place beyond my expectations.

All that day I waited for punishment, as much for the invasion as the drinking. He went to his room when he came home that night and I followed him. He was reading. "Whiskey has good and bad points," he said, never looking up. "Like anything. A man learns to use and not be used."

The window.

Above the stair landing, it glittered. Stained and leaded glass came together in a long, many-pointed star.

I asked him once what it meant.

"Not a damned thing," was what he said. "Seems like a joke."

The window was interwoven color, beginning on the outside with blues and greens, meeting in the center with warm orange and red.

At the top of the stairs I found a light switch that worked. The electric light destroyed the other light of the window. The hall was empty and echoed the sound of my steps, coated with dust, the floor strewn with trails of collected lint. Spider webs were stiff and thick in the corners.

My room was the same, remained to greet me, to be part of myself again. The bedspread, embossed with cattle brands, specially ordered for my fifteenth birthday, the board mounted with the tracks of my electric train: all the things I had forgotten: the coat I wore hunting, boots bought from the Pendleton Rodeo, where I rode bareback and bucked off every go-round the year I was sixteen, with the toes wore out and stained with the manure of some branding corral, the clothes I had outgrown.

I was again in the special thing it was to be my father's heir. For a long time I understood that someday my father and I would talk and then I would know what was expected and he would know what to expect. We never did.

I wanted no more of the house. I walked down the hill with my suitcase and found a clean motel and slept. In the morning I woke and could remember no dreams and was satisfied.

The sun was well up over the sand hills to the east. In the cafe a couple of old working stiffs were talking up a fishing trip and coughing over their first morning cigarettes. I listened, but knew it was too early for decent fishing in this country. So I smoked and walked up to the house.

The weather had changed. The sun was warm and strong and there was no wind. I stopped and looked over the slanting roofs of town. The valley was the same, laced with willows and cut by sloughs that flood out of the creek in late spring, carrying snow water and irrigating the meadows. The fields were brown and specked with snow, showing just a tinge of green where things were changing into spring. Cattle milled and spread and I got to wondering who was looking after the place. Somebody had to see about stock water and salt and feeding and make sure everybody wasn't up town drunk. Pretty soon they had to be trailing those cows out through the edge of town to the summer range.

Then I saw the man was me.

A thin smoke was rising straight from the cook house.

This was my old world, easy and familiar as if I'd never left. But staying here would be saying I was like all the rest, blind as a sheep and falling into whatever came. Nothing but what my old man made me. I began to walk again.

The streets were about the same, the trees didn't look any bigger and the houses not much older, but in places the roots had pushed up the sidewalk and I didn't remember that from when I left. The house looked pretty much the same as it always had.

The dust beside the cement walk ran into dead, year-old weeds and the weeds into brush. The walls were three foot thick native stone, decorated with chips of glistening obsidian set in the mortar, black slick obsidian that shone in the sun on a bright day. Sometimes the old man would stand across the street and simply look at his house in the afternoon light.

"Only fool thing I ever did," he said. "So I made it a good one."

The house was worn and dirty inside. But I figured I could clean it up, get a woman to come in and paint and refinish the furniture and hang new curtains. I knew I was going to stay. I guess the idea of money and being somebody was part of it, but there were other things too.

I looked out a front window and watched a bunch of dogs chase a bitch in heat through the yards across the street and remembered climbing in those trees and throwing a football, dodging parked cars and shouting in the twilight. I could see the ball, black and perfectly timed, dropping from the late purple sky. I remembered wishing, as the first mothers began to shout it was time to come in, that I hadn't lost my own mother in the process of birth, a victim, so it was said, of her past life. I didn't understand that at the time.

Now the street was empty. No children. I wondered where we had all gone. Those times were better than any. I don't know where things started to change. We would lie by the creek and fish and talk of what was coming. Then, without warning, we were committed to nothing.

The last year. In the spring my father bought a mortgage and evicted a man with eight children from a ranch that controlled water rights he wanted. I was in school with three of the boys, dirty, hard-nailed and thick-headed boys who had never done anything but work and scrounge. They cursed me publicly the day they left, then followed me to the lot behind our house. I beat the oldest in a half hour fight and felt that I had betrayed myself when they left, sullen and bewildered, as was I, that righteousness had lost.

That night I went to my father's room and stood in the doorway while he looked up from one of his books. "You're wrong," I said. "A dirty wrong sonofabitch."

I waited for wrath and what I hoped would be an explanation which could satisfy the shame I felt. "You don't know anything." He spoke easily and didn't move. He knew what I was talking about.

"Nobody has the right," I said. "It's wrong and always will be."

"You'll learn," he said. "That right has nothing to do with what happens to people. The sooner you learn, the easier you'll have it."

He went on without giving me time to say anything. "You'll learn not to worry about people. Anything can happen to people." He smiled, as if he had said it right, as if there could be no possible way for me to misunderstand.

Those were old times and gone. I started for the back of the house and ended in his room. It was the same as

I remembered, except he had a big potbellied stove in the middle of the floor, sitting in a box of sand, and a pile of split wood beside it. The carpet was rolled against one wall and there was a butt can half full of water next to the bed.

It was the same old camp bed. When he went to the desert he would roll up the tarp with the blankets and pillow inside and tie it with a leather strap and throw the bundle in the back of the pickup.

I pulled back the canvas, half expecting to see the old man frowning and hiding there, like it was a test and nothing could ever kill him. It was all gone. Nothing left but faint blood specks on the bare canvas to mark his passing. I pulled the canvas back up.

It had finally come to me. I walked down to the courthouse and told the sheriff my father had cut his own throat. Ben said they were glad I saw it that way, that they had been figuring on calling it that.

I drank awhile that afternoon and talked to some boys I knew. Finally I got tired of listening to their day dreams and went up to the house. The evening was calm and cold and I stood on the porch and looked down over the lights of town toward the darkness of the valley beneath the rim. Then I went inside.

JIM FINLEY

LEAVING ON THE WIND

The day we buried Hadley Strickland was the kind of day that made people around Judd burrow down inside themselves and not talk much. A bad norther had blown in across the West Texas flats kicking up topsoil and turning everything in sight a hazy brown. The old-timers said a person could get accustomed to the sandstorm miseries if they stayed long enough. I never did believe that, and neither did Ben-Oliver. I guess Jesse didn't know what he believed anymore.

There weren't many people there that day, hardly enough for a decent funeral. Besides me and Ben-Oliver and Jesse Tuckett, there was Jeb Lewis and the McClures and Nat Sudder and Hugh Yoakum. And of course, Hadley's mother, Minnie. The drought had pushed one family, then another off the land until nothing much was left but a few empty buildings, and what Ben-Oliver called "a lot of lonesome."

I always did think it was a hell of a place for a town. Out in the middle of nowhere. No trees. Nothing. Except maybe a few tumbleweeds or a scraggly jackrabbit popping up now and then, racing off in the distance with his ears sticking up like a giant cactus in a desert. Just flat land as far as you could see, and the gray-brown sky and the wind, always the wind, and the sand swirling up around us, cutting us off from one another, making us feel like there wasn't another living soul on earth.

Ben-Oliver didn't like it any better than I did. He was always complaining about how Judd wasn't even on the map.

"If you ain't on the Conoco map," he would say, "you ain't nowhere. Just wished I lived some place that was on the fuckin' map."

Minnie Strickland had waked me up that morning all in a tizzy about how bad the weather was and how she couldn't hold her mind on nothing for long and how sick to her stomach she was over poor Hadley and that he must have suffered a lot because he didn't look like himself and how sad it was that Mr. Strickland had been dead for years and didn't get to see Hadley in his Marine outfit. She wanted to know if there'd be any Marines at the funeral and I assured her that they'd send an honor guard over from Abilene and they'd be dressed all smart in their uniforms and shoot off their guns and play taps and give her a flag. She said that would be real nice and it'd make Hadley's dead daddy right proud.

I dressed and walked out of the back of the old Buckaroo theater and up the aisle toward the double doors. They had fancy clowns carved an inch deep above the wooden handles and they made a swishing sound when you went through. Creed Mays had left everything that Saturday after the credits rolled the last time for Marilyn Monroe in the *Misfits.* Creed liked Marilyn Monroe and refused to send the reels back. He said he got a lot of threatening letters about it, but that didn't bother him much. Finally, the letters stopped coming and Creed kept showing the film over and over again.

"Just look at that," he said. "That ain't acting. She's hanging out there raw, living every bit of it all down inside."

"Guess I never thought about it like that," I said. Creed went right on talking, like he would've kept talking about her even if nobody was standing there.

"Not another soul could do that, 'cept maybe Montgomery Clift or James Dean."

"Hmmmm," I said, shaking my head, thinking how I'd known Creed all my life and even worked for him in the picture show after school and on weekends before I went to war. I thought about how I'd never seen him act like this and then I noticed his cheek jumping and twitching, jumping nearly all over his face.

"Don't ya see?" he said, looking at me real serious.

"See what?" I said. He ran his fingers through his thick hair and screwed up his face between twitches, like he couldn't believe I didn't know what he knew.

"Well she ain't gonna make it, that's all." Creed threw up his hands. "Shoot, she won't even last out the year." I couldn't say a thing. I just stood there with my mouth open thinking about how Marilyn Monroe had died back in 1962, and how Creed had shoved that out of his mind. I wondered what coming back to Judd would do to me and Ben-Oliver. I didn't reckon it mattered much to Jesse.

That was the Saturday I got back from the war, the same day Creed tossed me the keys and said he was going to Abilene, had a job in the Post Office over there. Said if I could sell the building or anything in it to send him half.

Out back the old red brick resembled all the other buildings on Main Street. But in front it was shaped like the Alamo, kind of ornate like a Hollywood movie set. Inside, everything was like it was before—the seats, the projectors, the concession stand, the popcorn machine, the small room Creed had built in the back to live in, even the smell of popcorn grease and sticky Royal Crown syrup still hung in the air and made me remember things I thought I'd forgotten.

Me and Ben-Oliver and Jesse had grown up in the picture show and lived all the fantasies of being movie stars and great lovers and heroes, and then the war came along and we got our chance. We went half way around the world to some place we'd never heard of to do what was right and fight for our country and save innocent people's lives and get decorated for bravery and come home to a hero's welcome, just like it always happened up on the screen in the Buckaroo Theater.

I huddled from the cold against the ticket window wishing I had a bigger coat. I watched a tumbleweed run the only stop sign in town like it didn't matter any more, the same stop sign me and Ben-Oliver and Jesse got drunk and pushed over on the night Jesse was fifteen years old. Then we put our arms around each other and swore that no matter about the future we'd stick together and that whatever happened to one of us happened to all of us.

The north wind pushed the tumbleweed on down the street, out past the school building that seemed to be sinking into the ground where the sand had piled up on one side. I could see Ben-Oliver's old Dodge pickup coming up the road and I knew he and Jesse were coming in, just like always, to play a few hands of dominoes and tell some stories and wait on Nat Sudder's green Ford to deliver our government checks.

Except today, we had to bury Hadley.

Even though me and Ben-Oliver and Jesse were older and never ran around with Hadley, I couldn't get my mind off him dying so young and what the war had done to all of us, especially to Jesse. Ben-Oliver said that sliver of Asian grenade blew Jesse back to when he was ten years old. He was about that age when the Tucketts moved down off the Caprock to Judd. They left because the pay Zack Tuckett got at the Shallowater Cotton Gin wasn't enough to keep Jesse's sister, Romania, in food. The price of Caprock land had jumped sky-high once irrigation wells sprouted all over, so Zack moved his family down to Judd and bought five acres of cheap peanut land and lots of chickens and a hog or two and put in a big garden. Romania was twenty-seven then and weighed over four hundred pounds. She couldn't fit into the house, so Zack built a room in the barn with a floor and double doors. He strung a rope to the kitchen window and tied a cowbell on the end and Romania jerked on the rope when she needed something.

Me and Ben-Oliver made friends quick with Jesse. He was awful cock-sure and he got depressed a lot, but there was something about him that just grew on a person.

"No bigger'n a piss ant, is it," Jesse said that first day, biting off a chew of Brown Mule and pointing it toward me.

"What's that?" said Ben-Oliver.

"Judd." Jesse spit. "That's what you call this place, ain't it?" I took a plug of tobacco and tossed it back to Jesse.

"Well I sure as hell never heard of no Shallowater," I said. Jesse spit again and wiped his mouth on his shirt sleeve.

"Just a frog jump from Lubbock."

"Is it on the Conoco map?" asked Ben-Oliver.

"What?"

"The Conoco map. Is it on the Conoco map?"

"Damned if I know," said Jesse. "Don't matter noway, a person can get famous even if they don't live in no big place. Take my sister, Romania, she got famous, got real famous traveling with the Tri-State Circus up in Amarillo. County fairs and all, you know."

"How'd she get so famous?" asked Ben-Oliver.

"Ate," said Jesse. "Ate like a teenage rhino. Hell, they even showed her over't the state fair in Dallas one year. Hauled her around in a flatbed cattle truck 'til they busted an axle and the Circus went belly-up. That's when Romania come on back home and we moved down here.

Me, I'm countin' on gettin' famous myself someday, just like Romania."

"You right sure 'bout that?" said Ben-Oliver.

"Sure as I'm chewing this plug. Yessir, I'm gonna put Judd on the map."

I edged up closer against the ticket booth out of the wind and looked up the street. The feed store was vacant and so was the pool hall and May's Cafe and Ferguson's Drugstore. The Dodge was coming past the old cotton gin now. It had been the first to close down. Every day or so the wind would blow a sheet of tin off the roof, leaving another gaping hole. I listened to the Rexall sign rocking back and forth screaming on its rusty hinges and wondered why me and Ben-Oliver had come back. We never talked about it much, but I knew it was because of Jesse and how we'd grown up together and how he didn't have anyone after the '61 tornado blew his family away and how he got all nervous when we took him to a big city, like over to Abilene or up to Wichita Falls. And then there was that night when Jesse turned fifteen and we all got drunk and pushed over the only stop sign in town and swore we'd always hang together, no matter what happened.

Ben-Oliver was with Jesse when they got wounded in Quang Tri. I tried to talk to him about what happened back there, but he'd act like he didn't hear a thing I said and he'd just start telling another one of his stories. When he did that, I'd forget all about Quang Tri because Ben-Oliver could really tell good stories, especially when he was in the mood. And he was usually in the mood when he was with Jesse and me, although I suspect the stories were mostly for Jesse's benefit, not mine. But just the same, I had to be there to make it work, to somehow complete the recipe.

Ben-Oliver liked the idea of me living in the picture show. He said it made a good place to tell stories, up there on the stage in front of the big screen where we had the domino table set up. That's really about all we did back then, just hung around the Buckaroo Theater shuffling through endless games of slow dominoes and listening to Ben-Oliver tell his stories. At first he stacked our heads full of war tales, laboring under their weight, halting and sweating behind his red beard, making Jesse and me live all the worst parts over again. These stories were pretty much the same—all about the stifling heat of the Mekong Delta, the heavy shelling during the Tet offensive and then the fear and boredom getting all mixed up in the middle of your guts. And there were always the children dressed in explosives and the holidays and the hoochie women in the bars of Saigon, the pagodas and the shaved heads and the futility of all bloody wars. We were there at the same time and shared the same feelings and talked our way through it again and again, and finally Ben-Oliver didn't tell any more war stories. That was about the same time Jesse and me stopped listening anyway. Ben-Oliver went into one of his moods and didn't say anything for a long time. He was like that. He just sat there staring at the dominoes and drinking one Lone Star after another and not smoking his Chesterfields. Jesse kept on winning all the domino games. To him, yelling DOMlNO was winning. He couldn't count the dots, so we didn't bother to keep score. He'd scream DOMINO, then he'd knock them all down and shuffle again.

Finally, one morning Ben-Oliver sauntered through the double doors with the clowns carved in them. He had a Chesterfield dangling from his lips and Jesse was right behind him marching in place and pulling at the hair on the back of his neck. He always did that when he got excited and me or Ben-Oliver would have to hug him to make him stop.

"Did I tell you about my Aunt Cora?" Ben-Oliver said, squinting his eyes against the smoke snaking up his face.

That was the first of a new batch of stories. They came out in startling colors; browns and golds and tones of red, blue and silver. They rolled off his tongue like balls of mercury—quick and beautiful. Humorous stories, powerful stories, stories that glittered with charm, stories with plots and characters that laughed and cried and danced out of his mouth. Those were the best times, especially for Jesse. He would drag his chair up close and follow Ben-Oliver's words with his lips and change his face with the cadence of the story, at times looking as if he might dive into Ben-Oliver's mouth and swim in the words.

"Tell it again, Ben-Oliver," Jesse would say. "You know, the part where the man's standing up on the flat mountain looking down at the Sycamores and Maples in the breaks and then remembering all them things. Come on, Ben-Oliver, tell it again." And Ben-Oliver would smile real warm and laugh and ruffle Jesse's hair and start all over again and Jesse would enjoy it just as much as he did the first time. That's when I'd lean back and watch Jesse's face light up and remember the good times we'd had together and, for a minute anyway, forget that the war ever happened and that Jesse took all that shrapnel in his head.

I heard Ben-Oliver cut off the motor and watched them pull in up next to the curb. The old Dodge didn't have any brakes, so Ben-Oliver always had to coast to a stop.

"Goddamn, that wind's cold." He sat a can of Lone Star on the hood of the pickup and pulled up his collar and hunched his shoulders under his ears and put his back to the wind. "Hell-of-a-day for a funeral." Jesse had on his uniform. I hadn't seen it on him since the war.

"Hold on there, Jesse," I said. I walked around him, talking on about how sharp he looked in his dress outfit and that he'd make a West Point pass-in-review forget to turn eyes right. I guess I overdid it a bit and Jesse began to march in place and pull at the hair on the back of his neck. I noticed there wasn't much hair left back there.

"Dominoes!" yelled Ben-Oliver, hugging Jesse. "Go set up the dominoes." Jesse grinned unnatural-like and cut his eyes back and forth under his heavy brows before he ran through the double doors. Ben-Oliver looked at me and nodded toward a row of seats at the back of the theater.

That's when he told me he was leaving. Just like that. Said that after we bury Hadley he was taking off.

"What the shit you talking 'bout?" I said. I noticed Ben-Oliver didn't have his Chesterfields with him. He turned up the Lone Star and finished it and took a long look at me.

"He can count the dots."

"What?"

"The dots on the dominoes. Jesse can count 'em as good as me or you. Always could." I stared at Ben-Oliver with my mouth open. "Don't matter," he said. "He's just as dead as Hadley and I reckon he aims to stay that way as long as I'm here to take care of him."

"You talking at me serious, Ben-Oliver?"

"You heard me, I ain't helpin' him none. Figure if I leave, he'll have to back out of that world he's livin' in."

"C'mon now, Ben-Oliver, me and you and this side of Dallas knows Jesse's carrying a junkyard full of metal behind his ear." Ben-Oliver just sat there shaking his head no, not saying a thing, just like when I would ask him about what happened in Quang Tri.

I looked at Ben-Oliver, then I looked at Jesse standing up on the stage in front of the big screen. I thought about how Minnie Strickland just knew that Hadley's dead daddy would be proud of him in his Marine outfit and how Creed Mays wouldn't believe that Marilyn Monroe died back in 1962 and how Ben-Oliver believed that Jesse could count the dots on the dominoes.

I watched Ben-Oliver's lips not moving and listened to the wind blowing in gusts down the street outside the double doors, carrying away another layer of topsoil, exposing the bare earth below.

We all huddled in the cold above Hadley's grave and stared at the gray coffin cleverly draped in a flag with the corner stripes whipping in the wind. Poor Jesse never moved. He stood there with his uniform drooping off his shoulders, looking all shriveled up in his old man's body. Ben-Oliver kept nudging him and saying he didn't need to salute no more, but Jesse left his hand up there and acted like he didn't hear a thing. Even when Minnie tried to hug him, he stood real stiff with his hand still cocked up smart beside his head. A Marine, looking wooden like his uniform had been painted on, blew taps.

About two hours before dark when the sun was hanging like a giant beet behind the dust in the air, we put Jesse between us in the old Dodge and headed back to town. Then for the last time Ben-Oliver did what he always did. He coasted to a stop in front of Ferguson's Drugstore and rolled down his window and listened to the Rexall sign rock back and forth on its hinges.

"Hear it?" he said. Jesse leaned over and stuck his head in the window.

"I hear it, Ben-Oliver. I hear it real good." Then Ben-Oliver said the same thing he said every time.

"That's the future leaving on the wind."

"Yea, Ben-Oliver," Jesse said, "Leaving on the wind. Just leaving on the wind." Ben-Oliver yelled loud and grabbed the air and made like he caught a piece of Juicy Fruit. Jesse grinned like always and cut his eyes back and forth and stuck the gum in his mouth and started stomping his feet and pulling at the hair on the back of his neck.

The wind died some that night, but it sleeted off and on and a light snow covered the ground. Nat Sudder came by in his green Ford the next morning and told me that

Ben-Oliver and Jesse were gone and that he'd found a note telling him where to send Ben-Oliver's checks up in Wichita Falls.

"You didn't see Jesse?" I asked. Nat looked at me funny and said he figured Jesse was wherever Ben-Oliver was.

"You right sure Jesse wasn't out there?"

"I'm sure," said Nat, tilting his head to one side and wrinkling his brow like he just discovered he'd lived all his life without really knowing what was going on.

I finally found Jesse late that afternoon. The clouds were hanging low and the wind had picked up again, piling the snow against the north side of everything. It looked like somebody had spread a dingy white sheet over the mound of dirt that was Hadley's new grave. Jesse still had on his uniform and his hat was pushed down on his ears, making them stick out, like a jackrabbit's ears do sometimes when he's not scared and running off somewhere in the distance. He was saluting and I could see his fingers turning blue under the brim of his cap.

"Jesse, Jesse, ain't ya cold?" He stood there and didn't say anything. "Jesse, you can't stay here. You got to come on with me." I put my arm around his shoulders and tugged a little bit and started walking him back toward town. The snow was swirling up around us making everything real quiet, like it was trying to cut us off from everybody else.

The flurry had let up some by the time we got back to town and we could see the Alamo-shaped front of the old Buckaroo Theater and Ferguson's Drugstore and we could hear the Rexall sign rocking on its hinges. It didn't seem to be so loud anymore. Jesse stopped short and stood still. Then he looked at me real lonesome-like under his dark brows and tears came up in his eyes.

"Leaving on the wind," he said. "Ben-Oliver's just leaving on the wind."

Standing there in the middle of Judd looking at Jesse with his uniform hanging off of him and his cap shoved down on his ears and hearing him say that made me feel all empty, like somebody had just ripped my insides out.

I dug around in my pocket and found a stick of Juicy Fruit and acted like I grabbed it out of the air. Jesse grinned and wiped his eyes on his shirt sleeve and started marching in place and pulling at the hair on the back of his neck. I hugged him and thought about that first day when he tossed me the plug of Brown Mule and kept spitting and wiping his mouth on his shirt sleeve and telling me and Ben-Oliver about how he was gonna get real famous just like his sister, Romania, and put Judd on the Conoco map.

"Dominoes," I said, trying to remember some of Ben-Oliver's stories. "Go set up the dominoes, Jesse."

MARK STEVEN HESS

WHERE YOU HAVE BEEN, WHERE YOU ARE GOING

I shut the door of my car. I can hardly hear the noise it makes. All sounds are sifted here, broken up by the prairie, digested and dispersed in fine pieces through the air. The color is brown—brown plains of brown dirt, brown weeds rolling off north, south, east, west with a brown road slashing across them. The sky contains no clouds. It is a solid blue sheet meeting brown prairie in one straight line as if someone had pasted two pieces of colored paper together.

I walk north across a ditch, and I thank God this is not my home.

This is my grandfather's home. He was born here. He spent his life here before he died seven miles away in a rest home in a town called Arickeree. There are five paved streets in that town, each lined with elm trees on both sides. It looks like an oasis as you approach it from the state highway—122 miles straight east of Denver by counting mile markers. When you get there, though, you can see that the trees are only a cover for more brown—brown-faced people with lines of brown underneath their fingernails from working in their brown yards.

I only saw my grandfather once. I was four years old. One day an old man appeared in our house. Dad said, "Son, this is your grandfather." The old man shook my hand and laughed. He slapped my back. He kneaded my shoulder. He wrestled me close to him and squeezed my knee until I squirmed and laughed and wrestled his big hand to get loose and finally he could say, "You're just about one of the girl-craziest persons I ever seen."

He stayed only for a week, and when he left I kept expecting to see him still in our house. I thought I'd see him just around the corner in the hallway, smoking cigarettes at night in his bedroom, or brushing thick lather onto his face as he whistled to himself in front of the bathroom mirror. I have never seen a man since who has whistled so often or so well.

I continue north now, keeping to the right tire rut—the same rut Dad and I followed to the old homestead I have only seen once before. The ruts lead up and down the swells of the prairie to the homestead. Each swell is like a tiny horizon, and there are places where the swells are so abrupt and so close together that I do not know what is ahead of me thirty yards away. When I walk I feel as if I am climbing over ocean waves. I am surrounded by waves, and though the waves don't move, I still feel threatened. I walk on. I walk on because I know that soon I will rise up over a swell and there will be the windmill—there will be the lighthouse that tells me the homestead is not far away.

It is forty years before. Grandfather has just died. I am five years old. After the funeral Dad stops at a store with a green-and-white-striped awning. We go inside and there Dad buys me a pair of black cowboy boots. I wear the boots out of the store and run down the street to try them out. They are exactly the kind I want. "Yes," Dad says, satisfied, "those are very fine boots."

Dad says he wants to show me something. We get in the car and drive on dirt roads. On the way, Dad tells me of Indians and arrowheads and how he used to go hunting arrowheads after big rainstorms when the dust on the ground was newly melted away by the drops of rain. By the time Dad stops the car, my feet have begun to sweat in the leather boots. This can't be what he wants to show me because there is nothing here. I guess that he has to pee. He gets out of the car and motions for me to follow. He takes my hand, and we walk north along tire ruts. "Just watch for the windmill," he says. "When you see the windmill we'll be there." We are going to see where my grandfather grew up, a place where there were real cowboys and real Indians.

My grandfather stretches his legs out in front of him. He is a big man. He takes up two spaces on the sofa just getting comfortable. He tells us a story about a windmill.

The windmill has stopped turning. They have had no way to get water for three days. They try greasing the windmill; they try replacing the gears. Nothing works. Two Indians pass by. Grandfather offers them a shotgun and a pint of whiskey if they will make it rain. They ask why doesn't he just try greasing the windmill. Grandpa throws two extra pints of whiskey into the deal. Finally they accept. The Indians dance all night, and the next day it rains—a thunderstorm. Lightning strikes the windmill, and the windmill begins to turn. It continues to rain for twelve days. No work gets done, and all the people around Arickeree get scared because they have never seen so much rain. The sheriff comes from Arickeree and arrests Grandfather for negligence in giving rain dancers too much whiskey.

Dad has dropped my hand. He walks looking straight ahead and does not notice me. Now and then I have to skip to keep up. "Can't we drive?" I ask. "Ain't no vehicle could make the trip over this land," he says. He is talking like Grandfather. The new boots hurt my feet. "Is it far?" "Not far." "Are were almost there?" "Look for the windmill," he says. "Dad . . ." I say. I pause. I make him see me. "My feet hurt." He looks solemn, slightly hurt, slightly pleading. "We'll try going slower," he says.

He stops, points, and turns, indicating the horizon. "Right there," he says, "settlers used to come on covered wagons. It wasn't easy out here. Sure there were Indians . . ."

"Indians?"

"Indians. And you had to watch out for them too, but getting lost out here was just as dangerous. You might think it's hard getting lost in such an open place, but that's just the problem. There's nothing out here to look at to see if you're going in a straight line. And then there are these swells. You get down in between two swells and you can't see where you're going or where you've been. The only thing that can keep you going is hope and that next swell—hope that soon you'd come over a swell and there would be a river you could follow, or maybe there would be the Rocky Mountains and you could head straight out to them."

"There was Indians here?" I ask, walking again, forgetting now my discomfort.

"Indians? Sure."

"Bad Indians?"

"Well, some were bad, I guess. But most of them your Grandpa knew were good."

"Grandpa knew Indians?"

"Sure. Don't you remember his stories? He knew as many Indians as you might ever want to know. He could name all the tribes, Sioux, Cheyenne, Papoose, Squaw, Hermoso. In fact . . . not far from here, just on the other side of your Grandpa's homestead, is an Indian grave."

"Can we see it?"

"Yes, I suppose a fellow could walk to it. No . . . it really isn't too far from here."

We walk faster.

There was the windmill, just above the horizon, pushing up higher and higher over the next swell with each step as if it were growing up out of the prairie. I remember now the way I yelled the first time I saw it, how I ran ahead of Dad and laughed, feeling like a real cowboy in my black cowboy boots. This day, though, calls for silence.

I walk, hands in my pockets. I feel my pocketknife there, cold, familiar. The knife has no color anymore, though it was once shiny gold, and the end of the longest blade is chipped off square from using it as a screwdriver. Every family has an heirloom—a sort of talisman. This knife is ours. Somehow . . . when I touch it—when I fold my hand around it—I can feel Father's strong hands, and as I hold the knife now I do not want to let go.

I am certain that Dad must have been relieved, even satisfied that day with all my running and yelling as we approached the homestead. I am certain because I know what it is like to lose your father. I am certain because even now I want someone to fill this place with laughter. If I could have any wish right now, it would be that I could fill this place myself.

"How long were you in jail?" I ask through everyone's laughter. Grandfather keeps an even expression. "It was two weeks," he says, "two weeks and then the sheriff let me go." He talked while his fork rested on his plate. He talked with his fork poised in front of his mouth. He talked through mouthfuls of scalloped potatoes. He talked through bites of strawberry shortcake.

When Grandfather returned to the homestead he found the two Indians waiting for him. They had set up a teepee and had waited there two weeks for Grandfather to return for the sole purpose of learning from

Grandfather how to operate the shotgun he had given them. There was never a time when it had rained for twelve days before on the prairie. It was as if the ground didn't know what to do with all that water, so for a while the water just stayed there, and the prairie was dotted all over with small lakes. Grandfather wasn't going to let an opportunity like this slip away, so he grabbed his shotgun and his bird dog Scooter and took the Indians out to see if they might be able to hunt a few of the ducks that flew in off the lakes.

Grandfather was a bit worried that Scooter might not quite know what to do with a duck. Scooter had never seen a duck before, nor a lake for that matter. But right away they saw some ducks and one, two, Grandfather gets off two shots and two ducks fall to the ground. Scooter brought the ducks back, not even hesitating, and neither duck so much as had one tooth mark on its body. Meanwhile the Indians were shooting wildly with their shotgun and coming closer to killing themselves than any duck. One would shoot and the kick of the old shotgun would knock him all the way to the ground. Before that one had time to swear, the other one would grab the shotgun and fire. Then both Indians tried holding the shotguns at the same time, but both barrels shot off and knocked both the Indians to the ground. Pretty soon the Indians got more than fed up with all this, and finally they asked Grandfather to come along with them; they'd show him the real way to hunt ducks.

When they arrived at the next lake, the Indians walked up close without any noise and crouched down low into their own shadows. Now Grandfather can't figure out how the hell the Indians are going to catch a duck this way, but soon the Indians start making sort of low and throaty duck noises with their palms cupped over their mouths. Sure enough, within five minutes four or five ducks swim up close to the edge where the Indians crouch.

Suddenly one of the Indians springs into the water and grabs a duck by the neck, twisting its head nearly off before the duck has time to quack even once in surprise.

An hour of crouching, springing, and twisting passes before the Indians relax. The result is a pile of a dozen ducks with broken necks lying on the ground beside the Indians. Grandfather was so happy at this that he forgot himself for a moment and shot a duck sitting on top of the water. He completely forgot about Scooter and his ignorance about duck hunting and water. Before Grandfather could do anything, though, Scooter was off and running on top of the water just like Jesus Christ. Scooter was there and back even before Grandfather had time to tell him he would drown, and just as always the hound laid the bird in Grandfather's hand without a solitary tooth mark. From then on the Indians never did get closer than a careful arm's length to Scooter in fear that whatever demon that made the dog run on the water might suddenly let loose and jump inside of one of them. Grandfather's brain was swiveling around faster than a weather cock in a tornado, but he never let the Indians see he was affected. Later, though, when Grandpa got the chance to fill up a pipe and sit down to think, he worked it all out in his head. After then, he wasn't troubled anymore because it was all just a matter of finding a logical explanation. And it didn't take Grandpa too long to realize that the reason Scooter could walk right on top of the water like that was because Grandpa never did teach the dog how to swim, and the dog was too dumb to figure out for himself that trying to run on top of water was likely to result in drowning.

It is getting darker. The prairie is silver; the prairie is grey. We stand by the windmill. It is just an old windmill, nothing else. There are no lightning marks, no buffalo hides tacked to it. I don't know why we have to stay here so long. Perhaps Dad sees more to this place than I do. Maybe he can still see what used to be here, the sod house, the turning windmill, my grandfather at the window, his face, his hands. I look at the windmill. I want to ask where the lightning struck it. I want to ask how it brings up water. I want to ask how long it will be until we can go to the Indian grave. But Dad does not notice me, so I turn sideways and try to make myself thinner. I don't want to get in the way.

Grandfather is wearing black cowboy boots that he and I polished the night before. He is boarding the bus that will take him back to Colorado. He shakes my hand. He tells me I have a strong hand. He slaps my back, kneads my shoulder, and then he gets on the bus—black boots clunking up the steps.

Dad says we will have to hurry to make it to the Indian grave before dark. He starts east, each stride a mountain. I nearly have to run to keep up. At first I am eager, but it doesn't take long for me to remember my boots. "My feet hurt," I say. Dad keeps striding. "It is only a little farther," he says. "But they really hurt," I say, letting a whine slip into my tone. "Watch the horizon," he says, "that next swell. We make it to the next swell, maybe there will be that grave on the other side."

It does not work. I feel the blister anyway.

Dad is striding—flying—and I keep falling away, my arm getting longer, his hand holding tighter to mine until he is almost dragging me with him. Tears come now. My feet drag and stumble over the hard mounds of dirt. No wagon full of settlers can stop the tears; no promise of an Indian grave can keep me silent. I let the tears force my mouth to open, and I cry.

I reach to feel the pocketknife. For an instant my hand does not find it, and I imagine the knife already lost—already buried in the dust somewhere on the prairie. For an instant my body, neck, and head shrivel together, my trachea constricts and I cannot breathe; for an instant I want to let my body fall, fold together, and collapse onto the prairie. But then I find it. I hold the knife tight in my hand and do not let go. It is my turn now to stand at the windmill and remember. Jesus . . . they were handsome men.

We are almost back to the car again. Dad carries me on his shoulders, my cowboy boots bouncing off his chest. Dad is striding still, now happily, now jokingly telling me stories of rattlesnakes, cowboys and cattle drives, and how Grandma used to make lye soap. I try not to be happy. I try not to smile, but it is no use. My tears are already dry.

Before we get into the car, Dad crouches low in front of me. In his hand is a pocketknife. He wants me to take it. In my hand the knife seems much larger. "I got that knife on my tenth birthday," he says. "Your grandfather gave it to me." I put the knife in my pocket, feeling on the outside to make sure it is safe there. We get in the car. I feel older now, grown up because I have my own knife. I look at my father and somehow he too is older.

"Dad," I say, "I really wanted to see that Indian grave."

"Yes," he says, "yes . . . so did I."

I turn and walk east, away from the windmill. I watch the next swell of prairie in front of me. I walk until I am on top of the swell, and then I stop. You can see both ways here. I stay there only a moment; then I continue east knowing that over the next swell will be the Indian grave.

GLADYS SWAN

LUCINDA

The night before, Alex had come, arriving sometime after midnight. Pilar had sat up in bed, first hearing the car door slam, then the sound of the key in the lock. She slipped out of bed without turning on the light, hoping not to wake Lucinda, who lay in a warm curl beside her, her small chest rising and falling with her breath. When Alex was gone, Lucinda slept in his place.

"You are here," she said, going into the living room, blinking against the light. He had thrown his windbreaker across the chair, and was sitting on the couch, taking off his tennis shoes, grunting and groaning like an old man.

"I'm beat. All the fucking trucks on the highway. Crowd a man. Have to take up the whole goddam road. Oh, God, I am fucking tired."

"Do you want me to rub your back?" she asked.

He worked his shoulders around, heavy, muscled shoulders. "Nah," he said. "I'm too goddam tired to stay up for it. Gotta get me some shuteye." He heaved himself off the couch and into the bedroom, Lucinda's room.

Pilar stood in the doorway, watching him take off his shirt and undo his belt. He looked fat and tan, as though he'd soaked up all the sun he could find out there on the coast, put some of it on his shoulders and the rest on his belly. He was a burly man, thick, carrying a load at the middle. Too much food, too much beer, Pilar thought, as she looked at him. Now he was there—back. She did not know exactly where he'd been and what he'd done—that is, what he had brought back with him, and what she was supposed to do with it.

"You just gonna stand there?" Alex wanted to know. "Look, kid, you ain't getting nothing out of me tonight. Right now, I'm no more good than a spavined horse." He flopped heavily onto the bed, made it groan.

She turned out the light and went back to Lucinda. When she slipped under the covers, Lucinda turned over, murmured something in her sleep and nuzzled against her. Pilar touched her on the shoulder, not enough to wake her, and lay in the dark for a moment, taking in the warm, sweet scent of her childhood.

Alex was home—for how long this time? It was his way, to come in like a change of weather, like a cloud of dust on the desert, or a cloudburst that sent the rivers roaring through the arroyos. Without warning. And when he came, it was always different, and when he left something changed with him. She lay in the dark wondering how this was, and how it would be now with his coming.

It did not always happen, it was true. His dealings took him away for days or weeks at a time. And things went on the same. She was used to his comings and goings, to the many conversations on the telephone, often in Spanish, of which he knew enough to take care of things. "Tiene usted el dinero?" she would hear him say, with an intensity she had come to recognize. And the amount of pesos he mentioned was more than she had ever seen. So much money. She did not know all the numbers even to count it. What would anyone do with so much money?

She could not tell how it would be this time. A month he had been away, in Los Angeles. Making deals. Buying, selling—she did not know what. She never asked him, he never told her. Sometimes he came back, singing at the top of his lungs, smirking like a well-fed tomcat. Then he'd pick her up and swing her around, and say, "Well, my chiquita, we'll do the town up brown. Do some of them nightclubs over in Juárez." But he'd never taken her back over there. She was just as glad.

Other times he complained about the fleabag hotels he'd put up in or the time he had spent waiting for José or Gary or Fulgencio or some other stranger to turn up, but these were the only clues she had as to where he'd been or how he'd spent his time. She did not want to know—

Once, not long after he'd brought her across the border, she'd been frightened nearly out of her head. When she was alone, she kept the door locked, as Alex had told her to do. And she seldom went out by herself. But this time somebody kept banging till she had to open it. Maybe it was La Señora who'd rented them the room. But no, a policeman stood in front of her in the doorway, demanding to know where Alex was. She could not tell him, nor could she understand what he was saying, though he tried a few words of Spanish, and she tried to use the English words Alex had taught her.

She was afraid the man had come to take her back to Juárez. But she had been wrong. He ended up by writing on a piece of paper, *The feds are wise,* and disappeared. So did Alex for nearly a month—and so she came to understand what the words meant. That was the first change, her worrying that he was gone and would never come back. And what would she do then, when her money was gone? The rent was paid, but there was only a little left for food. Then one day he was back. They moved out of the little room in the barrio into another part of the city. After that, she never asked him any questions. There was money, she did not care how he got it. She had a good place to live, with electricity and running water, and food on the table, and clothes to wear. But that had begun the changes. They had moved many times now, from one apartment to another. This was the best—clean, and the toilet worked, and there was a yard for Lucinda to play in. If she needed something, Pilar asked him for it. At first, she asked timidly, afraid he would be angry. But he would reach into his pocket and pull out a five dollar bill, or even ten and give it to her, as if he didn't care. Sometimes he gave without her asking. But unless it was to buy some present for Lucinda, she had little to ask for.

Now, for the first time, in this place she had a friend, Sarah—Sally, as she liked to be called, and it was good to have a friend. They were all Americans in these apartments, and Pilar was shy about speaking to them—her English was not so good, although she had learned a lot by listening to the television, repeating what it said. But Sally did not seem to mind her having to pause sometimes to reach for a word. She was alone as well, had just gotten a divorce from her husband—"the no good son-of-a-bitch. He screwed me over plenty, let me tell you." She talked a lot about him. She was teaching Pilar some new words.

That morning Pilar got up early and went into the kitchen to see what she might do to make a surprise for Lucinda. It was a game they had. Sometimes she peeled an orange or a banana and made a little figure out of the peelings. Or she arranged slices of fruit in a design on Lucinda's plate. After she had made her surprise, she would go to wake Lucinda. The child would be lying there, breathing so softly, the flush of sleep on her cheeks, her eyes closed with the long fine fringe of her lashes, her lips slightly parted. Asleep, she was like a creature from another world. Pilar found it hard to believe this was her own child. She would wake her, and watch her yawn and stretch as she came into the morning from wherever she had been. For a moment the sleep would stay with her. Then her eyes grew bright, as she remembered. "What is my surprise?" she demanded, and without waiting a moment longer, she ran into the kitchen to see.

"A bird, you made a bird—qué bueno pájarito."

Today when Pilar went to wake her, she put a finger over her lips. Lucinda caught on immediately:

"Papa está aquí?" she said, in a whisper.

"Sí," she said, whispering too. "Muy cansado."

"I will be very quiet," Lucinda said, her eyes lighting up. Whispering was a game too. She would play the Whisper Game. And the Tiptoe Game, and the Moving Very Quietly Game. Pilar watched her elaborate pantomime, and her expression, all very exaggerated. Such a clever little rascal she was—her little parakeet, her mouse, her bee.

"Come into the kitchen, mija," Pilar told her.

"Do you have a surprise for me?" Lucinda wanted to know.

"I have a surprise," she said. "A small surprise. And maybe there will be another," she said. "A special surprise."

"Something to eat?" Lucinda wanted to know.

"No, something else."

"When?"

"Later." Sally had bought it and brought it over to give to Pilar last night when Lucinda was asleep. Sally had brought other things, candy and books with pictures in them that Pilar and Lucinda had sat and looked at together. "I love that little kid," Sally said, and that made Pilar feel very proud of her. She wanted to give Lucinda her surprise right then, but Alex would be waking soon, and it would not be the right moment. It was different now that he was home — she had been alone with the child for so long, she hardly knew how to act now that he was there. They had their special ways. She would save her surprise until the right moment. For now, she had an orange on which she had made a face, with raisins for eyes and a smile cut out of the skin. She'd made a little paper cone hat to put on its head and set it up on a glass. Lucinda didn't want to eat the orange man — she named him Pepe.

As soon as Lucinda finished breakfast, Pilar let her go outside to play. In the center of the apartment complex there were swings and slides for the children. Usually, when they came home from the grocery store, she stayed outside with Lucinda and watched her play in the sandbox or pushed her in one of the swings. But when Alex was there, her whole routine changed. Otherwise she would have gone first to the store with Lucinda. Lucinda loved to shop in the grocery. They went every day when Alex was not home. Lucinda would pick out the vegetables and fruit and put them into a bag. She took boxes of cereals from the shelves, and picked out the kind of soap they would use, sniffing different ones till she found a scent she liked. It always took a very long time for them to do their shopping, most of the morning, in fact. And then the swings and slides. Sometimes now, though, Pilar spent time with Sally.

Just as Pilar finished making the coffee, Alex came into the kitchen, dressed in a faded checked shirt that he liked to wear and a clean pair of blue jeans. He still hadn't shaved, but he was feeling good, she could tell, punching his fist into his hand, as though he had new energy he needed to get rid of.

"Did you sleep well?" she asked him.

"Like a goddam brick," he said. "Boy, was I beat. Christ a-mighty. Today I'm just going to re-lax, have me a few beers and lie around. I don't wanna see no inside of a car."

She gave him a cup of coffee—she'd made a big pot, because he would drink many cups of coffee. She poured one for herself, half coffee, half milk, and sat down with him.

"You know," Alex said, "that Los Angeles is quite a place. Lots going on out there."

She had heard him say so before. And there was a program she watched on TV that had interested her because it was set in Los Angeles. She liked the palm trees and the ocean. Once she had even felt a desire to go. "All the movie stars live there," she said.

"That ain't the half of it," he said. "Everytime I go out there I think, What am I doing in a dinky place like this? Out there they've got some style."

She wasn't quite sure what he meant, but she wondered if this was to be a new change. Did he want to move again? After they had come to this apartment with a place for Lucinda to play and even a friend for her to talk to? She could not imagine going to another place.

"I like it here," she said, trying only to sound pleased with the apartment. But she felt a sudden panic. If Alex were to take her somewhere else, she would have to find her way again—learn new streets, find out where the grocery was. Maybe they would not have a playground. It was such a big city—so many cars.

"Yeah," he said, "it's okay. If you got to have a place to come back to when you need it." He seemed almost to be talking to himself. "But one of these days I'd like to live it up a bit. That's what it's all about."

She said nothing. She did not want to go against him. Now she could think only of Lucinda. In the beginning it did not matter to her where they lived. First the little room with a hot plate and a television and no backyard. Then after moving quite suddenly, half a duplex on a dusty street with weeds and cans in the backyard, and many stray cats in the sheds around—lean and hungry and fierce in the eyes. And they moved from there too, because Alex said too many wise guys were trying to nose into his business. And they had stayed in another set of rooms for a few months, then moved to this place.

At first she was alone in the room all day, watching the television. When Alex came home, she sat on his lap on the sofa, and they watched it together. And he taught her to heat up food on the hot plate and how to say words in English.

Then an extraordinary thing had happened to her. The change had come upon her more powerfully than any change in the weather. She had not thought about it until it had happened. In the beginning she did not even know what it was, her breasts growing, her waist thickening. Then her ripening belly, her shape enlarging like that of women she had seen on the street. It had been an astonishment to her to find herself like one of them, with a baby inside her, feeling its kicking there in the dark when she was lying alone, awake while Alex lay asleep beside her or while he was gone. It was like a secret growing in the dark, a surprise that would come when it was ready. And she wanted to laugh because a surprise was coming to her.

How she had wept and sobbed during the labor. It had frightened her very much when the pains began, and Alex wasn't there. He said he would be home, and finally he came and took her to the hospital. She had never been in a hospital before, had never felt such pains tearing her apart, not even when she was hungry. But afterwards there was the baby. Her child: with golden skin, lighter than hers, but with her own dark lustrous hair. Alex had been the one to name the baby: Lucinda. At first the name sounded a little strange in her ear, as though it were trying to be Spanish. But it was made in America. She liked the sound of it, its music. She made up little pet names to call her—Lita and Lulinda and Lucita. And she carried the baby around everywhere and sang to her and talked to her and watched her while she slept.

She had no thought for anything else while the baby nursed at her breast, filling up with milk till she got drowsy and fell asleep. Or when she fed her with a spoon or held her or shook a rattle until she grabbed it. Alex let her alone with the child. He was gone more and more all the time. And Pilar was glad to be alone with Lucinda. If he was at home, he sometimes looked at Lucinda, as if he were wondering where she had come from, as if she had not been made in America, but in a strange place and not by him. She did not look like him at all. Sometimes he picked her up and swung her around by her arms or held her upside down. And Pilar was filled with terror that he would hurt her. But Lucinda usually squealed with delight. Sometimes now she ate with them. But usually it was late when they had their meal, too late for her, with her active body and her young appetite, to wait for them. Pilar would feed Lucinda in the kitchen and put her in her playpen. Now Lucinda could go out to play with her friends. Lucinda was five.

After he had had his breakfast, Alex sat on the couch and watched the game shows on television, and flipped through a magazine that was lying around. Around noon, he got up, said, "I'm going get me some beer and talk to some guys and come home and watch the ballgame."

After she had done the dishes she found Lucinda and they went to the grocery store. The car was still gone when they came back, so they went over for a little while to visit Sally.

"See your man's home," Sally said.

"He came in the middle of the night."

"Well, I'm glad to get rid of mine—lying and cheating like the bastard he was. I tell you, I don't know what it is with men—only know I got to get me a new one. Somebody who'll take care of me and treat me right."

"I hope you find somebody," Pilar told her. "It is hard to be alone."

"You're lucky, you know. You got one that's not underfoot overmuch, that's the main thing—and you got that sweet little kid. That Lucinda," she said. "You want a cookie, honey?"

Pilar smiled, proud of her child.

"Guess she'll be starting school one of these days," Sally said.

"She is too young," Pilar said. She did not want to think about it. Lucinda going away from her. School seemed as far away as Los Angeles. Lucinda would go to school and learn how to read, and soon she would know more than her mother. Pilar had gone as far as the second grade, but she had forgotten most of what she had learned. She could read Spanish words, some of them. Lucinda already knew more English than she did, for the children she played with did not know Spanish.

"I better go now," she said, seeing Alex drive up.

Sally came out of her apartment with her and when Alex got out of the car, Pilar said, "This is Sally."

"Glad to meetcha," Alex said and gave her his hand, a big hand. "Just got back from L.A."

"You have a good time?" Sally said.

"You bet," he said. "Just got me some beer there in the car," he said. "Why doncha come on over later on and have one?"

"Sure," she said, looking at Pilar. "Sure thing."

When she and Alex went back to the apartment, Pilar told him how Sally had moved in while he was gone and how kind she was to Lucinda. It was the first time she had talked to him about someone he did not know. This time he did not seem to mind. Once a boy on the street had come up to her and asked her if she lived in the neighborhood. When she came home, Alex told her not to speak to strangers.

Sally came over with a bowl of popcorn she had made and Pilar set out some tortillas and chile sauce to eat while they drank the beer. For a while they all watched the ball game, then afterwards a comedy. Pilar didn't understand some of the jokes, but it didn't matter. Afterwards Sally and Alex started talking about L.A. Sally had lived there for a year way back when, and together they talked about the places they knew, the best bars to hang out in, and how bad the smog was.

"Used to work in a music store out there on the Sunset Strip," Sally said. "Nice place. That's where I met my ex, damn his hide. He was trying to be a country singer, and he used to buy all the albums. Me, I was just trying to get by."

"Ain't we all?" Alex said. "Time you get done working to get from one day to the other, you're about all wore out."

"You can say that again," Sally said.

Alex liked Sally, Pilar could tell. Sally laughed a lot, and it was nice when she laughed. She was not young, and her face had gone hard in a way, especially when she talked about what her man had done. But now she was enjoying herself. And pretty soon, she and Alex were joking with each other as if they'd known each other a while, and Alex was telling her things he'd done in L.A. How he had a friend who had a Harley-Davidson, which was the only kind of motorcycle to have—none of your crummy Jap machines—and he used to go out and really ride the thing, even on the freeways. He was fixing to buy one. "How'd you like to go out for a little spin?" he said to Pilar, pulling a bit of her hair. "Bet that would give you a thrill." Then they drank some more beer and laughed some more. Pilar laughed with them, for the air was light around them. He and Sally could speak very well to one another, Pilar thought. She admired how they spoke English. Lucinda was lying on the floor watching television, not paying any attention to them.

"By the way," Sally said, "How did Lucinda like the coloring book?"

Flustered, Pilar said, "Oh, I forgot. I haven't given it to her yet."

"Oh, well," Sally said, "It don't make no nevermind." And she took another drink of her beer.

"It was a nice surprise," Pilar said. She did not know how to explain.

"Well, give it to her now," Alex said. "No law against it, you know."

She went to get it. "Here," she said, giving it to Lucinda. "It is a surprise from Sally."

Lucinda looked at the box of colored crayons and the book.

"You can color any of the pictures, honey," Sally said.

Gravely, Lucinda opened the box and looked at the colors, then at Pilar. "Me gusta mucho," she said, excitedly, and for a long time she sat looking at the pictures in the coloring book and putting the crayons in different order in the box, taking them out again and laying them on the floor, putting them back. She asked Sally to tell her how to put them back the way they had come, then she closed the box. Pilar could tell she was sleepy and led her off to the bed, putting the crayons and the coloring book on the shelf till morning.

Pilar felt happy. She didn't listen any more to what Alex was saying, she just ate popcorn and drank beer till Sally said she had to get to bed early—next morning she had to go out to look for a job.

"Hey, listen," Alex said, "the night's young. No need to rush off. Hey, why don't we go out on the town and do it up brown. Take in some of those night clubs over the line."

Sally hesitated. "Well, I really . . . ," she said.

"Come on," Alex insisted. "The three of us. Have some fun."

"But Lucinda," Pilar said.

"She's asleep," Alex said. "We'll lock the door. She'll be okay. Nothing's gonna get her."

But Pilar did not want to leave her. Things could happen. But even if they didn't. . . . She might wake up and if no one was there, she'd be frightened.

"You go," she said. "I will stay here and you go—you and Sally."

"Hey, I don't like to do that," Sally said.

"It's okay," Pilar insisted. "You go and the next time I'll go."

"Suits me," Alex said.

That night Pilar slept badly. In her dreams she was traveling somewhere, but she did not know where she was going. She was alone. And when she woke up, she wasn't sure at first where she was. She found Alex asleep heavily on the couch, still in his clothes, his arm flopping over the edge to the floor.

Lucinda was still asleep. She opened the door softly and went outside. A bank of clouds extended over part of the city, but beyond it the sky was a rich blue, so filled with light that everything stood out in it with a sharpness that made it seem caught there forever in utmost clarity. The dark blue mountain closest and the pink mountain farther away, so clear, so bright it was like looking at a picture. For a long time she did not move.

She thought of the colors of Lucinda's crayons and she remembered her time at school. The teacher had given her a piece of paper and a little box of crayons, but she could not think of anything to draw. She had made a yellow mark on the paper, then a red one. She had made a little box out of the red, and a little circle out of the yellow. But some of the children had made flowers and cats and people. That was long ago, long before her mother had sent her out of the house, when the neighbor had told her mother Pilar was no longer a virgin. For a time she had slept under bridges and in abandoned cars, begging for coins from the tourists and rummaging through the refuse barrels behind the restaurants. Till some other girls told her about the hotel, where she could come and they would give her food and a place to stay, and even pay her money. And there Alex had found her. She was fourteen then.

When she went back inside, Alex was already up and dressed. He didn't want any breakfast—he was going out for awhile, didn't know when he'd be back. She wondered if he had asked Sally to go with him. Once she had seen him put his arm around a woman that he was talking to in the street, and they had gone off together. Perhaps he would go off with Sally—even as far as Los Angeles. She did not know if that was the change he had brought this time.

She went into the kitchen to make breakfast for Lucinda. Soon she would wake her. This morning she had fresh cherries to give her, and after she ate, she would give her the coloring book with the pictures already drawn. And together they would open the box of crayons and make blue dogs and red horses and green houses, with a blue sky and a yellow sun shining over all.

TOM McNEAL

GOODNIGHT, NEBRASKA

Before the day began to dawn—a full hour in fact before his alarm was set to go off—short, round-faced Meteor Frmka woke up happy. He sat up and in the darkness wiggled his toes. All but the big ones were wrapped in Band-Aids. Under the Band-Aids were tattoos, a message to Merna Littlefield. This as well as other things made him happy. Things were going good for Frmka. He'd just got his own car. Merna was kissing him with her mouth open. And he was beginning to make notable friends.

Just last Sunday, for instance, Frank Loomis and Leo Underwood, men Frmka hardly knew, came by to look at his car and, before Frmka knew it, they were all three on their way to Scenic, South Dakota. Frmka drove, Leo rode up front with a cooler at his feet, chatting happily, and Loomis sat in back never speaking at all except when he was out of beer. Then he would say, "Loomis needs another unit," which, with each repetition, seemed funnier and funnier to Frmka, and made his spirits soar.

In Scenic, they visited the whorehouse and tattoo parlor both. Frmka didn't tell Merna that. "We just made ourselves seen," he said to her, swelling up, trying to sound like Leo. It was Leo who on the way back from Scenic had turned from staring out at the flat and treeless plain and said, "I meant to tell you, Frmka, four or five of us are shooting birds next Sunday. Me and Loomis. Eddie Evans, Yul, maybe Whistler. The whole bunch. So what-taya say, buddy, care to join us?"

Buddy.

Frmka felt as if he'd just received some kind of honor. His face glowed. His smile shot ear to ear. He glanced back at Loomis, who was gently and privately picking his nose. Leo, however, kept smiling chummily. "Okay," Meteor Frmka had said. "You betcha."

It was still dark this morning as Frmka drove slowly down Goodnight's one oiled road toward his father's IGA. He parked in the back, unlocked the delivery door, found the flashlight in its place atop the fuse box. He went to the liquor aisle, unfolded the list Leo had given him, trained the beam of light upon it, and began filling the order. Supplying their liquor wholesale was part of the deal.

Frmka's contentment, as he poked his car down 2nd Street, was almost complete. The order was boxed and safe on the back seat. The darkness was just beginning to peel away. Full unbroken leaves lay in the street. It reminded Frmka of that moment as a kid when, just before breaking the seal on a new toy, hopes and outcome finally came together.

Frmka turned east onto Highway 20, made note of a certain blue VW bug at Yul's place, and of the prices at Goodnight Gas-for-Less, and then, at the county road where he was supposed to turn north, Frmka began to hum a melody of his own making and turned blithely south.

They stood around, the five men and the boy, waiting for Frmka. Of them, Loomis was the most impatient. Finally, he said, "So where's your little delivery boy, Leo?"

Leo, scanning the horizon, didn't answer.

"He still going out with Merna Littlefield?" Eddie Evans asked, and when no one replied, he said, "She's got no tits whatsoever."

The hunters had collected just after dawn at a widening in the road beyond Horse Creek, near enough to the Petersen place that the breeze carried the tinkling sounds of his pigs rooting creepfeeders. The idea was to shoot Petersen's cornfields, which had a reputation for pheasant. But nobody liked the idea of a liquorless day, and Frmka had the liquor, so they settled into waiting. They sprawled on warm motor hoods or leaned against trees, rubbing their hands and quietly smoking cigarettes and drinking coffee with a little whiskey that Leo found behind the seat of his cab, though it was almost gone now.

Loomis, when he saw that, led away his two black Labs and squatted alone. Loomis had long concave cheeks that made him look wolfish. His eyes slid side to side and when he raised his hand suddenly to flick at something in the air, his dogs, habitually expecting the worst, shied and hunkered down.

There was another dog, too, off to the side, a part-poodle who scooched its hind end urgently through the dirt while its owner, a man called Whistler, watched indifferently. Nearby, a kid with a candy bar watched with concentrated disgust. "Dog's name is Rat," Whistler said when he noticed the kid staring. "He hasn't got good manners, but he can work up birds like nobody's business."

The kid said, "I guess I just don't like red-assed poodle dogs, is all."

Leo, standing nearby, laughed so hard Whistler could smell what he had for breakfast or at least the ham part of it. Whistler took a step away and regarded the kid. He'd never seen him before and already he didn't like him. "Do I know you?" he said.

"Couldn't say," the kid said. He looked twelve, but his voice sounded older. He broke off another inch of Baby Ruth.

"My sister's kid," Leo explained. "Only nobody knows where my sister's gone to."

Whistler, who always went to the standards when he was feeling unsatisfied, began whistling "Stardust."

Minutes passed. Finally, Loomis in a low voice said, "That'll be your errand boy, Leo," and nodded toward a cloud of dust moving *away* from them on a county road to the east. Loomis said, "Five minutes. Then we go. Liquor or no."

Leo, to change the topic, nodded across at Eddie Evans, who was wearing a flourescent pink vest, staring off through heavy black-rimmed glasses, lost in his thoughts. "Nice vest, Eddie," Leo said. "Would you call it hot pink?"

Eddie Evans, brought to, blushed and pushed up his glasses.

"Julie dress you up in that?" Leo said. He was referring to Julie Lewis, the girl Eddie meant to marry. Julie's tight clothes had pulled Eddie close, at which point her eyes took over. They were the color of coffee beans and had a smoldering quality. Eddie found himself looking into them whether she was there or not.

"So she bought me a vest," Eddie said. "Something wrong with your girlfriend wanting you not shot at by dipshits with guns?"

Fifty feet opposite, the man everyone knew as Yul spat into the dirt, rubbed it in with his boot, and didn't look up.

"One minute left," Loomis said. He began getting his gear together. Others were doing the same when Meteor Frmka's dust began to bear their way.

"Finally reckoned west," Leo said.

Frmka, upon arrival, jumped out of his car apologizing.

"No need," Leo said soothingly. He eyed the boxes in the back seat of the car. "Get everything?"

Frmka grinned and nodded. "You bet. In pints. As ordered." He got out the register tape. "Came to thirty-two dollars and—"

"Buddy, buddy, buddy," Leo said, loosely draping an arm around Frmka's sloping shoulders. "The way we—"

"Everything strictly at wholesale," Frmka said, still beaming.

"Which is dandy," Leo said, "but the way we work it is the two with the fewest birds divvy the bill." Frmka glanced around. Already the others were pulling the pints from his car, sliding them into their pockets, and Leo was saying, "So you can see why we have to wait for the end of the day to settle accounts."

The others were setting out down the road. Frmka began walking with Leo to the rear. They'd gone a little distance before Leo, deadpan, said, "You bringing something to shoot with? A firearm, maybe, or a Kodak?"

Frmka stopped. Leo kept walking. Over his shoulder he said, "I'll be up with the others."

By the time Frmka had gotten his gun and gear, the rest of the party had disappeared from view. He broke into a dogtrot and, when finally he caught up with the others, his face was pink and his skin was wet and a misgiving he couldn't name was throbbing in his ears.

Within the first of Petersen's cornfields, the party fanned out along the fence line and, intending to make pheasants take wing, began crashing guns-up through the cornstalks, whooping and whistling. The Labs heeled alongside Loomis, waiting to retrieve while, out front, Whistler's part-poodle scooted about trying to rout the birds, without result.

When they reached the opposite end of the quarter-section, Leo said, "I am god-damned. 'Lousy with birds,' they told me. This very field." He looked around at big grins.

"I am unamazed," Eddie Evans said.

"Here's to the Hoochinoo!—only hostiles I'd care to know," Yul said, and began to gargle a mouthful of bourbon.

Leo did his Sam the Sham routine. "Uno dos, uno dos tres fartro!" he cried, and let fly.

Frmka was smiling, not so much because he felt like smiling, but because he didn't want anyone to see how lost he was feeling. The party again began to move. Loomis shouldered the loop from the gatepost and let the wired gate fall. The last one through reset it. Again they fanned out, set up a racket, headed west.

"When they said you was high-classed," somebody sang out, "well that was just a lie!"

Eddie drew within range of Yul and yelled, "Int this about the best thing you can do with pants on?"

Yul looked at Eddie and thought of thumbing Eddie's girlfriend's nipples into soft bullets. He wondered how long seeing Eddie's black glasses would make him think like that. Yul lifted his Red Sox cap, ran his hand over his smooth scalp, slapped the cap back on. He'd had his head shaved the first time when he was twelve, for lice, though he never admitted that. He said he liked it that way, and in time he did. He shaved it Wednesdays and Saturdays. It got him attention, and a nickname, and certain girls liked it.

"Dancing's fun too though," Eddie was yelling. "Julie claims she could square dance with me till kingdom comes!"

Yul decided this would be a good time to deal with his boot. He sat down and was left alone. The din, which was beginning to bother him, moved on, and he was left with a steady little wind shuffling the dry corn. He smelled his hand. Her smell was still on his fingers. It wasn't his fault, though. He'd been asleep, in fact. A horn had honked. It was after midnight, he'd turned on the yardlight, and there was Julie Lewis's VW. She wasn't in it, but a pair of pale green underpants hung from the antenna. "I'm thisaway," she'd said over at the edge of the darkness. She was coming toward him wearing a pair of black-rimmed glasses he recognized as Eddie's. Julie Lewis was a happy drunk. "Tonight your buddy Eddie asked me to join him in matrimony," she'd pronounced. "I told him I might, and I might, too, but first I gotta take care of a couple things—" she'd grinned big—"and you're one of 'em." She'd been square dancing at the Elks, Yul figured, because she was wearing a bright-trimmed turquoise dress, which, within a foot of Yul's door, she'd stepped out of. So all she was wearing was Eddie's black-rimmed glasses. "Well, how do you like 'em?" she'd said and Yul, staring, barely had the sense to say they were the nicest glasses he ever saw.

Yul unhooked the laces and pulled off his boots. It was a nail working through, and the heel of his sock was red with blood. Somebody probably had moleskin if he wanted it, but he didn't. He let a long gulp of bourbon settle over his thoughts, then put the boot back on and began again to tramp ahead. It needled him every step of the way. He figured that was fair.

For October, it was warm, and most of the party had pulled off their shirts. When the kid slipped out of his, it left only Frmka who hadn't. Leo, tired of Frmka hanging close to him, asked why.

"Happy as is," Frmka said. The truth was his back was hairy.

Leo nodded and grinned, something mean sliding into it. He winked at Frmka. "How 'bout you spreading out a little?"

Frmka, stung, while moving off began to think of Merna in the Littlefield kitchen putting up apples with her mother. She said she was going to do that today. The windows would be open, the breeze would be moving the yellow curtains, she would be wearing a dress. He wished he were there. Sitting at the table and eating gingersnaps, telling corny jokes and watching Merna's legs.

When the party came upon fallowed ground, they bunched up and took stock. "Think the birds're winning," Leo said.

Most of them nodded. Most of them were uncapping pints. The kid worked on an Abba Zabba. Eddie Evans climbed atop a cottonwood stump and looked around. Leo stared across at Yul and said, "Yul, my man, you're sulking. What've you got to sulk over?"

Yul didn't look at Leo. He just slipped an unlighted cigar into his mouth and said, "The standard shortcomings."

When Whistler started up on "Heartbreak Hotel," Eddie Evans, from his stump, pantomimed a guitar, gave it a deluxe pelvic thrust and crooned along.

> *If your baby leaves you* (thrust)
> *And you have a tale to tell* (thrust)

Leo chunked a dirt clod at him which, when Eddie Evans ducked, flew by and landed six or seven rows deep in the cornfield, and there, with a sudden shuffling of wings, four pheasant screeched and rose and swooped low over the cornstalks, three hens, which were protected, and a brilliantly feathered cock, which was not. The birds had settled again in cover before a gun was shouldered.

"Brer Pheasant safe with this company."

"Pretty though," Whistler said. "Wudnee pretty?"

Loomis slipped his pint into his vest, wiped his mouth with his hand and his hand on his pants. "Prettier on a platter," he said. He turned to Leo. "What about the Macy place?"

"Asked. Answer was no-can-do."

Loomis grimaced derisively and Leo, seeing this, turned back to the others, passed a grinning look all around and said, "Though I guess we could just sort of sally off in that direction."

West. They'd followed the county road past pastureland and then winter wheat, a brilliant green, when they began to hear faint music ahead of them. They followed the sound of it until eventually it brought them first within sight of a shiny, undersized pickup truck and then into the smell of burning marijuana. The pickup was parked where the dirt road crested. The music was loud.

"Jimmy Biddle," Leo said.

The party drew closer.

"And his faithful injun companion."

Albert Sharp Fish was slouched to one side of the cab surveying things the sleepy way the Oglala do.

When Leo and the others approached the truck, Biddle tuned down the music and smiled serenely. Sharp Fish smiled, too. So did Leo, but less naturally. He noticed Biddle was holding a joint in the low space between his knees. "So what're you two assholes doing way out here?" he said, trying for cheeriness.

"I don't know. Just sitting here planning . . ." Biddle's voice trailed off and his face went blank. He looked at Sharp Fish. "What is it we're planning again?"

"Our next trip to France," Sharp Fish said straight-faced and Biddle exploded into solitary laughter. Sharp Fish grinned and took the joint from Biddle's hand, drew from it, and passed it back. Biddle, composing himself, presented it to Leo.

Leo looked at it. There it was, limp and brownish and slobbery with their different salivas. "I don't think so," he said.

From off to the side, Loomis looked at Biddle's twinkly little truck, and then at Biddle and Sharp Fish themselves sitting there with their skinny little necks and their smug little grins. He spat. He grunted to his dogs. He'd seen enough. He was leaving.

They all were.

As they were going, Sharp Fish said, "Vaya con Dios," and when Biddle again burst into a laughter all his own, Loomis stopped. The others did, too. But Whistler in a coaxing voice said, "Shit, Loomis, we got better things to do. Let's leave'm be."

Loomis shot a scowl toward the heavens and walked ahead, his anger not so much diffused as divided, half directed toward the wimps in the truck and half toward his wimpish friend Whistler.

For a while, the party was silent, just drinking and walking, but Leo finally broke into it. "God-*damn!*" he said, and raked his hand up his crotch. "Worse comes to worse, we come back and shoot the legs off Biddle's candyassed mini-truck!"

All of them nodded or laughed or in some other way agreed, and they began to walk faster, as if somehow their muscles suddenly had more jump to them, and short-legged Meteor Frmka, to keep up, broke into an occasional trot.

Macy signs, painted in white on blackwall tires, seemed to hang from every fence rail:

NO HUNTING
L. O. MACY

Yul let his unlighted cigar poke jauntily from the side of his mouth as he streamed urine at one of Macy's signs, then walked about shaking it dry to what the rest of the party viewed as unmatched comic effect. Most of them were as tight as he was.

Loomis stood apart, sullenly regarding this merriment until finally he had to cut it off. "We need blockers," he said. "Least one."

He looked at Frmka, and the rest looked at Frmka, and Frmka looked back at them. When they weren't laughing, their faces were bland from drink. Frmka said, "Okay. Sure. Might be fun."

Leo said, "You know what to do, don't you?—just wander down the other end and set up a commotion so they won't go that way."

"Blow your nose or something," Eddie Evans said. Eddie wasn't a mean man, but he kept a little meanness handy, like a pocketknife.

Frmka alone blocked two quartersections, then Frmka and the kid blocked another, and after that nobody mentioned it again. They got off just one shot, Loomis's, upon reaching the shelter belt at the west end of the second field. Yul had been muttering to Loomis about the generally fucked-up state of this hunt when, directly behind Frmka, Whistler's part-poodle barked once and a single cock pheasant suddenly screeched and got up. Frmka froze. Loomis snapped his gun to, swung it past Frmka's head, and fired.

The bird swooped safely away.

"Missed," somebody said after a moment, and somebody else said, "Which one?"

Nobody could keep from laughing, either out of relief or because of some arousing scent that hung in the air with the smoke from the gun. Even Frmka, who didn't hear the joke for the ringing in his ear, made himself laugh and, when the party began again to move, he made his feet move, too.

The line kept travelling west, Loomis and his labs in the lead. After a time, Whistler drifted back to Frmka. "Ear okay?"

"I can hear fine, yeah," he said. He kept his eyes ahead.

From up front, Leo called back, "Anybody seen my sister's kid?"

Nobody had.

"Probably with Rat," Whistler said. "He's also vamoosed." In a lower voice he added, "Though it's not exactly like him."

Leo, for his part, wasn't worried about the kid. "Hey, Whistler," he yelled back, changing the subject altogether, "while you're conversing with the Meteor, ask him how his toes talk!" He grinned at Frmka, whose round face had suddenly pinkened, but Leo left it alone, as if it were something he liked having there to come back to.

"Talking toes?" Whistler said, still friendly.

Frmka felt burned down. "Ask Leo. Leo brought it up."

Ask Leo? What kind of answer was Ask Leo? Whistler picked up his pace a little, not much, but enough so Frmka caught on, and lagged behind. He looked back south at the squiggles of smoke from leaves burning in Goodnight, and soothed himself by imagining one of them rising from a leafpile in front of the Littlefield place.

The hunters walked and drank and wiped sweat and fell silent under the afternoon sun. Loomis in a snarl asked Whistler if he knew anything but death dirges and Whistler, without missing a beat, slid from "Baltimore Oriole" into a mocking version of "Zip-A-Dee-Doo-Dah"; Leo Underwood urinated as he walked, indifferent to spattering his boots; and Yul, who wasn't used to mixing pain, bourbon, and tobacco, bent over his knees and vomited copiously. They stopped securing gates after themselves, and they leaned a little forward as they trudged ahead, but so gradual was the incline they were mounting that none of them took any real note of it. Corn gave way to stubblefield, stubblefield to pasture. Pasture rose to woodlands.

Faraway, a dim yipping, and a squeal.

Whistler stopped and cocked his head. They all stopped. The squealing came again, this time trailed by a small shout—was that what it was? It sounded miles off. "Rat and the kid," Whistler said, almost to himself, but everyone heard. Without realizing it, they'd bunched together as they'd entered the timbered hills, where the land made a difference, where it rolled and gave way under the feet, rose and fell, and seemed, to Meteor Frmka, as he stood listening with the others, to breathe in and breathe out.

They spotted the kid eating a candy bar atop a gaunt boulder along the creekbottom. When he saw the line of men dipping toward him, the kid jumped down, waded knee-deep into a beaver pond, and pulled something out of the water. He held it up dripping and threw it into the mud on the bank. "Your rat-dog found himself a coon!" he yelled up to the party.

Whistler began to run. He knelt close to the animal on the bank but didn't touch it. The rest of the party gathered up behind. It was his dog Rat. On the back of his head was a bloody gash shaped like a smile. "Coon drownded him right here," the kid said.

"Smart coon'll do that," Leo said.

Eddie Evans studied the dog, then the kid. "You watched?"

The kid gave him a level look. "From a distance."

"Coon went off that way," Loomis said, pointing at tracks.

"And the dog was dead when you got here?" Eddie said.

The kid didn't flinch. "Whattaya think? I come down here, found him half-dead, and finished the trick?" Then, "And not that I did, but what if I had? It was a dog, not somebody's mother."

With one hand Whistler lifted the dog's head from the mud, and with the other he covered from view the bloody gash.

People were milling. "God-damn," Frmka said. From him the words sounded funny. "Maybe we oughtta call this one a day." It was a good idea, more than one of them thought so, but its coming from Frmka made it impossible to admit.

Whistler gently lowered his dog's head back to the mud and stared at him. "I knew he was funny-looking," he said in a low voice, "but I would've sworn he was smarter than this."

"Shoot the coon dead when we find him," Yul said.

Loomis whistled up his dogs, who had been sniffing at the muddy carcass, then began walking. The others followed. Whistler, in the rear, looked back just once.

To the north, clouds began to pack. The air seemed to thicken. The party weaved through the pines up toward the ridge, not talking, just looking for something moving to shoot at. By the time they reached the ridge, they'd put on their shirts and zippered their vests. They threw long shadows and began to grouse about whatever came to mind. When Loomis stopped to get his bearings, Yul said, "Where in holy shit are we?" and looked around at faces full of *Who cares?* "How come nothing lives here? How come there aren't any sounds? Or crows?" He thought about it. "Anybody even seen a single fucking *crow?*"

Silence.

"Well," Yul said, "I got a bootnail gnawing on my brain and I'd like at the fucking least to fucking shoot a fucking crow."

Leo, who'd been chucking rocks at an empty pint he'd set on a log, said, "Fucking Yulie's fucking cranky."

Eddie Evans stood studying Yul. He knew he wouldn't look back at him. Yul hadn't looked back at him all day, and Eddie was beginning to feel a little funny about it. He began to sort through all the things he could think of that would keep Yul from looking him in the eye and when he got to Julie his stomach fisted.

And Yul, vaguely aware of Eddie's eyes boring into him, turned the other way and muttered, "What kinda place is it that even fucking crows don't go?"

A chill passed through Frmka. Of the others in the party, only he grasped that Eddie Evans and Yul were beginning to understand what was between them. Partly he knew this from seeing the blue VW parked before dawn at Yul's place, but partly his knowledge came from a lifetime spent keenly tuned to other people's rising resentments. And he knew that though Eddie wanted to hate Yul, he was going to have a hard time of it because Yul was already hating himself.

Yul was going on about crows. No one else was saying anything. Then, after a while, Whistler did. "*Is* something queer about this place." He tilted his head. "You can feel it. It's like something's missing."

Leo, looking for another rock, said, "Think it's women."

Nobody laughed. Nobody was laughing at anything.

It was while this silence deepened that Meteor Frmka made his mistake. He opened his mouth and reminded them of himself. He let them know he knew something they didn't. "Old guy named American Horse told me Crazy Horse was buried up here someplace," he said. "On a ridge east of Beaver Creek that nothing grows on. Did his vision quest here. Where you fast till it comes."

Frmka felt everybody turning toward him with stilled faces. It was like how when he was little his whole family stopped chewing their breakfast and turned toward the radio set the morning Arthur Godfrey fired Julius La Rosa on the air. Quickly Frmka said, "Maybe it wasn't here. I don't know why I thought it was here."

The others just stared at him. Leo Underwood felt something pleasantly evil coming out inside himself. He worked a finger in his ear and grinned. "Meteor, buddy, I believe it's time you show us them toes."

Frmka looked stricken.

It was Yul who armlocked Frmka from behind and slammed him to the ground, where his head in the pine needles made a small crater. Yul kept him pinned there while Leo tore off Frmka's boots and socks, and lifted Frmka's tiny feet for viewing. The toes were the attraction, all wrapped with bandages. Leo ripped each off slowly.

L E T S

was tattooed on the knuckles of the right toes, and tattooed on the left was

U S D O

"Whatzit say?"

"Let's us do!" whooped Leo. He let Frmka's feet drop. "It's how Frmka plans to propose to Merna Littlefield. He's going to whip off his boots and show her them toes!"

Most of the others made a point of a big laugh. Frmka sat on the ground pulling on his boots, his face gathering around his mouth. He wasn't going to cry, but he wanted to. In a low little voice he said, "Tattoo was your idea, Leo."

Leo spread a wink all around. "This is what happens," he said. "Loomis and me are outta gas money so we in our wisdom let the meteoroid drive us to Scenic. He gets fall-down drunk. We visit the cathouse. He feels remorse, wanted to save it for Merna. So when he sees the tattoo parlor, he barges right in. I ask what he has in mind. 'Message to Merna in a private location,' he says. I think he's talking pecker so I say, 'Better make it short.' "

More loud, bitter laughter.

When it quieted, Eddie Evans in a baiting voice said, "So, whad she say when you peeled off your socks and popped the question?"

Frmka stared down. "Haven't yet." When he looked up again, the kid was staring at him and sucking on a Sugar Daddy at the same time. Frmka took himself a distance away and stared off.

"Let's us do!" Leo chortled.

When he saw nobody else would, Whistler said, "Leo, you're an asshole for about twelve different reasons."

Leo turned and, in a tight voice that was impressive for all the meanness he was able to squeeze inside it, said, "Maybe you'd like to try to drill me a new one."

"Screw you, Leo," Whistler said, lamely.

Yul, jumping in, said in falsetto, *"Screw you, Leo,"* and sorry Whistler would do nothing about it, shot a menacing sidewise look at Frmka, who was still staring off, but fixedly now, and Yul realized the episode with Frmka didn't feel complete. "See a dime down there?" he said.

Frmka started. "What?" he said.

"What?" Leo croaked and, folding his hands into his armpits, began to flap his elbows and croak raucously. *"What! What! What!"* Then, while staring at Frmka, he said to Yul, "Now there's your crow you was looking for."

Leo cast a look at Yul, who was grinning unpleasantly, and then at Loomis, who was studying Frmka, and trying to follow his gaze to the valley below. Finally, when Frmka moved again, Loomis walked over to him. "Whaddaya see?" he said.

All his life Frmka would wonder why he did what he did next. He'd always had the idea that when the time came, when honor was required, he would act decently, maybe even nobly, but when the time came, he couldn't. He led Loomis to a place where the view was unobscured. From there he pointed down to a small clearing. Others clustered to look and then all of them were looking.

It was a couple, on a blanket in a square of pale sunlight.

"Maybe they're doing the work of increase," Whistler said, but nobody else spoke. The party stared as one, slow-focussing eyes in wide slack faces. The man was stretched out on his back and the woman was turned into him, one leg swung over the man's, her head nestled into the crook of his arm. She wore long pants and a denim jacket and maybe was asleep. But something wasn't right. Finally, Loomis, tweezing violently at his cheek, said, "What am I seeing or am I seeing things?" When he untweezed his fingers, a small, perfectly proportioned half-globe of dark blood formed on the skin.

Leo went to one knee, fumbled his field glasses out of their case, looked into them for a few moments, and shrank back. He started to stand, and threw his arms out to steady himself, but sat heavily back down anyway.

"Feeling punk?" the kid said, in that voice.

"Lord God," Leo said, and held the glasses out to Loomis. "Sharp Fish," he said, "and Jimmy Biddle. Biddle's doing the snuggling."

Everyone looked through the glasses except the kid. Faces changed. Cheeks lost color. Jaws slackened then went tight. They all backed up, below the ridgeline, out of view from below.

Loomis in a stiff whisper said to the kid, "Scoot now," and pointed off. "We'll meet you back at that stand of trees, so git."

The kid merely withdrew steps enough to recede from their notice. Frmka withdrew too, but went further. He kept walking south, away from the shooting party, toward town, the Littlefield place, shelter from his thoughts.

The hunters collected without a word, squatted in an arc, and Loomis began glancing around, making his eyes felt. He liked what he saw.

Whistler started to say something, but Loomis said, "Another time, buddy," and rose to a stoop. They all did, a single file of stooping men, Loomis in the lead. The kid hung back but kept coming. Walls of air pressed in from all sides. They moved along the opposite side of the ridgeline, then down a steep-sided coulee, toward the couple in the clearing, without specific purpose, just moving ahead unawares, dreams walking like men. From behind, there came floating among them a whistling of "Blue Moon" that was soft and slow and seemed already to issue from deep regret.

If, in the twilight of an October Sunday, in a high meadow north of Goodnight and east of Beaver Creek, emotions swelled and good sense fell away and lives jumped course . . . well other less unlikely things happened that day, too, before night fell. During the Lutheran social hour, for example, Elanore Tyler unveiled her just-completed ceramic reproductions of the forty U.S. presidents, and made no bones whatsoever about her belief that Ike was the best of the lot; Robert Jackson shot dead a large badger he said had been molesting his chickens in broad daylight; Harmon Smith made that very morning's *World-Herald* with a photograph of a double radish shaped like a heart; and Meteor Frmka, without taking off his shoes or socks, sat in the darkening kitchen of Al and Esther Littlefield and proposed marriage to their daughter Merna, who, while giving way to tears, whispered, "Yes, yes, a thousand times yes."

CHARLES FRAZIER

LICIT PURSUITS

The language of the law is strict. And it is the law for which I travel. I sleep on my saddle beside the trail. My horse steams in the rain. My black wool coat finds another hole in the woods. On good days I travel to the sounds of light torn apart by foliage. Great grey birds with breasts big as hams sit staring at me from the limbs of black balsam. The clatter of the horse's hooves on flat stones in the trail is the chant of the law that keeps me moving.

In the slack time after harvest, when the ruby apples are all locked away in dark storehouses, the outlaw is everywhere. He comes down into town from the mountains. He speaks in the tongue of knives. He enters the merchants' stores and gazes over their stocks with muzzle eyes. To our women he extends his lust, his hands groping in the watering troughs for something solid to grasp. At the end of the week he kills or steals or rapes and retreats along muddy trails into the high mountains where he pulls the altitude about him like a cloak and disappears into a dream of blue mists and black stones. And I must gather my weapons and follow him on the usual autumn journey.

There are days when my senses fail me, when my perceptions seem to have been bumped hard overnight and won't function all day. Voices shift and blur and words have no more meaning to me than the sounds of stones clicking against one another on the bed of a fast-moving creek. I cannot leave the office because the eyes of the electors in the street look large and pale as duck eggs set pupilless in their heads. Every robin passing overhead seems a circling buzzard sending me searching for the carrion and the carrion-maker. Those are bad days for a lawman, dangerous days when I wonder if I am fit for my job. But the true lawman knows that to lose self-control is the greatest of his temptations. So I clamp down. I tighten. There can be no middle ground. No temperance. When I walk the streets of town I imagine that I look as much like the citizens around me as a lone hatchet in a boxful of hammers.

Last year the outlaw was large and dark, as dense-looking as a sledge. He bludgeoned a man to death in broad daylight on Main Street. I caught him in the hills two weeks later after a hard pursuit and brought him back to hang. When my horse bolted from under him, he fell like a dropped hammer, pulling the tree limb down until his toes just rested on the ground. The shock of the fall had sucked consciousness from him, but his dark face turned only a little red. He was far from executed. I had to force two of the spectators to hoist him while I climbed the tree to shorten the rope. This year, though, the outlaw was young and pale, a handsome kid with a wispy, glowing blond beard. He rode into town on a little over-fed bay mare and wandered about for days drinking peach brandy and eating cherries. His eyes were the blue of high mists, and no matter what he was doing, he seemed always to be looking in a kind of intricate affinity north to the mountains. The odor of his clothes was the dark smell of leaf mould, and by the third day it had permeated the town. He sang a little song over and over like an incantation. The tune was dissonant. It would have made no sense to play it on any instrument but the bagpipes. It gave me pain deep in the bones of my fingers. The words were, "That possum meat am good and sweet,/Carve him to the heart."

The victim wore an ordinary suit of black clothing. He had come into town to have a hat made. The outlaw chose him in some obscure pattern of predation that transcends randomness to carry the force of fate. After the victim couldn't get the back door of the hat shop closed and locked between him and the outlaw he simply ran like perfect prey into a corn field. And the outlaw walked out the door and shot him calmly in the hip. But the victim didn't flounder a bit there in those broken stalks that went down with him. He lay there with his old hat still on his head until the outlaw walked over and shot him in the face. Of course, I only heard that, never saw it. What I did see was after. And it was rectangular. At the top, above the corn tassels, the sky ended. At bottom, sun-baked red clay, rocks, particles of unabsorbed compost, flecks of mica reflecting light. To the left a pine branch intruded with what seems to me a dual purpose: (a) to create foreground, establish depth, serve as a point of reference, and (b) to balance the frame, shoulder some of the burden of the dead weight which lies to the right, off center, recumbent in a nest of fallen stalks. He lay feet foremost, clay ground into the weft of the black pants, torso set at an exaggeratedly, even extravagantly, acute angle to the legs. One arm is bent under his back. The other lay on the broken corn. Often the smeared face was hidden by the shadow of the backlit hat. Not always.

After a few days in the blue mountains my hatred for the outlaw became less personal. I held myself aloof and distant from it, and I no longer took pride in thoughts of his hanging. Instead I envisioned his death as a static event, imagining his eyes glazing in the last moments, spending their light like a blown-out lantern wick still glowing and smoldering with one or two faint sparks along a charred edge. In that last instant I wanted him not to fear me or even to feel the completion of what he himself had set in motion. All I wanted was simple recognition in those last glowing moments of that power of the law I had somehow come to control. I held on to that idea for a while, turning it over and over in my hands, lifting it to my mouth and breathing warm breath onto it while it sang its old song, hanging it on a string around my neck like an amulet. Later, when the fire had died down, I fluffed it back up, tucked and folded its corners, and rested my head on it to sleep. And when I awoke before sunrise, its shape had stabilized in the cold morning air, becoming firm and strict as an axe blade.

I had eaten but little before I left town and nothing on the trail. The fast had begun to affect my senses in a way beneficial to pursuit. I experienced the world like a passing vision. In a high clearing, a bald, I came upon a man standing under an apple tree. He held aloft a pole, and on the end of that pole was tied a small pig with a head as long as the remainder of its body. The pig feasted on the high apples above ladder reach that had escaped picking. The man looked to be the kind of tow-headed mountain trash who plant popcorn and watermelon instead of beans and potatoes. "What are you doing there?" I asked. "I'm fattening this pig for the wedding," he answered, "We gonna take him an' strip off the skin and lay him outside til the frost hit him and bring him in the house and put him in a pot and parbile him and stuff a apple in his mouth and put sweet taters all around him and lay him in the oven and let him lie till he gets right brown and then take him out and put him on the wedding table." When he finished he cackled like a guinea. My head swam from my self-imposed fast. I could see the interrogation would not be easy. "I am in hot pursuit of the outlaw," I said. "A murderer. You would be wise to help me." He lowered the pig to the ground. I continued, "I have reason to believe he has passed this way. You may have seen him, a kid, blond and dreamy. He is complected like fog. In the face he looks like the kind of person who would wear a tiny flower carved from a human tooth on a leather thong around his neck." "Hell, I've never seen nobody like that," he claimed, though I suspected differently. "But," he went on, "if you're gonna be in Toxaway Thursday night you're welcome to come to the wedding and eat some of this pig here. Everybody's coming. Just everybody." "I'll make a point of it," I said. A lawman knows a tip when he hears one. The informant lifted the pig back into the apple tree and began singing a song of food: "Trout, mullet, puppie-drum,/Them's the things I'd founder on."

The Six Mile and the Twelve Mile are narrow and muddy piedmont creeks, but the Keowee is pure and sweet with its origins deep in the blue mountains. I followed it to Toxaway. For the trained, fasting mind the signs of the outlaw were everywhere along the way: (a) ignoring gravity, water ran out of its usual course and flowed among the stones of the trail; (b) the horse failed to shy at a panther's scream near a blowdown high on a ridge; (c) five downed limbs formed a pentagon across the trail; (d) the sun rose late and all day the sky was the green of a fading bruise.

As I approached, descending toward it from a near ridge, it did not seem to me much of a town, only a group of unpainted houses, a store, and two churches clustered in a bend of the Keowee. Heavy mist from the river blurred the edges of the buildings, and blue smoke hung low in a band over the rooftops. The big mountains and the heavy foliage stole the light and left the town in deep gloom, always moving down toward night. It seemed an insubstantial place, a town ready to rise up after dark and move through the woods with a smoking lantern looking for kindling, a town with a good many hard stories to tell in a voice of rust. I did not trust Toxaway.

I stopped at a sinister uphill turn before the buildings began and turned the horse into the woods and slept there between the trail and the river until dusk. I dreamed the dream of willed starvation. When I awoke, tree trunks stood out black and solid in the grey twilight. My head was clear from hunger and contrast ruled my perceptions. I saw everything sharp and distinct as a drop of blood on a wedding dress. The horse I left hobbled near the river. I threaded my way through the trunks toward town. There I eased among the dark buildings looking for the dull yellow glow of lamplight. I knew he could be harbored by kin in any one of these houses, could be nodding in a rocker by a hearth dreaming the fire like a legal citizen. I circled the houses in the dark, anticipating. One by one, I examined the golden windows before me, but they framed nothing but uniform domesticity—women ironing Sunday clothes in preparation for the wedding, men smoking pipes, children making toys from spools. Every frame was a scene from a gallery of lawful pastimes. I was not needed there. But in an outlying house near the edge of the forest I found what I knew must be the bride. I looked in a side window and saw through to the fire. She sat in profile to me with just washed dark hair spread across the back of her chair to dry. The face was pale and intense with the force of pale spring foliage, of a new leaf pushing past dark loam. On the floor beside her sat a glass of warm foamy new milk. She drank from it and then wiped the white foam from her lips with the back of her hand. The wedding dress hung behind her from the ceiling. It was, for such a girl, a crude thing, a failed attempt at finery, a great hooped construction that hung there like a corpse that life had just fled. I heard bob-whites call in the woods beyond the house. Then, from nowhere, the hollow sound of hooves. The horse and the rider skidded around the corner of the house and made one pass by where I crouched against the stone foundation. I heard above my head the deep sigh of a long blade passing through air. The horse wheeled, its hindquarters clenched under it in the spin, ready to dig for purchase and accelerate out of the turn for another pass. But I was off running into the ebony forest. Flight and pursuit are part of the deep structure of my life. I know it as well as most of my countrymen know the wooden end of a hoe. But this flight was profoundly desperate. I ran as if with my head in a croker sack. I could see nothing under the trees and expected at any moment to open my skull against a trunk or hanging limb. The horseman was drawing near. I could feel through my boots the force of the pursuit. I had never felt more alert, my perceptions on fire from hunger and danger. As I ran, I saw ahead the sick malignant green glow of a stick of doddy wood rotting phosphorescently on the damp ground. The pale light was the only form I could distinguish from the darkness. I ran for it, the horseman bearing down from behind. The doddy stick could have been far gone, rotted to a useless soggy mass that would crumble at the touch. Or it could be near solid, only the bark damp and glowing. I bent, grabbed it, and spun. The stick felt satisfyingly heavy and solid in my hand. As I whirled, the glowing club became a green arc in the darkness, an arc that would have gone on to describe a circle had it not smashed against the head of the horseman. At the moment of impact, the doddy stick shattered, throwing a halo of pale light around the head. I swear that in that instant I caught a glimpse of white hair. The halo faded and the body fell heavily to the ground. The blade clattered brittle against a stone. The horse ran on blindly into the dark woods. I stepped behind a thick trunk and watched as the man rose. Damp fragments of the shattered limb clung to his hair and clothes. The faintly glowing figure moved erratically, fleetingly. I heard a hammer cock and he began firing randomly, the yellow blaze from his revolver momentarily overwhelming, dissolving the green glow. But in the dark following the muzzle flash, the figure slowly reasserted itself. I could see his outline if I looked not directly at him, but just off to the side instead, like looking at a faint star. I could have killed him anytime, but I turned quietly into the woods and left him there firing into the night. The fasting predator husbands the prey.

Hoping they would take me for a distant relative from the lowlands, I entered the church with the wedding party. I sat in an empty pew in a dark back corner on the bride's side and began to scrutinize the celebrants. The force of hunger made my vision acute. Though the room was dim, almost windowless, lit only by the fire of six lanterns lashed to joists, I could see, already seated near the front, the fool with the pig I'd met on the trail. He sat on the groom's side amidst a group of clear defectives, the kind of pale-skinned tow-headed folk who slept all winter, getting out from under a pile of greasy quilts only to piss off the porch, toss another log on the fire, and throw a few more potatoes in a cast iron pot. My man was not among them but he was of them, was in a sense the tow-head elevated to a state of outlawish beauty. The tiny choir began a song to start the ceremony. They sang *a cappella* an intensely dissonant high-country hymn called "Will You Be Among the Missing?" Their separate voices arched and writhed around each note in a grating keen, the very sound of deprivation and desire. Like wolves howling at the moon, the disparate voices began with a few solitary piercing yips followed by a chorus of deeper howls that built in pitch and volume and for a few seconds found harmony before disintegrating into a desperate clash. When the hymn died, the preacher, a fat pullet of a man, entered from a side door and stood before the altar. "Let us begin," he said. The pump organ commenced with a dire wheeze, like a consumptive blowing a harmonica. The groom and his second entered from the same door as the preacher had. The groom was him, dressed for a wedding or a funeral. I could make my move any time. The organ's wheeze continued, and the bride entered from the back door. The dress looked a little better with her in it; that new leaf face drew my eyes away from the mechanics of the hoops. Still, she seemed not so much to be wearing the dress as riding it. As she neared the middle of the church walking toward the smiling outlaw, I moved. You are taken, I screamed over the gasp of the pump organ. The second pulled from under his coat a derringer and let go. Whether it was his aim or the fact that those pistols are wildly inaccurate at any range beyond arm's length, I don't know, but the bullet severed the lashing of a lantern. It plummeted to the floor at the bride's feet where it shattered, throwing coal oil and lantern fire onto the wedding dress. Flames rose instantly from the belled fabric. The metal hoops kept the flames away from her body, and she stood serenely in the glow of her own light. The outlaw and I, from opposite ends of the sanctuary, ran toward her, but the crowd emptied the pews before we could meet. The fire now formed a perfect circle around the perfect face. A hint of a smile reshaped her broad mouth. Five of the tow-heads, dropping to their knees, attempted to beat out the flames with their hands. Like supplicants they circled the circle of flames, charring their palms in a failing attempt to extinguish the blaze.

The outlaw and I forced our ways toward her, he an instant quicker. He grabbed from an old grandpaw a cane, and with the crooked end hooked the top hoop and yanked, ripping fiery skirt from cool bodice, succeeding where the kneeling beaters had failed. The flames fell, collapsed to the floor in a much diminished blaze which the bride stepped over with a neat scissor of her bare, smokey legs. I eased behind the outlaw and brought my pistol up beside his head, touching lightly the fine white hair just behind his ear. You are taken, I whispered.

On the day, town was filled with spectators and hawkers of gingerbread, beer, and peanuts. The eating audience nauseated me. The outlaw wore the same dark suit as for the wedding, and when I stood him in the bed of a wagon under the tree, he looked thin and startled as a single black "I" on a white page. I bound his knees and ankles with long pieces of sisal and pulled a croker sack over his platinum head. When I snugged the loop around his neck, the thick knot tight behind his right ear, the cloth of the sack ballooned in front of his mouth, then sucked darkly in, over and over. As I made these preparations, I could see among the crowd the wide mouth, the dark hair, the new leaf face. I tried not to look at it, not to contact eyes. I vaulted from the wagon and in one motion smacked flat-palmed the scrawny haunch of the steer in the traces. The animal ambled slowly forward, and my man shuffled in an awkward dance step across the three feet of wagon bed moving beneath his feet. But when he hit the edge he didn't so much drop as float off, sinking as in water slowly to the end of the rope. Even after a minute, the sack puffed and sucked, puffed and sucked. I quickly tied to the ankle bindings a loop of rope that hung a foot below his boots. I stepped into the loop and bounced, my arms around his waist, my face against his chest, until I heard the snap and felt a great relaxation. The body hung for the legal hour at which time it was remanded to the relatives.

JIM HARRISON

HOW IT HAPPENED TO ME

From *Dalva*

Here is how it happened to me, how I had my child early in my sixteenth year. It has often occurred to me that I may be a grandmother at forty-five. I tried it out in front of the mirror, whispering "Grandma" at myself softly, but it was all too unknowable to be effective. But now I am drifting away from it again. My mother Naomi and my sister Ruth feel wordlessly upset that the land will go to Ruth's son, there being no other heirs in the prospect, another reason for the priest mating. None of us minds the name Northridge disappearing, but it would be a shame to see the land leave the family, and Ruth's son professes to hate it and has not visited since his early teens. Enough!

His name was Duane, though he was half-Sioux and he gave me many versions of his Sioux name depending on how he felt that day. Grandfather's place, which is the original homestead, is three miles north of the farm. The homestead was a full section, 640 acres, onto which the other land was added since 1876, to form a total of some 3,500 acres, which is not that much higher than average for this part of the country. Our good fortune was that the land was bisected by two creeks that form a small river so that the land was low and particularly fertile and could easily be irrigated. The central grace note, though, is that my great-grandfather studied botany and agriculture for two years at Cornell College before he entered the Civil War. In fact, an accidental traveler down the county gravel road near Grandfather's would think he was passing a forest, but this is a little farfetched as the farm is so far from the state highway that there are no accidental travelers. All the trees were planted by Great-grandfather to form shelter belts and windbreaks from the violent weather of the plains, and to provide fuel and lumber in an area where it was scarce and expensive. There are irregular rows of bull pine and ponderosa, and the density of the deciduous caragana, buffalo berry, Russian olive, wild cherry, juneberry, wild plum, thorn apple, and willow. The final inside rows are the larger green ash, white elm, silver maple, black walnut, European larch, hackberry, wild black cherry. About a decade ago Naomi, through the state conservationists, made the area a designated bird sanctuary in order to keep out hunters. Scarcely anyone visits except for a few ornithologists from universities in the spring and fall. Inside the borders of trees are fields, ponds, a creek, and inside the most central forty, the original farmhouse. Enough!

Duane arrived one hot late August afternoon in 1957. I found him walking up the long driveway, his feet shuffling in the soft dust. I rode up behind him and he never turned around. I said, "May I help you?" but he only said his own and Grandfather's name. He was about my age, I thought, fourteen, scarred and windburned in soiled old clothes, carrying his belongings in a knotted burlap potato sack. I could smell him above the lathered horse, and told him he better jump on my horse because Grandpa had a pack of airedales who wouldn't take warmly to a stranger. He only shook his head no, so I rode ahead at a gallop to get Grandpa. He was sitting on his porch as usual and at first was puzzled, then intensely excited though noncommittal. He had to wait at the pickup as I patted the half-dozen airedales each on the head before they jumped in the back of the truck. If I didn't pat each one in turn they would become nasty to one another. I loved these uniquely cranky dogs partly for the way they welcomed me and how wildly excited they became when I went riding and invited them along. I never took them when I rode into coyote country because the dogs once dug up and ate a litter of coyote pups despite my efforts to fight them off with my riding crop. After they gobbled up the pups the dogs pretended to be ashamed and embarrassed. Enough!

We found Duane sitting cross-legged in the dust. The dogs set up a fearsome howl but never dared jump out of the truck without Grandpa's permission. We got out and Grandpa knelt beside Duane, who wasn't moving. They spoke in Sioux and Grandpa helped Duane to his feet and embraced him tightly. When we got back to the house Grandpa said I should leave and to tell no one at our place of the visitor.

I'm sure I loved Duane, at least at the beginning, because he so pointedly ignored me. He came from up near Parmelee on the Rosebud Indian Reservation and though his looks were predominantly Sioux his eyes were Caucasian, cold and green like green stones in cold flowing water. Technically he was a cowboy—it was all he knew how to do and he did it well. He refused to live in Grandpa's house but took up residence in a shed that was once a bunkhouse. Two of the airedales decided to live with him of their own accord. Duane refused to go to school; he told Grandpa that he could read and write and that was as far as he needed to go in that area. He spent his time looking after the remaining herefords, repairing farm buildings, cutting wood, with the largest chore being the irrigating. The only other hired hand was Lundquist, an old Swede bachelor friend of Grandpa's. He taught Duane irrigating, and jabbered all day on the matter of his own Swedenborgian version of Christianity. Lundquist daily forgave Duane for the death of a distant relative in Minnesota who was murdered during the Sioux uprising in the mid-nineteenth century. The actual farm work wasn't that onerous, as Grandpa mostly grew two crops of alfalfa a year within his forest borders, and the bulk of the rest of our land was leased on shares to neighbors.

On New Year's Day of that first year Duane received a fine buckskin quarter horse from a cutting-horse strain, plus a handmade saddle from Agua Prieta on the Arizona border. Normally the gift would have come on Christmas, but Grandfather had lost his religion during World War I in Europe and didn't observe Christmas. The day stands out clearly: it was a warmish, clear winter morning with the thawing mud in the barnyard a little slippery. I had gone way over to Chadron with Grandpa the day before to fetch the horse, and the saddle had come by mail. Duane came riding in on the Appaloosa from feeding the cattle and saw me standing there holding the reins of the buckskin. He nodded at me as coolly as usual, then walked over and studied the horse. He looked at Grandpa, who stood back in the sunlight against the barn. "Guess that's the best-looking animal I ever saw," Duane said. Grandpa nodded at me, so I said, "It's for you, Duane." He turned his back to us for a full ten minutes, or what seemed an unimaginably long time given the situation. Finally I came up behind him and ran my hand with the reins along his arm to his hand. I whispered "I love you" against his neck for no reason. I didn't know I was going to say it.

That was the first day Duane let me go riding with him. We rode until twilight with two dogs until I heard Naomi ring the dinner bell in the distance. Duane rode across the wheat stubble until he turned around within a hundred yards of our farmhouse. It was the most romantic day of my life, and we never spoke or touched except when I handed him the reins.

One of the main sadnesses of my life at the time, and on occasions since, is that I matured early and was thought by others to be overly attractive. It isn't the usual thing to be complained about, but it unfairly, I thought, set me aside, brought notice when none was desired. It made me shy, and I tended to withdraw at the first mention of what I looked like. It wasn't so bad in country school where Naomi was the sole teacher and there were only four of us in the seventh grade, but for eighth grade I had to take the school bus to the nearest town of any size, which, for certain reasons, will be unnamed. There the attention was constant from the older town boys, and I was at a loss for what to do. I was thirteen and refused all dates, saying my mother wouldn't let me go out. I also refused the invitation to become a cheerleader because I wanted to take the school bus home to be with my horses. I trusted one senior boy because he was the son of our doctor and seemed quite pleasant. He gave me a ride home in his convertible one late April day, full of himself because he had been accepted by far-off Dartmouth. He tried very hard to rape me, but I was quite strong from taking care of horses and actually broke one of his fingers, but not before he forced my face close to his penis, which erupted all over me. I was so shocked I laughed. He held his broken finger and began crying for forgiveness. It was stupid and profoundly unpleasant. Naturally he spread it around school that I had given him a great blowjob, but school was almost out for the year, and I hoped people would forget.

If anything, ninth grade was worse. Mother insisted I dress well, but I hid some sloppy clothes to wear in my school locker. I played basketball for a month or so but quit after another unpleasant incident. The coach kept me very late, well after everyone had left, to practice free throws, and to play one on one. While I was drying off after a shower he simply walked right into the girl's locker room. He said he wouldn't hurt me or even touch me, but he wanted to see me naked. I was quite frightened when he came closer saying "please" over and over again. I didn't know what to do so I dropped the towel and turned all the way around. He said "once more," so I did it again and then he left. When I got in the car I almost told Naomi, but I knew that the coach had three children and I didn't want to make trouble for him.

In contrast to other males, Duane hadn't shown a trace of affection in the year and a half since his arrival. All that we shared was the love of horses, but that drew us together sufficiently to give me enough solace to keep going. At one point I had become so depressed I thought of maiming myself, burning my face, or ending my life. Naomi wanted to take me to a psychiatrist in the state capital, but I refused. One evening she gave me my first glass of wine and sent Ruth out of the room. I told her much of what was bothering me and she held me and wept with me. She said that what was happening to me was the condition of life and that I had to behave with pride and honor so that I could respect myself. When I found someone to love who loved me it would all make more sense and become much better. I didn't tell her I loved Duane because she thought him so rude as to be mentally diseased.

One Saturday I was hazing some young steers for Duane so he could practice his buckskin on cutting, which is when the rider allows the horse to enter the herd, select a steer, and "cut" him out of the herd. My job was to keep the steers from dispersing and running off in every direction. The oldest airedale understood the game and helped me to turn back especially recalcitrant steers. I think the dog stuck it out merely for the outside chance of getting to bite a steer.

That day it began to sleet so we went in the barn and practiced roping on some old steer horns perched on a pole. I was the "header," that is, I lassoed the horns, while Duane was the "heeler," which was much harder because you have to lasso the back hooves of a running steer. Duane seemed especially cold and removed that day so I tried to tease him about a necklace he wore. He wouldn't tell me what the necklace meant no matter how I badgered him.

"I heard two footballers down at the feedstore say you were the best-looking girl in school," he said, knowing how much it bothered me. "They also said you were the best fuck in the county."

"That's not true, Duane," I had broken into tears. "You know that's not true."

"Why would they say it if it wasn't true?" he asked, grabbing my arm and making me face him. "You never offered it to me because I'm an Indian."

"I would do it with you because I love you, Duane."

"I'd never fuck a white girl anyway. Not one who'd fuck those farmers."

"I'm a little bit Indian and I didn't fuck those farmers."

"There's no way you can prove it," he yelled.

"Make love to me and then you can tell I'm a virgin." I began to take off my clothes. "Come ahead you big-mouthed coward." He only glanced at me, then his face became knotty with rage. He ran out of the barn and I could hear the pickup starting.

When I rode home I couldn't stop crying. I wanted to die but couldn't decide how to go about it. I stopped along a big hole in the creek, now covered with ice, that we used for swimming in the summer. I thought of drowning myself but I didn't want to upset Naomi and Ruth. Also, I was suddenly very tired, cold, and hungry. It was still sleeting, and I hoped the ice would break the power line so we could light the oil lamps. After dinner we'd play cards on the dining-room table beneath portraits of Great-grandfather, Grandfather, and Father. I would think, why did he leave us alone to go to Korea?

After dinner Grandpa pulled into the yard in his old sedan, which startled us, because he always drove the pickup. Naomi and I had to go into town with him because Duane was in jail and they needed part of my story. In the sheriff's office I said I had never had anything to do with the bruised and severely battered football players. Grandfather was enraged and the sheriff cowered before him. The parents of the football players were frightened, perhaps unfairly, because Grandfather was rich and we were the oldest family in the county. When they brought Duane out of the cell he was unmarked. The football players tried to sneer, but Duane looked through them as if they weren't there. The sheriff said that if anyone slandered me again there would be trouble. Grandpa said, "One more word and I'll run all of you filth straight back to Omaha." The parents begged forgiveness, but he ignored them. I could see he was enjoying his righteous indignation. Out in the parking lot of the county building I said thank you to Duane. He squeezed my arm and said, "It's fine, partner." I almost fell apart when he called me partner.

I was not bothered by the boys at school after that, though I was lonely and I was given the behind-the-back nickname of "squaw." I didn't mind the nickname; in fact, I was proud of it, because it meant in the minds of others that I belonged to Duane. When he found out, however, he laughed and said I could never be a squaw because there was so little Indian in me as to be unnoticeable. This made me quarrelsome and I said, where did you get those hazel-green eyes if you're so pure. His anger seemed to make him want to tell me something, but he only said he was more than half Sioux and in the eyes of the law that made him Sioux.

After that we didn't have anything to do with each other for a month. One summer evening when Grandpa was over for dinner he took me aside and told me it was a terrible mistake to fall in love with an Indian boy. I was embarrassed but had the presence to ask him why his own father had married a Sioux girl.

"Who knows why anybody marries anybody." His own wife, whom I never saw and was long dead, had been a rich girl from Omaha who drank herself into an early grave. "What I'm saying is they aren't like us, and if you don't behave and stop chasing Duane I'll send him away." It was the first time I stood up to him. "Does that mean you're not like us?" He hugged me and said, "You know and I know I'm not like anybody. You show the same signs."

I felt it was all unnecessary as Duane showed not the slightest sign of being anything more than minimally my "partner." I tried becoming less pushy and doe-eyed, which did serve to make him friendlier. He took me to some Indian burial mounds in a dense thicket in the farthest corner of the property. I didn't tell him that my father had taken me there soon after I was given my first pony. Not far from the burial mounds Duane had erected a small tipi out of poles, canvas, and hides. He told me he slept there often and "communed" with dead warriors. I asked him where he got the word "commune," and he admitted he had taken to reading some of the books in Grandfather's library. It was the first cool evening in September and the air was clearer than it had been all summer, with a slight but steady breeze from the north. I mention the breeze because Duane asked me if I ever noticed that the wind in the thickets made a different sound depending on which direction the wind came from. The reason was that the trees rubbed against each other differently. I admitted I had never noticed this and he said, "Of course, you're not an Indian." I was a bit downcast at the reminder, so he gave my arm a squeeze, then he gave me my first real hope by saying there might just be a ceremony to make me a bona fide Sioux. He'd check if he ever got back to Parmelee. I hated to leave, but my mother insisted I be home before dark when I was with Duane. I went to my tethered horse and Duane said, "If I asked you to stay all night, would you?" I nodded that I would, and he came up to me, his face so close that I thought we were going to have our first kiss. The last of the sun was over my shoulder and on his face, but he suddenly turned away.

That summer I became friends with a girl named Charlene, who was seventeen and two years older than me. She lived in a small apartment in town above a cafe that her mother managed. Her father had died in World War II and this misfortune of war helped bring us together. I barely knew her at school, where she had a bad reputation. It was rumored that when rich pheasant hunters from the East appeared in late October and November, Charlene made love to them for money. Charlene was very pretty but an outcast, she didn't belong to a church or any school groups. The only time she had spoken to me at school was when I was in the eighth grade—she told me to "be tough" when the older boys were bothering me. We didn't get to know each other until we began talking in the town library.

On Saturday afternoons Naomi would drive to town to shop for groceries and do errands. Ruth would tag along with me to the saddle and harness shop, and then we'd have a soda and all meet at the library. We never saw Duane in town because he would do farm errands on weekdays, claiming it was too crowded on Saturday. The town was the county seat but barely had a population of a thousand. I had been reading *Of Human Bondage, Look Homeward, Angel,* also *Raintree Country* by Ross Lockridge. They were wonderful books and I was puzzled when I read in the paper that Mr. Lockridge had committed suicide. Charlene saw me with the books and we began talking. She was in her waitress uniform and said she came in on Saturdays after work to get something to read in order to forget her awful life. We met and talked on a half-dozen Saturdays, and I asked her to come to dinner on Sunday because I knew the cafe would be closed. She said thank you but she wasn't our kind of people, but then Naomi showed up and talked her into it.

Charlene began spending every Sunday with us. Grandpa liked her a great deal when I brought her over. It was her first time on a horse, which thrilled her. Duane made himself scarce—it was always difficult for him to deal with more than one person at once. Naomi gave Charlene lessons in sewing and made some clothes for her that couldn't be bought short of a long drive to Omaha. Naomi told me in private that she hoped Charlene wouldn't sell herself to pheasant hunters again in the fall. She said more than one upstanding woman in the area had done so, so it wasn't an item on which a woman should be judged unfairly.

One night when she was staying over, Charlene told me the rumors were true. She said she was saving up to leave town and go to college. I asked her what all the men did to her, but she said if I didn't know already she wasn't going to tell me. I said I did know but was interested in the details. She said she got to be very picky because they all wanted her, and one man from Detroit paid her a hundred dollars, which was what she made in the cafe in an entire month. The only embarrassing quality of her visits was the degree to which she was impressed by our house and Grandpa's. It was natural of her to be so, but it upset me. We had few visitors and I certainly knew that we were what was called "fortunate," but one tended to take it all for granted. Furniture and paintings in both houses had been accumulated on travels beginning with Great-grandfather, but mostly by Grandfather around the First World War in Paris and London, and later by his wife, and also by my parents. It was the time of life when you wanted to be like everyone else, even though you had begun to understand there was no "everyone else," and there never had been.

My bad luck, innocently enough, started with religion. We had always gone to a small Wesleyan Methodist church a few miles down the road. Everyone did for miles around except the Scandinavians, who had a similarly small church that was Lutheran. Once a year in July the churches held a joint barbecue and picnic. It was all quite friendly and social, our religion, and our preacher, though very old and quite ineffectual, was admired by all. On this particular Sunday we had to get to church a little early because Ruth served as the pianist. Charlene was with us—she had never been to church until she began coming to our house for Saturday night and Sunday, and found it interesting though peculiar.

I remember it was the first Sunday after Labor Day and it was very hot after the brief cool spell when I was out at Duane's tipi. Our regular minister was away on vacation in Minneapolis, and his replacement was a young, handsome preacher from theological school who was a fireball and aimed, according to the mimeographed announcement, to be an evangelist. We were accustomed to restrained homilies on the tamer aspects of the New Testament, and the substitute preacher swept everyone in the congregation off their feet, except Naomi, who was quietly tolerant. He thundered, roared, strutted up and down the aisle, physically grabbed us; in short, he gave us drama and we were unused to drama. The gist was that many of the inventors of the atomic bomb and hydrogen bomb were Jews, or Children of Israel. God had called upon his Chosen People to be his tool to invent the destruction of the world, which would call forth the Second Coming of Christ. All those who were truly saved would be drawn up in the Rapture before the Conflagration. Everyone else, no matter how sincere, would endure unbelievable torture with millions and billions of radiation-crazed zombies devouring each other's flesh, and the animal and sea world going berserk, and primitive tribes, including Indians, rising up to slaughter the whites. I remember thinking for a moment that Duane would save me. For the time being, the church moaned and wept. When the sermon neared its end and the wringing wet preacher gave the invitation to come forward there was a general rush to the front to give our lives to Jesus, including me, Ruth, Charlene, and more than two dozen others, including all the younger people.

In the confused but saner aftermath it was decided that we all should be baptized just in case hydrogen bombs were actually aimed at our part of the country. In the upper Midwest, no doubt due to the weather, many things are considered chores, including funerals, weddings, baptisms, that need to be accomplished with a certain dispatch. The plan was to meet at the swimming hole on our farm as soon as a picnic could be gathered (food is never neglected) and the proper clothing found, which was anything close to white.

We reassembled by mid-afternoon and the ceremony went well except for the appearance of a water snake. The weather was so hot that the water felt especially cool and sweet. Naomi looked at Ruth, Charlene, and me in our wet white dresses and said it couldn't have done us any harm. While I was wiping my face with a towel I heard a bird whistle that I knew had to be Duane. The others went off to eat so I snuck through a grove of trees to where I saw Duane sitting on his buckskin.

"What were you goddammed monkeys doing in the river?" he asked.

"Well, we were getting baptized in case the war comes, and the world ends." I felt a little stupid and naked in my wet white dress. I tried to cover myself and gave up.

He told me to jump on the horse with him, which surprised me because I had never been asked to do so. He smelled of alcohol, which also surprised me because he said alcohol was a poison that was killing the Sioux. At the tipi he put his hand on my bare bottom where my wet clothes hiked up sliding off the horse. He offered me a bottle full of wild plum wine from Lundquist. I drank quite deeply and he put his arms around me.

"I don't like the idea of you getting baptized. How can you be my girl if you're getting baptized and singing those songs."

His lips were close to mine so I kissed them for the first time. I couldn't help myself. He peeled the dress up over my head and threw it in the grass. He stood back, looked at me, then let out a cry or yell. We went into his tent and made love. After a while he fell asleep in the hot tent. Far off I heard Naomi ringing the bell. I went out into the late afternoon and slipped into my damp dress. I ran all the way except for stopping to take a quick swim. I wondered if I would look different to everyone. That was the last time I saw Duane for fifteen years.

I didn't tell Mother until November that I was pregnant. I told her I had missed only one period when it was actually two. That was so she wouldn't think it was Duane, who had disappeared. I told her it was a pheasant hunter. Her first reaction was a rage that I had never seen before, not against me—I was her "poor baby"—but against the perverted man. I had to add one lie to another because Naomi immediately called Charlene, who swore innocence in the matter. I invented a tale of being out riding and meeting a handsome man who was looking for a lost English setter. I helped him find the dog and he seduced me, which wasn't difficult because I was tired of being a virgin. Naomi took me in her arms and consoled me, saying it wasn't the end of the world I had lived in so innocently. She withdrew me from school in

November during Thanksgiving break, telling the superintendent that she intended to send me to school in the East. The only people who knew were a doctor in Lincoln, Ruth, Charlene—whose contempt for the world was so great she could share in any secret—and Grandpa.

It was hardest on Grandpa, perhaps harder on him than me because I had the resilience of my age, and he had none. A poet, I can't remember who, said there is a point beyond which the exposed heart cannot recover. I was fifteen, nearly sixteen, and he was seventy-three. I was the "apple of his eye," perhaps the feminine counterpart of my father.

From the time that Duane disappeared in late September until I was taken away the day after Thanksgiving, I rode over to Grandpa's every day to see if there was any news from Duane.

I never asked directly for news and he never mentioned directly that Naomi had told him I was pregnant. He was considered extremely eccentric well beyond the confines of our county, though never to me. In many ways he had been my substitute father for the nearly ten years since Dad died in Korea, the point in time in which he had ceased active life and retreated behind his successive walls of trees. He had had "too much life," he said, and wanted to think it over before he died. Not that there was grimness on my nearly daily visits—I had at least ten routes to ride over and back, and all of them were well-worn paths. He was grave if I was unhappy, and either went to the heart of the problem with subtlety or sought to divert me with talk of books, travel, or horses. Naomi felt that he spent far too much on horses for me, but then he had been a horseman all his life. Even in those days he thought nothing of spending $10,000 on a horse, while a car was nothing more than a vulgar convenience.

It is nearly thirty years ago and I still feel the pain of that October and November so that my heart aches, my skin tightens, and I can barely swallow. There was a stretch of Indian summer when I would sit with Grandpa on the porch swing watching autumn, then squeeze my eyes as if Duane were walking up the driveway back to me. There was nothing left of him, not a trace, in the bunkhouse, except the two airedales who dozed on his cot as if waiting. I groomed his buckskin but hadn't the heart to ride the horse.

One afternoon, the day before Thanksgiving when I cleaned out my locker and said a tearful goodbye to Charlene, I rode over to Grandpa's in a gathering snowstorm against Naomi's wishes. I asked him to light the soft oil lamps because they cast a yellow light around the room, but the light made him look old and quite sad. Behind his head on the den wall was a folio print from Edward Curtis of the warrior chief Two Whistles, with a crow perched on his head. Outside the sky was gray and full of snow, with the wind buffeting the windowpanes. He put his favorite Paganini violin solo on the Victrola. He rejected more modern record players, having grown fond of and used to the bad sound reproduction. I said something idle to the effect, "I could just shoot myself if Duane doesn't come back."

"Dalva, goddammit!" he roared. Then for the first time I'd ever seen, he began to cry. I rushed to him, begging for him to forgive me for saying something stupid. You must never say that, he said. He repeated himself. He poured us each some whiskey, a full glass for himself and a little bit for me.

In the next hour I was to become old before my time. He told me that my grandmother had been somewhat insane and had committed suicide with whiskey and sleeping pills. She had been a lovely and kind soul but had left him to raise the boys. Now that my father was dead, and my uncle estranged, wasting his life wandering the world, I had to live, and he had deeded me this strange corner of the farm. They all could have their goddamn wheat and corn. Then his face darkened and he held my hand. Just before the war my uncle Paul had come home from Brazil, and he and my father, Wesley, had gotten along well, so Grandpa had taken them to a hunting cabin he kept out in the Black Hills. They had a fine drive out, though they drank too much, and Lundquist had followed in a truck with the horses and bird dogs. Grandpa and Wesley had had a good time hunting, but Paul had disappeared for two days, returning with a lovely Sioux girl "to clean the cabin" he said.

"The girl didn't care for Paul at all," Grandpa said, "but fell in love with your father and he with her. Naomi knows nothing of this. Paul and Wesley fought over the girl and I gave her some money and I sent her away while your father had taken a horse to town to be shod. I liked her a great deal and told her to get in touch with me if there ever was a problem. Actually I sent her away because I was taken with her also. It was all a goddamn mess and I was relieved when we got back home. She wrote me a note with the help of a missionary saying she was pregnant. I sent a man out there to check and it was true. So I sent her money on a monthly basis for ten years or so until she disappeared or died of drink as many Sioux do, then I supported the child through a mission school. When Duane showed up here he didn't know who you were. Then he came back the day you were baptized and said he wanted to marry you and I told him he couldn't legally because you were his half-sister. He ran away. I know there is no pheasant hunter. Naomi couldn't bear to hear this. We're the only ones who must ever know this. You have done nothing wrong except to love someone. I would have told him earlier who you were except I thought you were helping to keep him here."

Grandpa embraced me. I told him I loved him and I meant to live.

It was the first of June in 1972 that Naomi called me in New York, where I worked as an assistant to a ragtag film documentarian who was obsessed with the poor. We worked and lived together, along with an English sound man, making cinema verité short films for Public Broadcasting. The afternoon Naomi called we were packing the van for a trip to West Virginia for some footage on a coal-mine strike. "I looked at this postcard for two days without calling," she said. "It's from Duane in the Florida Keys and says for you to come down quick. I don't feel too good." She added a phone number and the fact that I would be in her prayers. I called the number but there was no answer. I called Delta, made a reservation, and packed an overnight bag. I tried to explain myself to the director and lover but was summarily fired from an affair and a job.

I reached Key West before midnight, rented a car, and drove to a motel recommended by a Cuban girl on the plane who wore lots of jewelry. No one at the number had answered at either La Guardia or at the Miami airport. The air smelled like dead fish and rotten fruit and even at that late hour was sodden with humidity. Oddly, the airport bar doubled as a strip club and through the open door I could see a girl grabbing her ankles and bending over as far as possible. This was 1972, well before Key West cleaned itself up and became a tourist mecca.

At the motel I drove the desk clerk crazy by calling the number every ten minutes for the next hour and a half. It was the Pier House bar, crowded and nightmarish with what I thought was a convention. There were at least two dozen men and women around my age, thirty, who wore blue shirts that had CLUB MANDIBLE printed on them. They were getting quite drunk and some of them were smoking huge marijuana cigarettes out on the patio. I bought a drink and stood outside in the hall by the pay phone, watching the activity in the bar. Then a woman answered the phone. Her name was Grace Pindar and she sounded black. Yes, Duane expected me, and no, he wasn't there, he was out fishing until at least noon tomorrow. How can he fish at night? That's when they catch the fish, she said. Duane and Grace's husband were commercial fisherman. Bobby was the captain and Duane was the mate. She gave me directions to where they lived on Big Pine Key.

Now I was trembling and walked out the door, across the patio beside the pool, and down to the water. A slight breeze had come up and the palm fronds were rattling. Two burly men were standing in the water in their clothes fly-casting to tarpon that were rolling under a light attached to a dock. One of the men screamed "holy shit" as he hooked a huge tarpon, which jumped in the dark several times before it broke off. He waded back to the beach where I was standing and tied on another fly. "You want to have some fun?" he asked. He had a big twisted nose but a kind face. Now the other fisherman with one eye and brown moon face waded toward me and I felt a decided urge to go to my room. I asked again where Big Pine Key was and they offered to drive me there. I got the directions, thanked them, and went to my room. I must have awakened and fallen back to sleep a hundred times that night, listening to the wind rattle the palm fronds, the party noise of people jumping in the pool, the slurred shouts that the humidity and walls softened until all the words and dreams in the world became round.

I know in my heart there was nothing that I could have done for him. In the fifteen years since I had seen or heard from him he had punished himself and had been punished, as much as any human could and still be alive. There was the question of to what degree, and in what parts of his soul and body he was still alive.

I can see the house and clearing and trailer in a bare pine grove with dead stacked brush, a saltwater channel and pool hedged by mangroves. There was no one there, I thought, but a dog who became friendly, the house no more than a shack with the TV on but no one around. Gray chickens and three piglets in a pen. I went down to the tidal creek and there in a corral in the pines was the buckskin, and I jumped and the dog barked at me. I thought a ghost horse, but he was sixteen, not all that old for a horse but missing a hind hoof up to the pastern. I slid through the corral bars and looked. It was healed, a nubbin hide-covered, the horse sun-bleached but looked well brushed. The tidal creek was full and moving as a small river and there were egrets. A voice said, "He want a swim, that's all he want to do is swim." Grace was brown-black, Bahamian. "They'll be home soon." She took me to Duane's old Airstream trailer, which was implausibly neat inside with dozens of bottles of prescription medicine and pictures of me, his mother Rachel, and an old one of Grandfather on a horse. You're pretty, Duane is good with ladies, but now he's sick, you could take him to a good hospital not the VA hospital. Grace was hard to understand. We heard the boat coming up the creek. I ran down and Bobby Pindar, who was about forty but you couldn't tell really, yelled for Grace who caught the lines and tied off to the dock. Duane got up from where he was lying down on the cooler covered with canvas, shirtless, and I could see holes, indentations in him, also in his cheek and neck because they were whiter than his skin. Scar tissue doesn't tan well. He hugged me smelling like sun, fish, and salt. I got you down here because I want you to have my benefits. They said I'm dying. Rachel said you had to give the kid away. Maybe you can find him and give him some of my benefits from the Army. They unloaded the fish with Duane telling me the names of different fish. I couldn't quite talk. He hugged me again and I started to cry but he told me to stop. We're getting married so you can have my service benefits, he said, shaking from sickness. Grace set up a table in a grove of trees near the creek and started a fire. Bobby Pindar carried a tub of ice filled with beer. Grace had a bottle of rum, a bottle of hot peppers, Cuban bread, and the chickens she was going to cook. Duane got the buckskin who was excited. Bobby said that horse is the champion swimming horse of the world and should be on TV. Duane got on with just a halter and the horse jumped off the dock. Duane gave a big rodeo hoot and the horse swam up the tidal creek into the mangroves, then back to us and up a path. You try it, he said. I took off my skirt and blouse. It was wonderful, jumping through the air with a huge splash. Duane dove in the water and we swam with the horse up and down the clear, deep creek. We caught three hundred pounds of shrimp with a net across this creek, he told me. We got out of the creek and drank rum and beer. Bobby Pindar came down and said we got to have the wedding before we eat. Duane said he's looking at your tits and ass, so I put my clothes on. They had a license. What if I'm already married, I teased, but that only stopped them for a moment until I shook my head no. I am the full-fledged captain of a boat I marry you said Pindar. Duane took off his necklace and put it around my neck. Kiss her, Duane, you asshole, Grace said. He kissed me. I never been married how do I know? Duane said, I only know about war and horses. We ate some shrimp and drank a lot. Duane went off to pee and Bobby said Duane had the record for the most time spent in combat, almost four years before they shipped him home as good as dead. He had a sack full of medals for you. It don't look good for old Duane he said. We ate shrimp and chicken and drank more, then went swimming again without the horse. I was drunker than he was and I asked what all was wrong. Kidneys liver pancreas stomach, he would have to be hooked to a machine at the VA hospital to stay alive. I'll take care of you, I said. It was nearly dark and Grace who was quite drunk yelled at us to start our honeymoon, so we went to Duane's trailer to please her. He poured us big glasses of rum, I know now to get rid of me. We clicked glasses. How's it with you, little sister, he said, then I fell asleep or passed out with his arms around me. I'm with my lover and we'll take the horse back to the country I thought. Doctors will make him better and we'll live up in the cabin in Buffalo Gap with the horse. On the way we'll stop at the Missouri River, then the Niobrara and let the horse swim, and we'll dam the small spring in Buffalo

Gap and let the horse swim there. In the middle of the night there was a loud banging and a flashlight in my face. It was Bobby yelling that Duane and the buckskin were gone. He dragged me to the boat. Another fisherman called and said he saw Duane and the horse swimming out Bow Channel past Loggerhead Key toward open water in the dark, and when he pulled alongside, Duane pointed a gun at him. Bobby took the boat out the creek and into the channel. These same stars wavered and I rinsed my face and shivered. At a buoy we met the other fisherman who had called the Coast Guard. I heard the man whisper that he followed Duane and the horse at a distance out toward American Shoals and the Gulf Stream. He heard two shots and guessed that the first was for the horse and the second was for Duane. Bobby started to cry, then stopped, and both boats steered toward the oncoming lights of the Coast Guard launch. I looked up at the stars, which had never seemed so huge. I sat on my father's lap in a blanket to watch the shooting stars. Naomi said, there is the archer, the crow, and whale, and lion, shining in the black sky. Should I have been with Duane plunging in these waves that make the stars waver and sway, over the phosphorescent crests and down through troughs and up again. The three boats searched all night but we never found the horse or Duane. The Coast Guard said sharks and blood. I was not well after that and Uncle Paul came from Arizona to get me. Months later, in October, with the permission of Naomi and Ruth who saw no harm, I buried an empty coffin like my father's in our cemetery in the middle of the lilac grove.

RICK BASS

CHOTEAU

Galena Jim Ontz has two girlfriends and a key to Canada. It's the best hunting in North America, up the road, past the entry gate, where he has this key. The tiny dirt road going into Canada hugs a mountain face on one side, and the sheerest of cliffs on the other. Driving it, if you dare, you can look down and see the nauseating white spills of rapids in the Moyie River. There's not a dead-end sign or anything to warn you when you first get on this road, and you follow it straight up the mountain, around a few bends, then—as if climbing into the clouds—always, you keep going up, and the smart people who somehow find themselves on this road will stop and park, and get out and walk, if they want to see what's ahead (no place to turn around: you have to suck in your breath and back down, stopping to throw up sometimes—the jeep, or truck, slides when you tap the brakes, rolls on the loose gravel, acts as if it's going to take you over the edge and into space beyond; sometimes it does, and you can see wreckage on the rocks below). But Galena Jim guns his old black truck up the road without a care, and when he gets to the heavy crossbar gate with the padlock on it, no sign differentiating the United States from Canada, just a gate, he gets out and opens it with his key, and we drive through, and then he gets out again and locks it behind us, and we've left northern Idaho and are in a new country, pioneers, it seems, hunting in a country that has never been hunted.

"Oui," says Jim, grinning. He's got black hair, an old lined-looking face—he's forty—and light blue eyes, a kid's grin. "Oui, oui, oui." It's the only French he knows. He loves to hunt. I don't know how he got the key. Some sort of charm or guile somewhere, I'm sure. People only see that side of him. Though surely Patsy, who has been his girlfriend ever since she left Oklahoma with him, sees the other part. I do, too. He is still a boy, still learning to be a man, this in the fortieth year of his life. He doesn't always make the right choices—but he's still trying, he still has choices to make, at least—an odd, stubborn sort of purity. I like Patsy. She's forty, also. I'm not so wild about the girlfriend Jim keeps in Libby. The girl is sixteen, has yellow hair, and is a hard talker, ready to get out of the sticks, ready to go on the road. Except she's frightened, I think, and wants Jim to go with her. Which he won't, of course.

But he's got that choice. He still has so many! And who wouldn't want to have Jim Ontz, Galena Jimmy Ontz, on the road with them, that first time?

Everyone else sees just the boy in him, and is charmed, says, "That Jim," etc. chuckles, buys him a drink, or what-have-you, and they think that's how he is, that he's a wild man, the wild man of Yaak Valley, and are glad to have him, a legend living among them, like a damn motto or state flag or something.

They don't understand that he's still growing up, that he's just getting rid of things, and trying to keep other things out.

They call him Galena because of what he did to the road when he first moved up here, back when he and Patsy were about to get married. (They never did.)

It was about ten years ago, and they'd just made the big strike down near Thompsons Falls. Galena is usually found as an ore, mixed in with what they call "country rock"—and all sorts of processing and smashing and refining is necessary to separate it—but occasionally a vein of pure glittering space-blue slick and shiny heavy-as-lead galena will be discovered, and they can claw that directly out of the mountain with a bulldozer.

Jim had left the rodeo circuit, had come north. Most of the people living in the Yaak, then as well as now, were from Texas, but Jim was from Oklahoma, a little farther north. The country was and still is too tough for anyone else. It was when they were first putting a real road in through the valley—the last valley in the Rockies before you get up into Canada—and it's still the last valley in Montana without electricity, and probably always will be—and Jim was working on the road crew, helping cut and blade through rock and forest the little one-lane road that follows the Yaak River, which flows west into the Kootenai.

What Jim did was to steal a cement mixing truck from the road crew project, late on a Friday afternoon, after everyone had gone home—Jim was the only crew member who actually *lived* in the valley, all the others had gone home to Libby, or Bonner's Ferry, or even Eureka—and he took it down to Thompsons Falls, with me and Patsy along for company, and he backed it up to the roadside cut where they were mining all of this galena straight from the vein.

He climbed up on top of the mixer, so that he was right against the cliff, and with a hammer and railroad spike, he chiseled into the vein, spilling pebble- and cobble- and fist-sized pieces of galena down into the cement mixer's huge bowl. We held flashlights for him so that he could see, and whenever a lone car or truck would come driving down the road, we'd turn the flashlights off and hold our breath. Jim would keep chipping, though, banging away at the side of the mountain with savage, rooting swings, as if there was something *buried* beneath the galena.

It was a dark night, with the moon not up yet, but the galena was so shiny that it caught even the starlight, and Jim looked wild up there in the dark, his big arms and shoulders working frantically.

And when he finally had the mixer loaded the way he wanted it, half-and-half—it was about midnight—he climbed down, too tired to drive, and Patsy drove us back to Yaak, taking dirt roads, going up through canyons, cutting across meadows, taking all the shortcuts, skipping the few little towns between Thompsons Falls and Yaak. We got stuck in the last meadow outside of the valley, coming up along a dry little beaver-dam creek, and we had to dump some of the galena-and-cement to lighten our load.

By that time the moon was up over the mountains, and it shone down on us so brightly, lighting our every move, that it seemed unnatural, wrong—*too* bright—and as the galena splashed into the shallow creek, making a little dam, it sparkled with an eerie blue light that seemed almost to come from within, like some beautiful new electrified form of life, maybe even life being created, inside the mixer.

We got the big truck going again, and drove, sliding and groaning, all the way up through the pasture like that, leaving a wide trail of galena, as if some beautiful animal had been wounded and was leaving a glowing blue spoor.

When we got back out to the road, Jim hopped out and shut the sluice pipe, and no more galena was lost: but it's still out there, a hundred-yard stripe of it, and hunters call it Galena Meadows now instead of the old name, which was forgotten, and that's even how it shows up on the maps; and it's beautiful, in the moonlight, shining in the night like an electric blue blaze. Helicopters land on it, whenever they have to fly into the valley to pick up an emergency patient, because it's so easy to see, even in bad weather. The meadow is the safest place to land, and they aim for the galena, illuminated by their landing lights, shimmering, almost pulsing, as the winds blow snow across it.

What Jim did next was pretty self-incriminating.

He drove down the sidewalks of the little town of Yaak—a mercantile on one side of the street, and the Dirty Shame Saloon and a few houses on the other side—and with the cement mixer growling and tumbling, sloshing all that mixture around inside—lights coming on, from the cabins along the road—he poured galena sidewalks for the town, on either side of the new road that was coming through, and when he was finished with that he drove around and around in circles in the center of town, pouring a town plaza, right in the middle of where the road would be coming, so that it would have to fork left and right around this slick blue circle. And Dickie McIntire, the owner of the saloon, came out and with the snowplow on his truck graded and leveled both the sidewalks and the little plaza-circle, and by the time the sun was coming up, the men of Yaak were building a gazebo out of lodgepoles in the center of the large blue circle, and Jim and Patsy and I had returned the cement mixer and had gone home and were sleeping hard.

There aren't but twenty or so people living in the valley, and we all liked the new sidewalks and the new plaza, and felt they were at least what the road crew owed us for the inconvenience of the new road and the people it would bring—and so no one said anything on Jim, although he had poured a little strip of the galena mixture all the way up to his cabin before returning the mixer—and then, even after the crew started back to work on the road, working for several more weeks, bits and chunks of galena were still falling out of the shaker, being poured out onto the new road, and now, at night, in places all along the new Yaak River Road, your car or truck headlights will pick up sudden, flashing blue-bolt chunks and swatches in the road, blazing like blue eyes, sunk down in the road—the whole road glittering and bouncing with that weird blue galena light, if you are driving fast.

Jim says you need two of everything up here. Winters hit forty, sometimes fifty below, and the air as still as your sleep. Two trucks, two chainsaws, two girlfriends, says Jim. Two axes, two winches, two sets of snow chains. Mauls, generators, cross-country skis: two of everything, depend on nothing, and he's right, of course.

I moved up here from Fort Worth twelve years ago, and have given up trying to live with a girlfriend or a wife. I've gone through three of them, and the partings have always been wild and bitter, never pretty, always leaving great relief on either side after it was over. It's a rough country, and beauty doesn't do well up here unless it's something permanent, like the mountains, or the river, or even the great forests, century-old larch and cedar. Jim and Patsy have been together as long as anyone up here, though, so perhaps what he says is true.

The mean hard-mouthed girl comes into town sometimes, for a drink at the Dirty Shame, and whenever she comes in, Patsy gets up and leaves. The mean girl from Libby is named Wilmer, but Jim and everyone else calls her Tiger. She just turned sixteen in the spring; she used to be fifteen when she first started coming up here. It's a different country.

I watch Patsy going out to the truck, walking proudly, not looking back, whenever Tiger shows up. I really like Patsy. Patsy might be the best thing in this valley. She tans Jim's hides and pelts, helps him with his trapline. She's got long brown hair, down almost all the way to her butt, and a good, strong face. She's from Illinois, but you'd swear Alaska. Patsy makes what she calls "dream hoops" for the entire valley, beautiful wreaths of bird feathers, feathers she's found and not killed to get—grouse, eagle, crow, jay, owl—and the wreaths are small and thick, spiraling in on themselves, all feathers, with only a finger-sized hole in the center.

You're supposed to hang them over your bed, she says, right over your head, and all the bad dreams that would otherwise come to you in the night, making you anxious and tense the next day, instead get tangled up in the birds' feathers. The good dreams are free then to come in through the small hole. It works, strangely enough; everyone agrees that it works. It's spooky.

Jim says that in the absolute dead of winter—during the Wolf Moon of January—trees splitting, exploding like fireworks all over the valley, and deer and elk freezing in their tracks, frozen in upright positions, standing out in the bright white meadows like statues, with no place left to go, just *frozen,* finally, from the great cold—he and Patsy will get so cabin-fevered, so out of their minds and rage-crazy that they could *kill* each other with swords, if they had to. When they start feeling that rumble coming on, that low, slow kick in the back of their heads and between their ears—the itch starting up—then one of them will go lock the guns in the barn and throw the key into a snowdrift, where it will not be found until spring thaw; and then, when their hate for each other, and for everything, for the entrapment of the cabin, can no longer be stood, but when stepping outside might be fatal—lung-searing, at a wind chill of seventy below—they put on these huge red inflatable child's boxing gloves—"Rocky Boppers," they are called—and with these monstrously oversized balloon-fisted gloves, they'll stand in front of the fire and just let each other have it, whaling away, pounding and pounding on each other, jabs and hooks and uppercuts, all of it, fighting for over an hour sometimes, fighting until they can't stand up; collapsing then, exhausted, as if drunk, in front of the fire, where they will fall asleep, into the deepest of sleeps, with a dream hoop over the mantel, until the fire dwindles and Jim must get up and take the balloon gloves off and go outside and get another log for the fire.

Jim's a tough man, a little on the short side, but heavy, about 170, 175 pounds. Still, I wouldn't like to be on his end of it when Patsy gets crazy (though I can hardly imagine it, I have to go by what Jim tells me), because she's taller than he is, has pretty good reach, and is in such good shape. I have to say that Jim isn't.

I've been skiing with Patsy in December, when the snow is still soft and fresh and the woods are silent, and we're looking for feathers for her wreaths; and I can tell she has to hold back to keep from leaving me behind without even thinking about it. She's the best damn skier in the valley, and sometimes when I look out my breakfast room window, even if there is a heavy snow falling, I'll see her go trucking by, with a determined, wild, happy look on her face, and a Walkman strapped to her hip: lifting those skis and leaning forward and digging in with the poles, just flat-out racing, jamming to her old sixties and seventies rock and roll; escaping the winter, escaping her love for Jim, escaping everything.

Jim and I hunt in the fall, waiting for the snows to come down so he can run his trapline. He traps anything, everything—mink, beaver, badger, coyote, wolf, panther, bear; but in the fall, what we hunt is deer and grouse.

We don't go after the elk any more, which are still up so high, and too hard to get to. Jim says he has a bad ticker, and perhaps he does, because he stops and rests often, even deer hunting, down in the low woods, along the creeks. We do a lot of still hunting, where we sit camouflaged, waiting on a ridge for something to walk past below.

Jim doesn't own a horse; he's through with them, says he has gotten them out of his system. He runs his traplines on a snowmobile, of all things, loud and obnoxious in the winter stillness, but he says it's faster (though not as dependable: it can't tell where the ice is too thin, beneath the snow, the way a horse can; he's ditched several into frozen streams that way, has barely gotten out alive, miles from home and twenty below, with dark coming on, sopping wet). Galena Jim is the last tough man there is, for a fact—but it's because he's still got that boy in him, some part he flat-out refuses to let go of. . . . And so in the fall, when we shoot our deer, I am the one who has to pack it out, because of Jim's bad ticker and because he does not own a horse. He delights in shooting the biggest deer in the most remote places, places so far from a road that a helicopter with a winch-cable couldn't get the deer out. And sometimes, for two or three days, we'll pack the deer out, me pulling a travois-sled we've lashed together, dragging the cleaned deer out, Galena Jim walking beside me, or behind, whistling, smoking his pipe; *sauntering,* with his rifle strapped to his back, carrying a walking stick: out for a stroll.

I'll be lunging it up the hills—leaping forward in the harness we've fashioned for me, trying to get old Jim's big deer out of the woods; and he'll do his sharpshooting trick of knocking the heads off grouse as we come upon them on the trail, leaving them headless, spinning in the pine needles, fresh juicy meat for supper. And that's how we'll go through the woods, moving back down out of Canada, where the deer are larger and where there are no other hunters, and no roads—a hell of a good place to get lost—and we'll finally work our way back to the one thin road that goes up above the Moyie River, the one with the gate.

We'll load up, and turn around at the end of the road (about ten miles into Canada) and drive back out, locking the gate behind us. Another trophy deer for Galena Jim Ontz. Sometimes I get one too, though as I get older, I would rather pull only one deer, instead of two.

One year, when I was twenty-five—my strongest year—we got a moose as well as two deer. But now when we come across a moose in the woods, I shout and whistle and throw rocks at it, before Jim can shoot. Even at twenty-five, it took me a week to get the moose (and two deer) out of there.

But we did get them out.

"Man, you're okay," Galena Jim says at the end of each sled-pulling day. He's a good cook, the best: those grouse on sticks, and potatoes in the coals; gravy from the deer meat, poured over the potatoes, and mashed. Jim knows all the names of the stars and constellations, and the *precise* distance we are from each of them (unless he is making it up, which I do not think he is). He points out the stars, so many of them, with a branch, and tells me the distance, in light years, as if he's been judging that particular star for a long time, wondering if he could somehow get there. He likes the trapping season best, and that's when he goes out alone, when everyone else (except Patsy) is trapped by the snow.

We'll sit there, so high in the Canadian Rockies, and watch clouds pass over the moon, feel the bite of what feels like the edges of eternity, a certain forever-aspect to things, as if this is the way it should always be up in this country—frigid, locked-in and cold, with springtime and yellow-flowered summer only an accident, which will, one of these years, not even bother happening. . . .

When we hunt, Galena Jim drinks whiskey in the evenings, telling me about those stars, and he tells me other things, things that no one else knows, maybe not even Patsy. Jim has a son, Buck, nineteen years old, who is in the state prison in Choteau, a lifer, maximum security, for killing a man. Buck is his son from a long-ago marriage, his only son. Buck's closer to my age than I am to Jim's. I don't know if Patsy knows about it or not. Somehow, I don't think she does. Jim doesn't talk about it much. Usually he just talks around the edges, like: "Wonder what Ol' Buck's doing tonight?" or something like that.

Or he'll talk about what it was like when he was nineteen, and twenty—things he used to do, and all the things he's done since. He'll ask me some of the things I've done, some of the things I've seen.

Not much, I'll feel like telling him, because it *doesn't* feel like much, not yet. That's part of the reason I hang around with Jim Ontz. But I can't tell him that. I know it'll let him down.

So instead I'll tell him about brown trout I've caught in Idaho, doubling their size, and the amount of time it took to land them. I'll make up lies about beautiful women I've loved, married women, women who've done these unbelievable things, and it's what we're supposed to talk about, out there in the woods like that, and it seems to make Galena Jim feel both happy and sad—better, in a way—and he laughs, looks over at me and laughs, and I think it even makes him able to get to sleep.

Hunting in a land where no one else can get to; bringing deer out of deep canyons and gorges that no one else could get them out of. I've still got my legs, my lower back: those Octobers, those early Novembers, we can do anything. Galena Jim said once that he had been thinking about breaking his son out of jail, but that was the only time he said that to me, never again, and I didn't know what to say. I didn't know if I'd let him down by not volunteering, or what. I don't know what I'd do if he brought it up again, and asked me to help.

I think that I would have to help him.

What I believe is this: that when Jim was young, he spent a lot of time on the circuit, trying to make it big, and not enough time around the house. I think that he has had his fill of horses, that maybe he has made some kind of promise to himself about never getting on them again.

I think maybe too that in winter, when everyone else is trapped, bound by their cabins, he gets so far out into the woods, in such a blowing wind, that he forgets where he is, even who he is.

I think he imagines he is his son, twenty years old, running the snowmobile along the frozen river, then stopping and getting off and walking up to his deadfall or his line-set: pulling the chain up out of the frozen waters, his eyes tearing and blurring in the cold—lifting the chain up, out there so far away from anyone, where no one can see, to find out if his luck has changed from yesterday, and what lies ahead in the next trap, and the next, and the next.

I have seen Galena Jim ride a moose before. Not showing off for anyone, unless it was just me—I was the only one with him. We were driving up the part of Hellroaring Road where the old World War II asphalt ends from the logging days and it goes to weeds and dirt—up above Pete Creek Road, up above everything, almost into Canada—and it was near the pass, where you go over from Montana into Idaho. Jim was driving, we were looking for grouse, and we came upon this big bull moose standing in the middle of the road. He was taller than the truck: the largest I'd ever seen, with a spread of palm-antlers as wide as a breakfast table.

Jim had been talking about food, about his favorite recipes for grouse, and for trout, and everything—he was supposed to go into Libby and cook dinner for Tiger, and was planning the menu, deciding what kind of wine to have with the meal—and this moose was suddenly in front of us, looking like he wanted to charge us, but turning instead, and running down the road ahead of us, like a blocker, clearing a path for us across the state line or something—and the moose wouldn't jump off the road, wouldn't veer to either side. Jim was gunning the truck, we were going thirty-five, almost forty miles an hour, right behind him—and Jim told me to take the wheel and the gas pedal, and climbed out onto the roof before I could say anything.

No one was around to see any of this. I couldn't understand why he was doing it.

He gave me the thumbs-up signal, and we pulled even with the big moose, racing alongside him, forty miles an hour with his clumsy, hoof-floating gallop, and he looked fierce, angry, outraged; and that was before Jim leaped on his back, like something falling from the sky.

He clung to the big moose like a midget. The moose veered off the road and plowed through a bunch of low alder and fir, knocking Jim off, and then, like a bad bull in the rodeo, the moose came back up the hill, trying to gore Jim, to trample him; and I got the .30-30 out, and was firing it into the air, and honking the horn, but couldn't shoot the moose, because Jim was in the way, running and scrambling, diving around rocks and rolling under logs, clutching his heart.

The moose lost Jim then, somehow, and came after the truck, and I was free to shoot it then; but I did not want to shoot a moose out of season, and especially such a fine moose in this one, and I did not know what Jim wanted me to do—what he would have done—and so I did not fire, and the moose slammed into the side of the truck and shook it, rocked it on its springs, roaring and coughing like a bull, and then it ran back down into the woods and disappeared.

I gave Jim some water and held his head up, propped him against a rock. The left side of his face was drawn down and twitching slightly. He didn't have any color, and for a moment, broken and hurt like that, almost helpless, he seemed like my friend rather than a teacher of any sort; and he seemed young, too, like he could have been just anybody, instead of Galena Jim Ontz, who had been thrown by a moose; and we sat there all afternoon, he with his eyes closed, resting, saving up, breathing slowly with cracked ribs.

It was only late summer and did not get dark until around ten o'clock. By the time Jim finally felt strong enough for me to help him into the truck, a low full moon had come up, and I did not know how to make the ride down the Hellroaring Road any less rough, but I went as slow as I could, and looked over to see how he was taking it.

He didn't look to be in pain so much as just sick feeling, as if he had done something wrong, had made a mistake somewhere.

"You're a good boy," he grunted when we finally got down off the road and back into the valley. I knew that in Libby, Tiger would be cursing him, maybe throwing things because he had not shown up; and I knew too that when we pulled up the driveway, with his truck battered and me getting out first, that Patsy would be frightened, that it would be like the worst of the dreams she never had; fearing the worst, knowing about his heart, and knowing about Jim. We drove with the windows down and a cool breeze in our faces, all the pastures bathed in bright silver moonlight, and the mountains all around the valley like a wall, holding us in.

The road sparkled and glittered in front of us, a path of where Jim had once been; a road one might encounter only in a dream. It was a road he had helped make, and we flew across it, rushing to get home.

THE AUTHORS

RICK BASS is the author of *The Watch,* a collection of short stories, and *Oil Notes,* an essay collection. Another essay collection, *Winter,* is forthcoming in January 1990. He has had stories selected for inclusion in anthologies such as *Best American Short Stories 1988; Prize Stories 1989; The O. Henry Awards; New Stories from the South 1988; New Stories from the South 1989; New American Short Stories; Pushcart Prize XIII;* and the forthcoming *Paris Review Anthology of Fiction.* He lives in Montana and is at work on a novel.

JOHN BENNION grew up in Vernon, Utah, a town of two hundred people which lies southwest of Salt Lake City on the Pony Express trail. Within forty miles are three military installations where the weapons of war are tested and stored. He is finishing his Ph.D. in Creative Writing at the University of Houston.

ANN CUMMINS was born in Durango, Colorado, but lived most of her childhood through late teens on the Navajo Indian Reservation in Shiprock, New Mexico. She has an M.A. in Creative Writing from Johns Hopkins University and an M.F.A. from the University of Arizona. She teaches creative writing at Northern Arizona University.

LOUISE ERDRICH grew up in North Dakota. She lives in New Hampshire with her husband/collaborator, Michael Dorris, also a novelist, and their six children. She has published three novels and a volume of poems entitled *Jacklight.*

JIM FINLEY has been writing fiction for three years. His stories appear in *Other Voices, Chattahoochie Review, Greensboro Review, New Mexico Humanities Review, Sands—A Literary Review, Nebo, Snapdragon, Crab Creek Review,* etc. He lives in Texas City, Texas, and teaches politics at the College of the Mainland.

CHARLES FRAZIER grew up in western North Carolina and graduated from the University of North Carolina at Chapel Hill. He lived for a number of years in Colorado before returning recently to his home state, where he now teaches in the English department at North Carolina State University. He has written a travel book on the Andes of Ecuador, Peru, and Bolivia which has been published by Sierra Club Books.

OLIVE GHISELIN lives in Salt Lake City and says of herself, "My biography is like the desert, rather bare. I have had one husband and two sons, taught some classes at the University of Utah, traveled a little in Europe and Mexico, and tended a garden. Writing has been a way of getting to the end of a paragraph without being interrupted."

RON HANSEN was born in Omaha and has spent most of his life in the Great Plains and Far West. He is the author of two novels, *Desperadoes* and *The Assassination of Jesse James by the Coward Robert Ford,* a children's book, *The Shadowmaker,* and a collection of stories, *Nebraska.* He teaches creative writing at the University of California at Santa Cruz.

JIM HARRISON is a poet and novelist living in northern Michigan.

MARK STEVEN HESS received a B.A. in English Literature from the University of Colorado. He lives in Yuma, Colorado, where he teaches high school English and is working on a collection of short stories for adolescents.

DAVID HORGAN grew up in Reno, Nevada. He and his family live in Missoula, Montana, where he works as a professional musician. He plays a Fender Telecaster. His first book of stories, *The Golden West Trio Plus One,* was a recent winner of the University of Montana's Merriam-Frontier Award.

FENTON JOHNSON has held a number of fellowships in writing, including a National Endowment for the Arts Fellowship in Literature, a Wallace Stegner Fellowship from Stanford University, and a James Michener Fellowship from the University of Iowa Writers Workshop. His short fiction has received a number of literary awards, including the Joseph Henry Jackson Award and the Transatlantic Review/Henfield Foundation Award. He has published a novel, *Crossing the River.* He divides his time between his old Kentucky home and San Francisco, where he teaches creative writing at San Francisco State University.

WILLIAM KITTREDGE grew up on the MC Ranch in southeastern Oregon, stayed home with the farming until he was thirty-five, studied in the Writer's Workshop at the University of Iowa, and is presently a professor of English at the University of Montana. He held a Stegner Fellowship at Stanford University, received two Creative Writing fellowships from the National Endowment for the Arts, two Pacific Northwest Booksellers' Awards for Excellence, and the Montana Governor's Award for the Arts. His most recent books are a collection of short fiction, *We Are Not In This Together,* and a collection of essays, *Owning It All.*

TOM MCNEAL has published fiction in *California Quarterly, Epoch, Playboy, Redbook,* and *Quarterly West.* He was a Stegner Fellow in fiction and is presently a Jones Lecturer in fiction at Stanford University. He lives in Menlo Park with his wife, Cathy, and their three dogs.

KEN SMITH was born in Silver City, New Mexico, and spent most of his young life in the Southwest. He has worked at ranching, farming, bar tending, and operating heavy equipment in various copper mines. During the Vietnam War he piloted rescue helicopters for the navy. He did both undergraduate and graduate work at the University of Arizona at Tucson. He is presently on the writing faculty at the University of Tennessee at Chattanooga, and lives with his wife and two sons.

GLADYS SWAN grew up in New Mexico, the setting of much of her fiction. She has published two collections of stories, *On the Edge of the Desert* and *Of Memory and Desire,* and a novel in the Vintage Contemporaries Series, *Carnival for the Gods.* She teaches creative writing at the University of Missouri-Columbia and is on the faculty of the M.F.A. program in Creative Writing at Vermont College. During 1988 she was a writer-in-residence in Yugoslavia on a Fulbright Fellowship.

GORDON WEAVER, professor of English at Oklahoma State University, is the author of five collections of short stories and four novels, the most recent of which is *The Eight Corners of the World.* Born in Illinois and raised in Wisconsin, he has lived since 1975 in Stillwater, Oklahoma, a locale that has appeared more and more frequently in his fiction.